"A slew of family secrets, sisterly betrayals, and the suspicious drowning churn the Palm Beach waters in this wickedly entertaining novel by Susannah Marren."

—MARY SIMSES, author of *The Wedding Thief*

"With a penetrating eye for tribal nuance, Susannah Marren returns to Palm Beach, where wearing the wrong shade of lipstick can be social suicide. *Maribelle's Shadow* explores how a mother and three daughters transplanted from Nowhere play the ambition game with chilling skill. Get ready for a mystery surrounding one husband's death, and don't expect *Little Women*."

—SALLY KOSLOW, best-selling author of *The Real Mrs. Tobias*

"Another stunning novel from Susannah Marren set in Palm Beach. Exploring the intricacies and interplay of family loyalty, romance, and high society, Marren never ceases to amaze. This one will keep you turning pages!"

—JACQUELINE FRIEDLAND, *USA Today* best-selling author of *He Gets That From Me*

"The mystery catches your attention, but Marren's vivid characters seal the deal. Maribelle and her sisters are complicated and brilliant heroines, determined to be remembered and make their mark."

—TERESA SORKIN, co-author of *Lacie's Secrets*

"A great escape! Susannah Marren's newest novel set in Palm Beach blurs the line between "inner sanctum" and "creative wannabe," and will leave readers wondering if they would want to be part of the "in-crowd.""

—JEANNE MCWILLIAMS BLASBERG, author of *The Nine* and forthcoming, *Daughter of a Promise*

"Sisters, husbands, scandal, business and betrayal. This intriguing novel about deception, marriage, and the high society Palm Beach scene will keep you turning the page until the surprise ending."

—SONDRA HELENE, author of
best-selling novel, *Appearances*

"Susannah Marren returns to familiar territory in her new novel, *Maribelle's Shadow*, navigating us through the glitzy, cut-throat world of the Palm Beach elite. The sudden death of Samuel, the husband of the oldest Barrows sister, sends the wealthy family into a tailspin of suspicion, deception and uncertainty. Love, loyalty and wills are tested as the mystery begins to come clear. An insightful look and welcome addition to the literature of mothers, daughters and sisters — richer and more relevant today than ever."

—ANNE WHITNEY PIERCE, author of
Down to the River and *Rain Line*

Maribelle's Shadow

For Juliet

I love you as one loves certain obscure things,
secretly, between the shadow and the soul.

—PABLO NERUDA
"One Hundred Love Sonnets: XVII,"
from *The Essential Neruda: Selected Poems.*

All that I have I bring,
All that I am I give.

—CHRISTINA ROSSETTI
Twice

Maribelle's Shadow

SUSANNAH MARREN

BEAUFORT
BOOKS

Paperback 9780825310294
Ebook: 9780825309083

For inquiries about volume orders, please contact:
Beaufort Books
sales@beaufortbooks.com
Published in the United States by Beaufort Books www.beaufortbooks.com

Distributed by Midpoint Trade Books, a division of Independent Publishers Group
www.ipgbook.com

Interior design: Mimi Bark
Front cover design and digital imaging: John Lotte
Jacket design: Mark Karis
Photo of woman on deck and ocean: Conrado/Shutterstock
Photo of cloudy sky: John D Sirlin/Shutterstock

Printed in the United States of America

PART ONE

CHAPTER ONE

Maribelle

When is the right time to tell your husband you know he's a cheater? Over breakfast? When he comes home from a business dinner, or he pretends to work overtime? These past few months, I wake in the middle of each night, chilled or feverishly hot, wondering this.

In the predawn, Maribelle walked toward the floor-to-ceiling windows of their living room and looked across the Intracoastal. The darkness mixed with lights to the west while to the east a damp wind blew off the ocean. The only sound was the palm trees stirring along the A1A. The garbage trucks hadn't yet rolled out. No sirens were racing to save a dying soul. Utter calm as high season began in Palm Beach.

By daylight she was in the kitchen, starting breakfast when Samuel ambled in, whistling. The espresso maker hissed; light entered through the slatted shades. Why wouldn't Samuel be cheerful? Maribelle thought. He had come in past midnight, undoubtedly from one of his encounters. Now he watched his dutiful wife beating four egg whites. She whisked too vigorously as she rehearsed her opening line, her segue, what every wife might want to know: *Do you love her? Are you leaving me?* As Maribelle was cutting a slab of clarified butter for the omelet pan, she asked herself, *do I dare risk a confrontation today?*

"Are you heading to yoga?" Samuel was smiling.

"I plan to." She was not smiling back.

"Your favorite way to greet the morning."

Samuel said it like they were still "kindred." That was how he phrased it. They had always wanted each other; the consummate treasure was being together. No wonder Maribelle looked away when Samuel had his trysts. They, as a couple, subsisted on the far side of that. He had always come back to her. They had shed his misdemeanor and gone on together. Until this.

How can you be someone who knows what I care about? A betrayer doesn't get to pose as my best friend, Maribelle wanted to shout. She flipped the omelet over, the pan sizzled. She had burned the bottom.

His hands were in the pockets of his khakis while he jiggled a set of keys. "I might take the boat out."

"Now?" *To be with her, why else?*

She wanted to ask why this woman mattered enough that their plans were in limbo. Samuel's promise—that they would leave town, start anew—felt squashed. Instead, she lifted her phone from their white quartz counter and opened the weather app. "There's a wind kicking up, it's at sixteen miles an hour."

"I'll be fine, Maribelle." He looked away.

"Except it's going to get stronger, by nine it could be at . . ."

"Not in the next hour or two. I need a quick spin to recover from our marathon fundraising. We hit our goal, but Jesus, it wasn't easy. What a drawn-out night. I want to get out of my head," Samuel said.

"The Literacy Foundation is grateful," she said. "We're doing a piece on fundraisers, and Nadia is thrilled with her interview there."

Maribelle was proud of her husband's dedication to his favorite charities. He meant it. He was a front-runner for causes—a Palm Beach philanthropist who basked in gratitude and praise. She was as enraptured as everyone else; the parts she admired about her husband, she admired no matter what.

"Are they?" He ran his hands through his hair, it sprang back. "That's great. Especially after dealing with fussy Mrs. A and her sidekick, prissy Priscilla. What a committee—old biddies, a group of spoiled young mothers. The men who write the checks are caged animals."

"Samuel, please, don't belittle people. They're your fans, some are true friends. Besides, if you speak ill of them, who knows what you say about me and my sisters."

He paused, laughed quickly. "Yeah, I suppose, in theory. But, c'mon, Maribelle, did you see the look on Mrs. A's face when she presented me with the plaque?" He stood ramrod straight, wobbled his head like a bobble toy, and rolled his eyes dramatically. *"For your meritorious sir-vuce . . ."*

Maribelle didn't laugh. "Don't be mean," she said quietly.

She waited for him to resume whistling. His good moods were preferable. She knew better than anyone else.

Wind gusts rustled the banyan trees in front of the house. Along the bulkhead, waves were churning up.

"I don't know, it seems too whippy for a speedboat. Why not something else? How about lifting weights with Travis?"

Still the protective wife, wasn't she? Maribelle realized she should stop this line of talk—her worry about Samuel's safety.

"Ah, a more prudent outlet," Samuel said. "Travis and I will go at lunch time. The gym helps when we're crazed at our desks."

"Good idea."

She was about to accuse Samuel of using Travis, their brother-in-law, as his front. Working out wasn't an outlet—a panacea for a tense day at in the office—it was that Samuel had to be fit. For her, for his mistress.

"We could put a gym into the building," Samuel said. "There's room on the third floor."

She couldn't stand the idea of Samuel bench-pressing while on the premises of Barrows, her family's company. How lucky he and Travis were to run this chain of convenience stores around the country. Clean, modern spaces, some with eighteen-foot-high ceilings. People stopped in for their chai lattes, Polly-O string cheese, Advil. Customers liked the atmosphere; some settled in at the coffee bar and worked on their laptops for hours.

"I'm sure employees would find it convenient."

Maribelle slid the omelets onto their plates. A dainty flowered pattern that she and her two sisters were given by their mother. One of her corny, intentionally sophisticated, if dated, ideas.

"Do you have a few minutes?" She poured espressos into the matching cups.

Samuel filled two water glasses from the filter. "I do. As long as it's not a ploy to keep me from defying nature on the waterfront."

Politely they sat down at their kitchen island. Super Dog came in from the den and circled around Samuel's feet. Two years ago when Maribelle and Samuel had picked her up from Animal Adoption, they had to move quickly. They had gotten the call that morning, and because it was an unusual event to have a purebred yellow Labrador puppy arrive at the center, they cancelled their workday. Only four months old, Supy had slept on Maribelle's lap in the backseat of the car on their ride home—halfway across the state.

"She's super," Maribelle had said as she stroked her faultlessly crafted head and admired her liquid eyes, "Just super."

"That's what we'll call her. "Super Dog—Supy for short."

Samuel's eyes had met hers in the rearview mirror. They were in tandem.

Today their shared dog/child seemed more Samuel's yellow Labrador than Maribelle's. She tried to remember when this happened. Maybe in the past year, when Samuel began walking Supy late at night when she was already asleep.

Supy looked up sweetly. Samuel leaned over to give her a piece of his gluten-free bagel. Beneath his deep blue cashmere sweater, his arms were strong, brawny.

"Aw, Supy, Super Dog, I'm happy to see you."

In the earliest light, Samuel was as seductive as ever—his voice, how he raised his left hand, and the shine of his wedding ring. A fine gold band with an extra rim of gold below and above. When they had become engaged and were choosing their rings, Maribelle liked the idea of how it encased their love. She wasn't sure why, but she knew she would need it in the years to come. She was bottling her husband up, preserving and securing him for the future.

"I spoke with that broker in LA," she said.

Samuel became wax-like. Without moving, he waited.

Maribelle kept going because he seemed to be listening. "Our house, this house, has to be worth . . ."

"Maribelle, if we leave for a year, we shouldn't sell this. It's home, our base, no matter what."

Samuel pointed to the hedges and bougainvillea beyond the terrace. On the ocean side the bleached out blue-grey waves were rolling in. Supy was wagging her tail.

"Look at what we have. Your work, mine. What about the magazine? What you're doing with it . . . adding local poets, book reviews, opinion pieces . . . it's your baby. You need to be present. Isn't that best?"

"Except we have a plan, Samuel. Didn't you and I agree to try LA? I'd explore producing, scriptwriting . . . maybe I could find a more serious job as a journalist . . . a managing editor. You'd delve into projects, maybe that food chain start-up you mentioned."

"I care about my work at Barrows, you know that," he sighed. "We're opening—Barrows is opening—three new southwest locations next month." He was quite still, as if bracing himself.

Barrows, Maribelle's family's company. They both knew if her father, Reed Barrows, had not died eight years ago while playing bridge at the Harbor Club, Samuel wouldn't be the CFO of Barrows. Nor would he have his 'toys' such as the *Vertigo*, his Riva Rivamare speedboat. "Isn't that the most expensive of them all?" Lucinda, Maribelle's mother, had asked when Samuel bought it.

Maribelle breathed in. "How you feel about Barrows, how you love it there, well, I'm not sure I'm quite the same. I *like* the magazine, I'm pleased to have the work, to be an editorial director is meaningful. It functions on some level—as a steppingstone."

Samuel came back to the countertop in a sensitive pose. "A steppingstone? Maribelle, you're the architect for reshaping, re-envisioning, making the magazine into something substantial."

Somehow his insistence combined with his body language stopped her from detailing how she really felt. Beyond that, she wanted to leave to further her career and escape her mother—the constant calendar, the vying for social standing. If they left Palm Beach, it would save her marriage. What Maribelle couldn't admit to Samuel was that she had craved exiting ever since she learned about his affair.

Samuel was eating fast, hardly cutting the omelet. Weren't they always rushing toward what's next and better, wasn't that what their lifestyle has done to them? The distance they had come since they danced together Samuel's senior year at Pinestream. He was the most dashing boy in the gymnasium. The wood planked floors were polished for Homecoming, the room had smelled of sweat from pep rallies and basketball games. Twenty-one years ago, Samuel had twirled Maribelle around the night long, dipping toward her to hear over the din. Like they were dancing in a grand ballroom not in a place with dense pine forests and a parking lot filled with pickup trucks.

There were fishing fleets along the Gulf Coast where they had grown up. Samuel's father was a shrimper, and he had two Labrador retrievers. It was no wonder their life today on the Intra-coastal entranced Samuel or that they sought the dog they did. When it came to a boat, Maribelle wasn't blaming Samuel for his Riva Rivamare. He had bought it last year after eyeing it for ages. He treated it carefully.

Supy came close to Samuel, nuzzled her face into his palm. Samuel stroked her back lovingly. If Maribelle confronted Samuel, and he decided to walk out, would he take the dog, arguing she was more his than theirs? Then Supy would become the prize of Samuel *and* this woman who imagined herself as the next wife. Maribelle's apprehension was rising, today was the day to speak about it.

Outside the wind rustled again.

"Samuel, it has to be soon. We're not bound to this place. We have no children to keep us tied to anyone or anywhere. You and I could have a splendid run somewhere else. Please don't take our chances away." Maribelle's words sounded high, tight. That this notion was within their reach was heady stuff.

Samuel tipped his espresso cup toward his mouth and fin-ished it off in a one sip. Suddenly he was in his most persuasive mode. His eyes blazed. His shoulders were like barricades, strong. While in private he might have been cynical about people in Palm Beach, in public he offered himself as a known listener, a true friend. Few missed these traits. Maribelle was about to get the polished version of her husband.

"I owe your family so much," Samuel said. "You and I have spo-ken about this plenty of times. We shouldn't be going anywhere. Not right now. It isn't logical."

"You and I were planning to go until she came along. You and your fantasy girl," Maribelle said softly.

At the same moment, Supy started barking excitedly, begging for another bite of bagel. When Samuel shrugged and passed it to her, Maribelle knew he had not heard her.

She thought about repeating herself, shouting it out. Instead she said nothing. Samuel came over and kissed the top of her head. He thrust his chin forward, he was deliberate about leaving now. She needed to gather herself, she was ready to stand at the front door, angling the question. She had rehearsed it for enough hours, it blistered within her.

"Samuel, there's something else . . ."

He smiled ruefully and glanced at his Rolex, the one Maribelle had bought five weeks ago for his thirty-ninth birthday. "We'll talk tonight, Maribelle."

"We have the Artists' Foundation at the Four Seasons at six-thirty."

"Afterward, we will. We'll have time then."

In the wedge of daylight that came into the room, his profile was perfected. A profile that belonged to Maribelle, just as his promises did. *He is my husband, and we share this life,* she told herself. Had she the nerve, she would warn him this woman was nothing but a ragged shadow. Except she wasn't certain it was true. Before her, there were three women. Once while Samuel was in the shower, Maribelle read a text from someone named Rebecca. *Countdown to Thursday. XO.* Once a jewelry store in South Beach called their landline about a pair of citrine dangle earrings that he had special ordered. During his last tryst, he called Maribelle "Honey" twice, then seemed appalled at using the wrong endearment. Gradually Samuel returned to her each time. Now another woman was Samuel's focus—Marielle sensed it made her husband happier and more distant at the same time. When they went places in town, he was only filling a chair. His schedule was wavering, he didn't always have a convincing excuse. He had become preoccupied; a few weeks back, he'd forgotten to pick Supy up at the vet.

"I've got to head out." Again, that smile. Supy barked anxiously, Samuel leaned down to swoop her into his arms. "I'll take Supy with me, I'll feed her on the boat, take her to work."

"Are you sure? I can text Trish. I mean, she's willing to come any hour and walk her," Maribelle offered.

Samuel rubbed Supy's head. "Ready?"

Maribelle remembered how she and Samuel used to agree about such things, including dog care. How life used to be when he thought she hung the moon, when he listened to her.

"Sure, Maribelle," he'd say, "One day we'll leave Palm Beach, we'll go wherever you want." Only last Sunday, during brunch at Longreen's, she was tempted to confess to her mother and sisters: *He's slipping through my fingers. There's another woman. Tell me how to keep my husband at my side.*

Another kiss, this time near her mouth. His face up close smelled clean, there was none of the stubble that appeared by the afternoon. Maribelle remained very still, waiting for them to wrap their arms around one another, his face close to the hollow in her neck. They would start sloppy romantic kisses. He would carry her to bed like the old days. Wait, they would stop themselves—was there time? Could they ignore the dog, ditch the boat, forfeit yoga? They would forge on. Samuel would place his hands beneath her thighs like he used to. They would go at it frantically, a quickie. You feel so good, he would say to her. You too, she would whisper back, his body against hers, obliterating all else. All that separated them.

"Maribelle?"

Samuel gathered his briefcase, a windbreaker and a dog leash.

After he walked through the back door into the garage, the room felt chilly. She opened the panel that hid their car keys and lifted hers from a hook. For the briefest moment, before her husband marched back inside with Supy, Maribelle only imagined that he had returned, that he was reconsidering her plea and had noticed her despair.

"The Range Rover, it won't turn over. If we leave now, you'd have time to drop me on the way to yoga. I'll get a lift to the office from the Yacht Club." He appeared calm but beneath that, he was hasty. He was texting rapidly.

She tugged at the waistband of her yoga pants that felt tight.

"Well, I'll need my bag . . ." Maribelle moved quickly toward the hallway.

He was leaning against the doorframe to the kitchen, as important to her as ever. Samuel, who made each person believe she or he was the only person who counted. *Samuel is spellbinding, Mom used to say. Isn't he almost too dynamic? Shouldn't husbands be noticed second, not first?*

Two hours later Maribelle was back from Yoga Sunrise and showered, feeling calmer. She turned on the new flat screen in their "massive suite," as her mother liked to say with a slight dash of disdain. While Lucinda was pleased that each of her three daughters had a "lovely home," she revisited who had what to churn up competition. This morning the square footage of the bedroom shared with Samuel seemed lonely—too long and broad for one childless couple and their ardent schedules. *Morning Joe* came into focus in a millisecond. Maribelle peered closely at Mika Brzezinski and Joe Scarborough, co-hosts. This was her favorite. She appreciated their brand of journalism, how they didn't merely report events but delved deeper. She wanted *PB Confidential* to do a piece on Mika. Maribelle imagined lunching with her at Ta-boo, both in sleeveless sheaths, perhaps in raspberry and teal. They would trade thoughts about how life imitates art, what female agency looks like. Both of them would delight in the idea that featuring Mika could add gravitas and make the magazine less fluffy.

As Maribelle selected her own form of stylish—zipping up a purple print Erdem dress, searching for a cropped cardigan—her iPhone binged, then vibrated. When she picked up, Caroline, her middle sister, asked, "Why is it so peaceful at Barrows before my husband and your husband show up?"

"That's a rhetorical question," Maribelle said.

"I'm only calling about next Friday. Mom's been so intense lately. Let's invite friends to buffer things and move the family dinner out of her house. To a restaurant or Justine's. Yeah, maybe Justine's is better since she's a fan of eating clubs."

Either Maribelle had her volume on too loud, or she needed her pods. She held her phone at arm's length and walked into her closet for a pair of blush suede booties.

"What's scheduled now?" Maribelle dropped a hoop earring. It bounced along the hardwood floor, proving she was unable to dress while getting into the machinations of dinner with her entire family. "You know what—you decide, make Mom happy. We'll be better off."

While they spoke, Maribelle glanced at the mirrored armoire. She was prepared for her day. In fact, for thirty-eight, she looked younger thanks to the many facials, a bit of filler, Botox on occasion. Why didn't her husband appreciate the result?

She shook her hair out of a clip. It fell down her back as if it weren't hers, as if it were her little sister Raleigh's lustrous tresses. Raleigh was ten years younger in every way, including the weight of her gold-brown hair and how taut she would be in the outfit Maribelle had on today. The family creed was that Raleigh resembled their mother, who was only eighteen when Maribelle was born in Kesgrave, a town in the Panhandle.

Another life ago their mother, Lucinda, with great effort, reinvented herself into a classic Palm Beach lady, one who mesmerized whomever was in the room.

Maribelle's doorbell chimed.

"Caroline? I've got to go. I think someone's at my door."

"Isn't that unlikely?"

"Let me check." Caroline was right. Who would be ringing her bell in the Estate Section of Palm Beach at eight-thirty on a Tuesday morning?

Maribelle swept down the staircase. A storm was kicking up, the wind wrapped around the house from the east. The doorbell rang once more, she looked carefully through the front window.

"Caroline? It's your husband, and he's got our dog. I don't know what's going on—I'll call you back."

When she opened the door, her brother-in-law was ashen. Supy bolted out of his arms. Her coat was drenched, she shook water onto their legs.

"Maribelle, something's happened." Travis half turned away from her. Behind him, a sheriff's car was parked in the portico. Maribelle's skin prickled, her mind fogged.

Supy came close to where she stood and sniffed the tips of her booties. Maribelle kneeled and ran her fingers along the dog's scalp, she whined and stepped back. As Maribelle straightened up, the sheriff walked toward the house, holding down the brim of his Stetson. The sky had dimmed. A pelting rain began.

CHAPTER TWO

Caroline

Caroline almost skidded across the A1A as the squalls pushed her SUV down the road. She was speeding because while she and her sisters were capable of exaggeration, her husband was not. When Travis called a half hour ago to say "there was a situation," she knew to rush.

Raleigh was waiting at her front door, the wind tumbling around her ficus hedges and honeysuckle when Caroline arrived. Disheveled and balletic, she walked into the rain, opened the car door, and slid into the passenger seat.

"Hey. What's going on?" She took a sip from the bamboo tea tumbler she carried everywhere.

"Travis didn't say. Only that we should come right away to Maribelle's."

Caroline turned off List Road, back onto A1A, concentrating on the curve. Raleigh didn't know how they had been summoned, the misery in Travis's voice.

Her sister was gazing out the window at the Intracoastal. "That's odd." She sounded vague, on edge. "What is it?"

Caroline sighed. She resisted telling Raleigh that she was worried. Her sister was too suggestible. For the short ride there, they would be bathed in her fear.

"When will this rain ever end?" She turned up the windshield wipers.

They stood in Maribelle's empty, pale formal living room. Caroline was unable to grasp the sight of her husband in some weird in-charge mode—this had to be an elaborate hoax. He was standing in the corner, weathered and weary like his father and cousins who still lived in Kesgrave. When they were kids, they went hunting for geese. His younger cousin, Arnie, had shot two toes off one Saturday morning.

Behind him, the rain sliced at the French doors to the garden.

"Travis, what's going on?" Already she felt covered in a film of dread.

"Travis, tell us," Raleigh whispered, visibly anxious. "What happened?"

"Where's Maribelle? Why aren't we talking to her?" Raleigh walked nearer to the window, twisting her hands.

"She'll be here." Caroline tried to be matter of fact.

As Travis was about to start, Maribelle came in from the library, toward Raleigh. Although she was always agile, she was dragging, weighed down, her head tucked in. Her work clothes and hair looked rumpled.

Maribelle sucked in the air. "It's Samuel."

"There's been an accident," Travis said. "On the Intracoastal. Samuel drowned."

"I don't believe you." Raleigh looked at him as if he were to blame. "It must have been someone else."

"I'm sorry. There was a search and rescue operation that didn't last very long. They found his body. He was thrown off the *Vertigo* out on the waterway. The wind . . . he might have been speeding."

Although Travis was not up close, Caroline knew his eyes were bluish red around the rims, how they got in scary or sad times. Raleigh began to cry. Caroline reached out for both her sisters' wrists.

"Didn't he have on a life vest . . . or that personal flotation device? What's it called, a PFD?" she asked.

"He might have hit a sandbar," Travis said. "Or submerged rocks. We'll learn. We'll find out from the Coast Guard."

Caroline turned to Maribelle. "I'm so sorry. Oh, my God . . ."

"I know. I know. I think Samuel will come in tonight, won't he? He'll toss his keys in the tray by the front door. This is some joke, some mind game."

"Yeah," Raleigh said. "That works."

Maribelle began making wounded desolate sounds. Fragmented memories of her with Samuel filled Caroline's head. Taking tango lessons when they were first married, winning a blue water regatta when they were in high school, shopping at Vintage Tales on the Avenue for Maribelle's birthday. She put her arm around her.

"He was the best of the husbands," she whispered, hoping Travis couldn't hear. "The best of the Barrows sisters' husbands."

Maribelle started sobbing. "What does that mean?"

She was right to ask, even as Caroline uttered the word best, she questioned it. Samuel was the most charming and so handsome, but he had attitude. Since they were growing up, back in Kesgrave, he had admired and resented the Barrows family. Especially their parents, compared to his parents, who were too homegrown. Once he had told Caroline that they made him feel like less. Still, he was dead, they ought to praise him.

"Smart, athletic, popular," Caroline offered up.

Raleigh took the cue. "He was, Maribelle, he was the best."

Their sister frowned. Caroline glanced at the ice grey rooms that led into one another—the library to the right of the main entrance, the living room where they stood, the patio and pool, the kitchen straight out to the left. Vast, decorated spaces. Possibly Caroline wasn't being kind enough. She guiltily thought about the many times she had reminded Maribelle of what it was like with two young daughters, how she had pushed the dogma that life is incomplete without children. She had been harsh in that distinctive, competitive, middle sister style.

Raleigh took her phone from her pocket and squinted at the screen. "Mom's texting."

Caroline lifted hers out of a crossbody. "She's a minute from here."

Maribelle looked toward the ocean. The waves were smacking against the shoreline. "She won't like what we tell her. You know she doesn't like loss. Sadness." Her voice was wobbly.

"Is that what we're worried about?" Raleigh asked.

From the doorway, Lucinda held the same anguish in her face as when their father was suddenly gone. Her hair was gathered in that low braid she favored, and her makeup was dark and thick for the morning. It might have been too difficult for her to walk toward her suddenly widowed daughter; instead, it was Aunt Bryant, their godmother, their mother's best friend, who walked to Maribelle and placed her hands on her shoulders.

"Maribelle, I am so terribly sorry," Aunt Bryant said. "Aren't we, Lucinda?"

Their mother nodded and slid closer to Maribelle. Perhaps because she was so near, Maribelle fell into her arms and wept. She stiffly patted her back.

Alex came in. He and Travis lined up at the bookcase, a reminder that they had been a triumvirate—three husbands to the three Barrows daughters. While these brothers-in-law had scrambled to please their mother-in-law, they had also shared some great times together. Alex had been included in their guys only camping trips to the Everglades and bowling nights at Greenacres. For some reason the disco nights at the Harbor Club were popular with all three of the Barrows sisters' husbands. When it came to work, Travis and Samuel had decided to redesign every Barrows in the country, tracking how to grow the company, enthused with the results. Alex wasn't in that loop.

Near the baby grand were photographs, a narrative of every occasion. All of it documented, from Maribelle and Samuel's engagement party, to a recent trip to Cap Antibes, to deep-sea fishing in Miami last spring. Radiant pictures. How would Maribelle process that Samuel wasn't ever again walking into the library, seductively apologizing that he was late? What would happen to her sister?

The potted daffodils and tulips on the terrace blew harder, canisters were rolling into one another. Travis cleared his throat. Maribelle quieted down.

"Samuel was great," he said. "We'd play doubles on Sunday mornings at the Dales and psyched everyone out. We won every week. We had a good time together. I can't believe he's gone or what life will be like without him, what Barrows will be."

"It wasn't my idea to go birdwatching, but Samuel convinced me," Alex said. "I thought he was joking. It's not as if Samuel fit the bird-watcher mold. The others were in safari vests and floppy hats. Samuel looked like he'd walked out of the pages of GQ. But when it came to identifying a bird by its call or picking out a blue-winged teal hiding in the branches, he was better than the rest. Every birder loved him, including the nerdiest ones. He knew their names, the birds they looked for. He made them feel like they counted."

"Samuel was the least moody person working at Barrows. I loved how he brought miniature candy bars to meetings. He always knew exactly who liked milk chocolate. We all, we each, felt special." Caroline managed to say this without crying and making it worse.

Maribelle slid back and forth as if she were rewinding the morning, searching for a rescue.

"He came to everything 'uncle', like gymnastic classes for Harper and Violet. They adored him," Caroline said. She watched as Raleigh walked to the glass panels and opened them for air. Only last weekend Harper and Violet were here, on the grounds that sloped toward the pool. They were giggling as Travis and Samuel swung them around, paired off, while singing *All You Need is Love* by the Beatles.

Raleigh turned around. "I remember Samuel when I was little in Kesgrave. Maribelle would put her make-up on those nights before their dates and talk about how he was a wrestler, that he'd caught the biggest fish on the river and won a fishing award. They were so grown up, the two of them."

"These boating accidents." Aunt Bryant was crying. "How someone can be taken in a moment out on the open water. It doesn't matter if it's a fishing boat, a sailing boat, some kind of speedboat like Samuel's."

What a memory for Aunt Bryant. Weren't they all thinking this? Her fiancé, Bud Humphries, had drowned in a gunning boat decades ago, back in Kesgrave. Maribelle took a breath and glanced out, away from everyone.

"Maybe that's enough," Travis said. "We need time to absorb the loss."

Alex made a soulful grimace. Caroline thought her sisters hadn't heard Travis's suggestion.

"Did Samuel leave a will?" Lucinda asked.

Maribelle gasped. Caroline, guardian of the peace, rose to her defense. "I'm sorry, Mom, what did you say? Samuel *just* drowned. We only found out, and Maribelle is . . ."

"We should know this, Caroline," Lucinda said. "Maribelle, did he?"

"We did our wills a couple of years ago. Right after Allison Rochester's brother was in Palm Beach over Christmas week and died jogging. He was forty something."

"Did Samuel have a safe deposit box? Somewhere he would keep it?" Mom asked.

"Mom, please. Really . . ." Raleigh paced, her feet were making an echo, a tapping sound.

Lucinda pressed on. "We'd like to avoid probate."

"Please, can't we talk about this later?" Maribelle was crying.

"Maribelle, don't listen. You don't have to." Raleigh rushed over, quietly crying herself.

"That's enough, Raleigh. Maribelle, pull yourself together. This is important." Lucinda was insistent.

"Important! My husband is dead! *That's* what's important!"

Aunt Bryant moved between Lucinda and Maribelle like she was a first-grade teacher separating two trying classmates. "Let it go for now, Lucinda."

Lucinda ignored her, shifting toward Caroline.

"Caroline, a word?" she asked.

"With me? Sure."

She motioned toward the wet bar. They crossed the room together. Caroline knew every other family member was watching, dazed by their mother's vehemence.

When they were out of earshot, Lucinda whispered, "Caroline, I'd like you to find the will. Guide Maribelle, take her to the bank vault if need be. First, stand with her at the safe in her house and have her open it up. Whatever it takes. Tomorrow."

Caroline was tempted to say, *you're unstoppable.* Instead, she counted to ten. "Together Maribelle and I can call Daryl Dexter's office. I'm sure he's their estate lawyer."

"I don't want any problems," Lucinda said.

"Mom, Samuel drowned *this morning* . . . we're trying to understand, it was some freak accident. Travis was told that."

"People will talk. Was it deliberate, they'll wonder? Then there's his estate."

"Lucinda?" Aunt Bryant called, her voice watery and shrill. "Can you and Caroline speak later?

Caroline and Lucinda faced Aunt Bryant.

"I'm sorry, Aunt Bryant," Caroline said, knowing they had been rude or suspicious, maybe both.

Lucinda frowned. "We didn't realize we were holding anything up."

As they followed Aunt Bryant, Lucinda pinched Caroline's elbow. "Remember my request."

CHAPTER THREE

Raleigh

Raleigh thought Aunt Bryant would be a better choice to be the designated sleeper at Maribelle's since she was almost too kind. She had never married. Her life was about her goddaughters and being a social worker at the not-for-profit, *Mothers and Children*. Besides, Raleigh knew—everyone in the family knew—that comfort wasn't what she did best. Still, everyone, their mother, Caroline, Travis and Alex, liked the idea that she would stay with Maribelle.

The minute everyone left, Raleigh walked with Maribelle through her hallways, which felt cavernous.

"You must be tired, Maribelle."

"I can't do this, sleep in here, our bedroom." Her voice was quaky.

Lucinda always said that Maribelle's "suite" was "so spacious and carefully appointed—beyond chic." She had insisted Maribelle use Pratesi sheets because they—like "wearing the right underwear"—set a tone from the inside out. Raleigh pushed these thoughts out of her mind. Tonight, there was a spectral cast over the entire space. The two of them were in her giant closet as Maribelle searched for something to give Raleigh to sleep in.

"I understand," Raleigh was relieved. She didn't want to be there either. They were standing along the mirrored wall, wan and defeated. Raleigh realized this must be what shock felt like, when the person inside didn't feel present. It was like being invaded by some unknown force. The disbelief rushed at them.

Maribelle's eyes were desolate. Raleigh held her. "Maribelle, listen, today is hard to believe. Impossible to believe."

"Yeah, a nightmare." Maribelle leaned in, then pulled away. She stood like a soldier for a second, then handed Raleigh a pair of boxers and a camisole in white silk with red hearts. They stared at the print before Maribelle changed her mind and took them back. She handed over another in pale blue with white piping.

"Do you need a toothbrush?" Maribelle was trying, dusting off her pain to be normal.

"I'll look in the cabinet. I'm sure it's all there," Raleigh said.

They nodded at one another because their mother had them so trained. Whatever the occasion, bathrooms had to have supplies.

At midnight Super Dog followed them in to the larger of Maribelle's two guest rooms. She was whining and disoriented, unaccustomed to being in this part of the house.

"C'mon, Supy." Maribelle placed her hand against the dog's face. "You'll be with me, it's okay."

Supy froze, looking at Maribelle, then Raleigh, mystified.

"Super Dog, Supy," Raleigh said.

The yelping and crooning began. Maribelle patted the top of her head. "She misses Samuel. He always takes her out at night, any hour that he gets home."

"Do you want me to walk her now, a quick walk?" Raleigh offered. Supy heard this and backed away.

"No, she'll be fine. She's with us."

Supy looked at both their faces, trying to figure out the set-up. She grazed a settee and side table to the left in the entryway. The bedroom was completely neutral, there was no color. The throw pillows were eggshell or fawn. There were crisp, white bed linens with an antiseptic feel. Maribelle opened the sliding doors, the floor-to-ceiling drapes billowed. Next, she chose a few photo albums that were kept neatly on the dresser, the kind no one puts together anymore, and brought them to the middle of the king-size bed. She began sorting through them, pulling a few pictures out.

"Here, look Raleigh, this is our third wedding anniversary. We flew to Philadelphia for the weekend." She seemed manic, her voice was high, hurried.

Raleigh stared at a picture of Maribelle and Samuel in puffy winter coats in front of the Barnes Collection. Samuel's arm was around her sister's waist, and they were smiling very brightly.

"Hmm," she said. "Nice picture. You guys look young."

Maribelle peered closer. "We were. Young and dumb."

"Maribelle, don't say that," Raleigh said. "Please . . ."

She lifted a picture taken at Caroline's wedding. "See, by the time Caroline got married, Mom and Dad were chi-chi. They were into it being a Palm Beach wedding."

"Caroline and Travis fell for the rooms at Longreens," Raleigh said. "They were there for lunch or brunch or something with Mom. Caroline thought it was elegant, and Travis always signs on."

Maribelle was rifling through other photos. "Here, pictures of Kesgrave, in high school. Like this one from Thanksgiving when I was sixteen, so you're six. Caroline's fourteen."

"I remember Mom cooked everything that year. She baked the pies. She was teaching then, right?"

Maribelle nodded. "Can you believe it? Mom as a ninth-grade teacher."

She held it up. Samuel was there too. She stared at his face. "See how cute Samuel was?"

Raleigh moved a little closer to see. Wasn't she supposed to say something reassuring? That she remembered how Samuel was one of the guests, that Aunt Bryant had bought her the dress she wore. It was pale pink with tree branches and leaves splattered across it and a matching sweater, which she had despised. If she said this, it would be about herself, and that wasn't fair. For many reasons, Caroline should have stayed the night with Maribelle. For starters, Raleigh was constantly in need of being soothed and not very soothing.

Maribelle brought the picture closer to her face.

"That night, after Thanksgiving dinner when everyone was asleep, Samuel came back to the house. We sneaked out on the screened-in porch. When he took off his shirt, it wasn't like when we'd swam along the riverbank, everyone in bathing suits. It was about us. It was the first time we . . ."

"You don't have to tell me anything more," Raleigh said.

"It must have been my pheromones. I was hooked on him from then on. I couldn't live without him."

"Mom used to say you never knew anyone else, you just married your first boyfriend without meeting any other guys. That you and Caroline were as stuck as she'd been marrying a local boy."

"Well, in the end we weren't stuck, were we? Samuel being local, being familiar, that worked. I liked it. Except now, now my husband's . . . he's . . . I don't believe it. This house feels like it's been emptied out."

Raleigh knew what she meant, as if there had been a giant suctioning of their lives. "Wait a second," She padded into the guest bathroom and returned with her makeup bag. "Mom gave me Xanax and Aunt Bryant gave me Valium. Plus, I have a few Benadryl."

She placed the pills on the nightstand by her side of the bed.

As if they were at a five-star hotel, two bottles of Voss water sat on the desk. Raleigh brought them over and opened the caps.

"Valium. It's strongest, I bet," Maribelle said, selecting one. Raleigh handed her the water.

"I've never had either of them. I'll stick with this." Raleigh held up a Benadryl Allergy and swallowed a whole pill, knowing a third of one tablet was enough to knock her out. Then she swigged the water, wishing she were someone else, somewhere else.

Maribelle jumped off the bed and walked to the open window. To her left was a shiny spot on the floor, possibly a puddle. Raleigh suspected Supy had peed there but decided not to mention it. A wind gust folded around the trees and hedges. It slightly jangled the house. The waves were crashing into the coastline beneath a full moon.

"Samuel slept in here from time to time. In this room." Maribelle said.

"Really? Why?"

"Either he snored, or he'd been out too late. I was irked."

"Alex snores. Not all the time, but enough."

"Alex is alive, you're lucky. Here I am without Samuel." Maribelle's hair blew off her face, her profile was fragile.

Raleigh felt sick. Sick for what was ahead for her sister. The wind was swiping at their faces. She thought of what Travis said about the blasts from the east that had churned up the Intracoastal that morning. How Samuel had hit "a submerged object," according to the Coast Guard.

"I'm so sorry," she said. Was Supy lifting her left eyebrow at her? Did dogs do that?

Maribelle stared out at the ocean again. The moon had moved to the south. "We were married for twelve years. He was so scheduled. Samuel was always packing it all into the day—work, tennis, weightlifting. The boat. The fucking boat."

It was almost two a.m. Raleigh wondered if Caleb, who woke up around now every night, would miss her when he called out her name and Alex came in. Their house on List Road, in the middle of the block without any dramatic views, seemed like another planet.

There was a wrath about Maribelle that was filtering into their space. Her sister's hair was loose and bunching around her shoulders. Raleigh's anxiety was rising. She had no idea if Maribelle was about to whisper something revealing or take a book from the dresser and throw it at the wall.

Her sister stretched her arms over her head. "Of course, we were both out around town, his work, travels for Barrows, my schedule at the magazine. How much time does anyone spend in their house?"

Maribelle was right, Raleigh nodded nervously. Were she asked to paint Maribelle's life with Samuel, it would not be in their home. Raleigh imagined them at the trendiest restaurants, glamorous dinner parties, the two of them highlighted among other guests.

"This never happened—that's what I tell myself." Maribelle fluffed up the pillows on her side of the bed, she was almost in a sitting position, not quite. Her eyes were no longer brown; they had turned murky.

The AC purred through the vents, the sheets were glistening, the lamplight was low. Supy started to doze in the corner on a quilt Maribelle had put down. Raleigh thought *if only this were a sleepover we had decided on because we're sisters, if only the truth weren't the truth.*

"You know, later, once we were married, we ended up doing these paired things—playing tennis, mixed doubles, our Scrabble Club," Maribelle said. "Samuel would strategize before every activity. Before we went to someone's party, in case there might be lip-synching, he'd go through a few songs he thought would work. I'd push for Beyoncé, and he'd want Fleetwood Mac. He wanted to rehearse our dance moves, yet we didn't have to. We'd win the dance contests at the country clubs anyway."

"Last season's sixties night at Harbor Club, the Dexters won," Raleigh dared to mention this.

"I know, *mainly* we won," Maribelle said.

"Because of you. You're such a good dancer."

Maribelle seemed kind of drifty. Had she heard what Raleigh said?

"We should get some sleep." Raleigh pointed to their sections of the bed. They both settled in, they were like two seahorses facing each other.

"Raleigh, between us, he wasn't impeccable," Maribelle breathed deeply. "I'm not ready to tell Mom or Caroline, not Aunt Bryant either. Samuel, he'd have these trysts, they didn't mean much. He'd come back to me, confess, say he never wanted to hurt me, how much he cared about our marriage. I have tried to be calm, considering how Mom described Samuel. She said women threw themselves at him, people found him irresistible. So, despite what he had done . . ."

"Don't do this, don't do this now. There's no need." Raleigh reached out and tapped her sister's upper arm. Her skin was polished. "There's no reason to talk about . . ."

"No, no. You're my little sister, I'm always trying to be an example. There's no example here, obviously, still I'm confiding in you." Maribelle gushed, seemingly relieved to be saying these things out loud. "The others, those women, they faded away. Until recently when Samuel fell for someone."

"Let's not do this tonight. You're too upset. Look at what you've been through." Raleigh said.

"No, I'm okay talking with you, Raleigh. You believe me, don't you? That it was right to tough it out to be with Samuel? I kept asking myself what he didn't get from me that he found in her."

A moment later Maribelle fell asleep. Her eyelids weren't covering her eyes completely. Raleigh found it to be eerie, like her sister was watching out for her husband who wasn't coming back.

What was it they say about the spirit on the day someone has died? Was Samuel's spirit hovering over them? Raleigh, shaking, walked to the window where the moon had shifted. It was rising directly overhead.

CHAPTER FOUR

Maribelle

"**M**aribelle, please, you have to come," Caroline was pleading. "I can't tell Mom no for you."

"Why? Just tell her I'm back at work, I can't do it."

"Jesus, shit, c'mon, Maribelle." Caroline pushed back. "Mom was in the office the day after Dad died. She won't see it like that." Neither sister mentioned this was not a litmus test nor was it comparable. Barrows meant the world to their mother.

"I am not Mom—that's obvious," Maribelle said. "Besides, she wasn't interrogated by some Coast Guard officer right after Dad died, was she?"

"No, she wasn't," Caroline agreed. "How did that go?"

Maribelle thought of Officer Breeley's visit to her house yesterday, how he tried to convince her that his questions were pro forma. He sat in Samuel's favorite pull-up chair, calling her "Mrs. Walker." How he shifted his body weight in his dark uniform, his heft almost blotted out the paleness of the room. His features and face were square, his hands wide when he held up his notepad and pen. He asked each question in a deliberate, velvety voice.

"Could you describe what happened that morning?" he began.

"We had breakfast," Maribelle told him. "Samuel wanted to take the *Vertigo* out to clear his head before work."

"Clear his head?" Officer Breeley asked. "Was something troubling him?"

"No!" She was speaking too emphatically. Suddenly there was a surge of guilt, although she hadn't done anything wrong. "He wanted to take a spin. The night before, we'd been out late, he'd been emceeing a big charity event."

Officer Breeley scribbled notes.

Maribelle answered the next slew of questions on autopilot. What did she and her husband have that morning for breakfast? What was he wearing? Who had been at the event?

She had looked away, feeling drained.

"Mrs. Walker? Excuse me?"

"I'm sorry, could you repeat that?"

"Would you describe your husband as someone who would speed in his boat?" Officer Breeley asked.

"Sure, but also someone who follows the rules," she replied.

"Would you say his familiarity with the waterways included stormy conditions?"

"I always think of him as a seasoned boat person who knew what to do. He steered us through a sudden storm last winter, completely calm and collected."

"And a strong swimmer?" Officer Breeley kept writing in his notebook.

"He was a lifeguard in high school. Yes, a very good swimmer."

"Any enemies, any problems that you know of?" His pen was poised for her answer.

"None that I know of."

"Money problems, marital problems, work issues?" He squinched his eyes.

"No, there was nothing odd, nothing wrong," Maribelle sucked in her breath.

Officer Breeley waited a minute. She wondered if he knew she was lying—in part. Wasn't he trained to read a person's face and interpret gestures?

"Are you certain?" he asked.

Her gaze moved past him, to the windows that faced the ocean. Who was she protecting here? It wasn't Officer Breeley's fault, but Maribelle hated him.

"As certain as I can be," she had said. "Nothing was wrong."

"Maribelle, are you there?" Caroline's voice sounded far off. "Did it go okay with the officer?"

"Fine," Maribelle said. She felt numb.

"Well, then let me press on. It's important that you make an appearance today."

Maribelle closed her eyes. "Okay. I suppose. I'm actually too tired to face the consequences if I don't."

When she walked into the Barrows conference room, she assumed she would be first. Yet Raleigh was there by the window. Wasn't she always by a window, contemplating flight? She turned to Maribelle. They hugged quickly, sadly. "Isn't it incredible how cars drive along Royal Palm Way, off to a festive, sunny destination, while we're at family meeting? With Samuel's memorial service hanging over us?" Raleigh asked.

Someone had placed bottles of Fiji water at each seat at the conference table. Since Maribelle had never come by Barrows on a regular basis, she was trying to conjure up Samuel at his day-to-day responsibilities. She should have paid more attention, maybe.

Raleigh followed her. "Do you know what this is about? I hope Alex makes it. He's gone to Jupiter, to the inlet there, for his latest painting. A contemporary. I texted him to turn around." She fiddled with her hair, waves fell around her face, not in a studied, hair-salon sort of way.

"Caroline says we won't be here long, although I have no idea," Maribelle said.

Travis came in with his iPad under one arm and laptop under the other. "You know, I look outside and instead of being pleased it's golf weather, I feel like I've been trampled on. Samuel and I would have squeezed in nine holes on a day like this."

Raleigh looped back to the window, a few northern parulas circled overhead.

"Alex would join you sometime, Travis, when you're ready for a round."

"That's kind of you of you to offer," Maribelle said.

Travis attempted to straighten up, he offered an abbreviated smile. Caroline arrived next wearing an ecru, monochromatic affect, including her platform sandals. When she walked across the oak planks, Maribelle remembered how she had insisted on this particular floor. Samuel was pleased that vendors for new products appreciated the look. Especially younger companies, startup beverages, and snack foods.

"Does anyone know why we're here?" Maribelle knew she sounded anxious.

"Not exactly. Marketing isn't presenting." Caroline, in contrast, sounded corporate. She applied a mauvy plum lipstick.

After Raleigh looked at the seating arrangement, she placed her canvas bookbag on the middle chair in the lineup.

Alex rushed in, wearing sneaks and a black T-shirt. *The artiste.* "Hello, all."

He approached Raleigh, their lips brushed together for a dry, married kind of kiss. Maribelle watched as her little sister pulled away first. It seemed abrupt. Every few months Maribelle wondered what Alex thought about being married into the family. Her impression was that Samuel had liked it—at least he welcomed working at the company. Why hadn't she ever asked him if he had found it complicated to be part of the Barrows clan?

Travis walked to the thermostat, an ergonomically sound system that he had insisted on installing. He fiddled with it although the air was filtered and already felt fresh.

"Caro, did you hear from Lucinda?" he asked without looking at her.

At that moment, their mother swept in, "I'm here."

Lucinda spoke loudly; her words filled the entire space. She was safely stylish for early "season," suggesting she had another plan as soon as they finished the meeting. Perhaps a stop at Vintage Tales or an afternoon tea at Brazilian Court with Rita Damon and Dee Willis.

No one was warm or friendly. Lucinda placed herself at the head of the table, filling what Samuel and Travis called the Reed Chair, a seat no one else would dare use.

"I am channeling your father today," Lucinda announced. "We will be brief."

"That's fine," Maribelle sighed. "I've got to check in at the office." Everyone seemed impressed that she was directed, rather than unraveling. At least when it came to her work.

"As brief as I can be," Lucinda said.

There was a bit of glancing at their cell phones then back to Lucinda. Directly across the street at Surfside, Palm Beachers were having a quick Greek salad or BLT before spiraling around, browsing at C. Orrico or Classic Books, enroute to the Avenue. If a few of these shoppers had ever been bereft, they had adjusted. Maribelle needed to believe it, that this sadness lessened. That she wasn't going to end up stepping from room to room in their house, waiting for her husband to show up. She needed to accept that Samuel's desk, with the Brice Marden purchased by their father hanging behind it, would be empty from here on out. Framed pictures of Barrows openings from Tampa to Savannah to Maine were on the low, sleek bookcase. Like her husband was still in the room when he was indelibly gone.

Lucinda cleared her throat. Maribelle thought how well her children knew her temperament; what they weren't sure of was her intent. "I've come to talk about Samuel," she said.

Maribelle stared at her neck for some reason—maybe to see whether she was getting those cords that everyone else's mother seemed to have already.

"Why?" Maribelle asked.

"Because he was a member of the Barrows family. He was an attentive son-in-law."

Lucinda paused to look at her other two sons-in-law, the ones who were alive. They were scarcely breathing. Had their chairs been able to swivel, they would have swiveled away from her. Maribelle wondered what it might be like to have a mother who was not always bandying about the idea of whom she preferred. A mother who didn't continually evaluate her friends, her daughters, and their husbands.

"Except," Lucinda paused again. "I'm not certain that Samuel was trustworthy."

Trustworthy. Maribelle felt them waiting for her defense. She knew she was expected to say that Samuel was dependable and honest, dedicated to Barrows. Then again, the women, the affairs, Samuel had been unfaithful. Was he like that at work too? Completely disarming while something else at the same time? Had he secretly resented her parents from way back before they all got to Palm Beach? A sensation began, *what if she wasn't able to vouch for her husband?*

She sat on her hands. "Mom, what are you talking about? What are you *saying*?"

"The morning that Samuel died, I was planning to speak with him. I'd found out a few days before the accident—when I was going through the books—that there was a circumstance, one that was cleverly camouflaged."

Raleigh and Alex were listening carefully. Caroline kept trying to catch Travis's eye while he stared intently at his laptop as if seeking an answer.

"No, no," Maribelle said. "That makes no sense."

"A monthly payment went to a fast-food vendor by the name of Riptide Corporation."

Travis stroked the spot above his lip where a mustache would be. A nervous habit, something Caroline said he did only during the most stressful situations. When their daughter, Violet, was four and went into anaphylactic shock after being stung by a bee; when his younger stepbrother was in a motorcycle crash and in traction for months. And now. Maribelle could only imagine what her husband had confessed to Travis.

"Although we don't have all the details, it seems that Samuel was Riptide Corporation," Lucinda said.

"That's insane. Samuel was dedicated to this company . . ." Maribelle said.

"The leases, the traffic in and out of our stores—the numbers are up. The stores are packed. What's static is the revenue. It's been decreasing for over twelve months." Lucinda shook her head. "Travis, what do you have to say?"

Despite the soundproofing, there was the roiling of the street.

"Lucinda," Travis cleared his throat. "I worked with Samuel every day . . ."

"Me too," Caroline said. "Samuel did whatever he could. He kept bringing in new products to sell, researching microwavable foods that were decent. At meetings, he pushed the hardest—new ideas, outreach. He wanted more development."

"Samuel wanted what was best for Barrows. He was obsessed with it. Travis, you know this," Maribelle was insistent, she had to be.

"I thought so, too," Alex spoke softly. "From what he said at dinners, or when we were out on the boat."

"Didn't Samuel know every single company that stocked the stores?" Raleigh chimed in. "Someone, maybe you, Caroline, told me that."

A trail of sunlight filtered in through the blinds, almost dividing the family into two factions. Maribelle was aligned with her sisters; on the other side were Alex and Travis with Lucinda at the head. The light flitted around them.

"Maybe, just maybe, there's something in his will that indicates . . ." Lucinda began.

"Mom!" Caroline interrupted.

"He's left everything to me, that's all," Maribelle's voice was weary. "I spoke with Daryl Dexter. He said when I'm ready, we'll go over the details. I suppose that means we'll sit in his office and read the will together. Before the memorial."

"Stop it, please." Raleigh held her hands up to her ears as she always did when it was too much to bear. Her fragility coiled around the room.

A clock ought to have been ticking, but there wasn't one. Instead, there was the ding of a text coming in, then another. A few of them had forgotten to silence their phones. No one checked, it wasn't wise to do so.

Lucinda raised her eyebrows. "Did he talk about spending money on anything new, Maribelle?"

"No, he didn't. Samuel and I talked about Barrows—it was his favorite topic. I don't believe what you are saying." Maribelle said. She had begun to panic.

"The question is reasonable, Maribelle," Lucinda said. "He was your *husband*. What do you know?"

How Lucinda viewed things underscored her belief that

husbands were imperative. She swore by the concept that men required attention and frequent molding. In her rulebook, one needed a handle on what husbands do, how they were.

"Does anyone ever totally understand what someone else is thinking?" Raleigh asked.

"The wife is sometimes the last to know," Caroline said.

Maribelle glanced at the very cool mid-century furniture and remembered how she and her sisters worked together on this room, on all the Barrows offices, when they were redesigned three years ago. They had chosen a wood and Murano glass sideboard that their parents bought in Madrid. They wanted Wegner Kennedy chairs to surround a Nakashima dining table that worked as a conference table. There was Raleigh's painting of the three of them, an ethereal, post-Renaissance portrait, originally called *Barrows Sisters: Kesgrave*, which hung on the long wall to Maribelle's left. Lucinda nixed any memory of having lived west of the Apalachicola River, and since no one wished to incite her, Raleigh struck out "Kesgrave."

Lucinda stood up from her dead husband's chair and started pacing around the table. "Travis? You must have something to report as CEO."

The focus shifted to Travis, who paused before speaking.

"Samuel and I were in the process of updating Barrows. Taking the locations beyond a chain of convenience stores."

Maribelle twisted toward him, "You do know something, don't you?"

"I don't, Maribelle, I know nothing," Travis said.

She wondered if he could pass a lie detector test.

"Caroline, do you?" Lucinda asked. "I mean, you do have a position at the company. You've worked with Samuel for ten years."

"I'm in marketing, Mom," Caroline said. "I wasn't at the financial meetings."

A recollection of her parents' acumen for business popped into Maribelle's head. How they talked about what people needed when they were on the road and ran inside a store. Their shared perception of what to offer the customer. How life had become since Reed was gone and Lucinda was in charge. Suddenly, a greige cast fell over her sisters. She felt it, too, except instead of being refined, it was a sickly shade.

"Where is the money now?" Alex asked. "How can you find or prove anything?"

"Proof. We'll get to that." Lucinda scowled. "Let me tell you about the effect—the ramifications. Not just for the company, in terms of financial damage. But by hurting Barrows, Samuel hurt us personally."

Raleigh and Maribelle exchanged one of their youngest-to-eldest sister moments. The two of them entwined—that's how it was, whatever the occasion. Maribelle knew Caroline had picked up on it without emoting while Lucinda gave them another withering look.

"I have held this family, this business together," Lucinda said. "You know what Barrows means to me. My ideas, your father's talent at taking it out into the world. Dad and I mentored Samuel, we taught him and Travis what they know. I'm the one who has worked—no, *danced*, nonstop—not only for the company but to live in Palm Beach, as I do, as we do. To be regarded as we are. It's critical to each of you. We have fifty-two employees in this office, the Palm Beach office, who depend on us. To say nothing of people who work in each state in the stores. We have to consider how we are perceived around town, as 'players' in the cliques. Definitely, there is our collective reputation."

Raleigh started to sob—small, slurpy sobs—while Maribelle stared at her wedding ring, an emerald cut five-carat diamond from Graff with baguettes on either side. Yesterday she thought about when to stop wearing it, if she might sell it. Now this. Why would Samuel steal from the business when he, when they, as a couple, had so much? For his mistress? Maribelle stiffened. It was impossible to miss him, yet she did.

"I'll expect a game plan, a remedy," Lucinda went on. "We'll get through Samuel's memorial, the reception. After that, we will get to work. We'll track down the money—we'll get it back."

Travis was up, it was his turn to say something reassuring. Except he, like the rest, stayed silent. There was a knock, and Estelle, longtime major-domo and devotée of Barrows, came to the door.

"Excuse me, Mr. Sears, I noticed it's getting late." Estelle pushed her short, ash-colored hair away from her ear lobe with her left hand. In her right hand, she waved two menus toward Travis. "Would you like me to order from Cucina or the Colony? Caesar salads or sliced chicken sandwiches?"

Was this simply another meeting that resolved little, thought Maribelle, with lunch as the highlight?

"Thank you, Estelle," Travis said. "Is anyone hungry?"

Everyone shook their heads. "Are you certain?" Estelle was surprised, conveying this could be a first for her. She lingered a moment.

"We are certain," Travis said.

She closed the door, purposeless. Lucinda waited before speaking. Maribelle knew her mother would count to ten before she picked up again, measuring every word. That was her technique when she was on a rampage.

"However it can be done, I want the right answers. To that end, I'm in search of the smartest forensic accountant."

"Is that really necessary, Mom?" Caroline asked. "We have in-house number crunchers. Travis can do some . . ."

"I think it's absolutely necessary, that I assure you," Lucinda said.

"Why?" Raleigh fiddled with her pencil, tapping the eraser against the table. The light settled directly over her. The veins on her temples were showing—her skin was that thin. "Travis has an MBA in finance."

"I do. I can look into it, Lucinda." Travis's voice sounded like it had been dubbed. Poorly dubbed. The words and his mouth movements didn't match.

Maribelle felt queasy, it was too much. Another memory— of watching *Saturday Night Live* skits with Samuel—ricocheted through her mind. How they had laughed as Supy snuggled between them. Next she remembered a conversation with Samuel, a month ago at most. He wanted to put "sit-and-work" areas with prepared foods and more caffeinated drinks in Barrows. What had that meant? More fake corporations, more stolen money? *What was he doing? Who was he?*

"That's fine, an outside forensic accountant is fine," Maribelle said flatly. "Whatever's best."

Lucinda had stopped tallying their expressions. She waved her hands dismissively.

"As I said, we'll need a forensic accountant, independent scrutiny. We've no idea where this will end up. It seems that over seven-and-a-half million dollars is missing."

CHAPTER FIVE

Caroline

"This was a fine idea," Lucinda said. "It was yours, wasn't it, Caroline?"

"Well, Maribelle's idea really. She felt no one wanted a religious setting, she chose this instead."

Caroline didn't dare mention that The Church of Bethesda by the Sea would have been her preference. Since Samuel died, she had been on high alert, ultra-careful to not upset Maribelle. She watched her sister as a young widow with dread, determined to go along with any of her plans. When Maribelle decided on the Palm Beach Literary Society for Samuel's memorial, Caroline began arranging it at once.

"I only hope it's large enough," Aunt Bryant said. "Can that be checked?"

"Up to four hundred seats, isn't that right, Caroline?" Lucinda said. "Plus standing room."

Today the room filled quickly as Samuel's various admirers filed in. Business associates, clearly from out of town in their dark suits—so *not* Southern Florida—their hair artfully tussled in the new '60s throwback style. Philanthropy "stars." Women in their finest day dresses. Wannabe vendors in their hipster attire. And, tucked away in the back where Lucinda could ignore their presence, Kesgrave cousins. No matter what the occasion, Caroline knew her mother wouldn't allow a reminder of their past.

There were others, people whom Caroline had never seen before, who were more Fort Lauderdale than Palm Beach. They were followed by Miami types—women in tight, low-cut tops and men in bracelets and a few necklaces as if they were headed to lounges and supper clubs, although it was midday.

"I'm sorry, how did *these people* learn about this?" Lucinda asked.

"Mom, it was everywhere," Caroline said. "There was a blast to every Barrows employee across the country."

Ryana Delce, the event planner, was walking with precision up and down the aisles and overheard the conversation.

"Oh, Mrs. Barrows," Ryana said. She smiled as if Lucinda should be pleased. "Samuel was CFO of Barrows. It was posted on Facebook, people were tweeting, people from your company posted on Instagram. Some do still read newspapers—Palm Beachers, well, south Floridians, love *The Daily Sheet* and *The Palm Beach Post*."

Ryana oozed confidence in her stilettos, a style that gathered dust in Caroline's closet. She and her sisters had moved on to wedges and chunky heels. Ryana tossed her head like it was a charity black-tie, not a memorial service. As she stood at the podium, checking the mic and acoustics, her over-stacked bangles clanked together. She turned down the volume.

Maribelle sat stoically in the front row next to Lucinda and William, Lucinda's replacement husband. On Maribelle's other side were Caroline and Travis, their girls between them. Across the aisle were Alex and Raleigh with Caleb on Raleigh's lap, clinging to his mother as she sobbed. Alex put his arm around her. No one spoke. Caroline reread the handout of the program. Lucinda used it as a fan.

More people than they could handle had signed up to eulogize Samuel. Lucinda and Travis had decided to cut the list, making certain Samuel's cousins, whom they called "hillbillies," would have no chance to speak. The Walker family, comprised of Samuel's two sisters and his mother, had come to the private funeral four days after the accident, so they declined to attend today. Caroline suspected it was the "Lucinda effect" that discouraged them from returning to Palm Beach. Her parents had viewed Samuel's family as too local, too rural, even twenty years ago when they had lived five miles down the road. If Lucinda had considered Samuel's family tawdry back then, her present existence only magnified it.

Besides, Lucinda was getting her wish as one after another of stellar "islanders" delivered praise for Samuel. The memorial kicked off perfectly with Ryana motioning as if she were a maestro. Stenton Fields, head of the board of the Arts and Media Foundation and newly titled head of environmental awareness, was the master of ceremonies. His elegance—that shock of white hair, ramrod posture, and "healthy" tan—silenced the room. While guests were enraptured as he spoke, Caroline was too worried about Maribelle to pay attention. She glanced over at her sister, who seemed stunned, as if somehow she was *mistaken* for the aggrieved and not actually that person.

Stenton was wrapping it up in a persuasive tone. "Samuel's place in Palm Beach philanthropy, his largess, his generosity, shall never be forgotten," he said. "This young man's love of animals, his concern for the environment, his championing of the disabled . . . what a fine, upstanding citizen Samuel Walker was! A paragon!"

Travis was up next. In tears, he stood clutching the side of the stand, too sad to straighten up and be dignified. Caroline had an urge to pinch him into reality. Her husband needed to be stronger, to admire Samuel without being personally bereft. That was the standard, how could he not know? Yet as he began, she knew it wasn't possible. He was almost mewling as he began his finely edited remarks.

"Samuel Walker was my friend since we were boys. From the day we met in kindergarten, through high school, where we both played football back on the Gulf Coast—he was captain—to the day he died, he was like a brother to me. I'll miss him every day."

Nasty looks were coming from Lucinda. She was bending at her waist, her head forward, to let Caroline know that Travis's simplicity wasn't acceptable. That Travis was basic, that he revealed life back in Kesgrave to honor Samuel, was an affront to Lucinda. The Palm Beach ladies seemed curious. While arriving in Palm Beach with an amorphous past was common, the revelation of a backwater story was not.

Ryana was attuned enough to realize this. By somehow catching Travis's eye, she earned her extraordinary fee for managing this social gathering. Although Caroline only half heard her husband's words, she was relieved when he segued to current memories of Samuel for his finale. He and Samuel scuba diving, each hitting a hole-in-one, and bench pressing three hundred pounds.

Next up were the predictable men, whose wives will not speak today: tennis partners, golfers, friends from Longreens and the Harbor Club. Fungible men who were as effective as Ambien at putting the guests to sleep with their remarks and memories. Those who had known Samuel, those with their own slick boats and other trophies—Ferraris, Maseratis, double-sized lots on this island—looked off into the distance. For all their possessions, they knew an accident might befall anyone.

Ryana immediately summoned the eulogizers who were wait-ing their turn. A man in a blazer with thin brown hair was up. He introduced himself as Ray, a manager of three Barrows loca-tions in the Naples area. Samuel and he were tennis partners at a country club there. Whenever Samuel got to town, apparently, they were in a tournament. And won! "How he loved to win," Ray said. "But what Samuel Walker loved most was making money. He wasn't only industrious, he was genius at it."

Lucinda was giving Caroline a signal to cut them off. Caroline knew she couldn't manage it. These guests had given up their time—a coveted commodity—to be at Samuel's memorial. They wanted to praise him. She pretended she didn't see her mother's agitated gestures.

A very blonde and voluptuous woman, maybe forty-five, introduced herself as Eileen. Her claim to fame was that she had worked at the first Barrows in Tampa for over twenty years. "Sam-uel supported the eating disorder chapter near us," she wept. "He wrote such a big check. When I told him how I struggled as a single mother to find afterschool programming for my kids so I could keep my hours at Barrows, he wrote the check for that too. He became a local hero to the moms, and he wasn't even a local!"

The next woman eulogizer stood up, ready to take the podium. She and Eileen embraced as they exchanged places, both were crying and sucking in air. Nanette stood very tall and thanked Maribelle for the chance to be part of a "celebration of Samuel's life."

"Working at Barrows is a family affair." She stopped crying to smile at the room, her lipstick was very red. "That was my sister who just spoke and now, I'd like to talk about Samuel in South Beach, where I am assistant manager at the Barrows on Collins Avenue. Samuel started a gymnastics center for children two blocks away, then the South Beach Jazz club, and six months ago, he helped me with a campaign for Greener Earth Savior. Not only was this incredible, but let's face it—Samuel was the smartest and strongest, like Superman."

Superman. Caroline knew her mother was right, the speakers needed to stop. Maribelle looked stricken. Ryana and the audience seemed intrigued. That was the strangest part. She pulled in her breath and watched as the last and most surprising speaker teetered up the aisle. A twenty-something woman with a bad spray tan and a nose ring in a black mini-dress and shiny knee-high boots. Palm Beach eyebrows were raised; the memorial had become live theatre.

She stood in front of refined, placid faces, excluding Raleigh, who was sobbing. "Samuel was the best boss ever." This woman announced.

Caroline did not look at Travis. Weren't they wondering the same thing? Since when had Samuel instilled a hands-on presence at the stores? Carefully, they avoided Lucinda.

"I wouldn't have been able to take a full-time job without free daycare," the last speaker said. "Barrows in Atkinson County, Georgia, offered incredible benefits to staff. Even though he was super rich, he knew what it was like to be poor, and he was so kind to all of us." She shed a few discreet tears and looked at Maribelle. "Mrs. Walker, your husband was topnotch."

Travis squeezed Caroline's hand sharply, he wanted her to react, to stop the show. What could she possibly do? Lucinda had red blotches on her neck and cheeks. She seemed to be gauging her rows of friends. Mrs. A, Rita Damon, the Mercer twins, Veronica Cutler. Each woman was unreadable, they stared straight at the speaker. Aunt Bryant looked dumbstruck while Raleigh was delicately throwing up into a wad of tissues. Maribelle was waxen—was she getting enough oxygen?

Strangers not only extolled Samuel but *reported* on his out-of-town generosity. That it was lost on Palm Beachers meant little, it was dangerous information for the family. Everyone knew

Lucinda wanted blood for the missing funds from Barrows. Now they knew—Samuel was a secret Robin Hood, wherever he went. *With Barrows money.*

And the causes? Ones that Lucinda disdained. Caroline suddenly understood. Her mother didn't believe in daycare and afterschool activities for grade-school children because they weren't an option in Kesgrave when her girls were growing up. Lucinda wasn't keen on anyone getting a free ride on her dime. Her view was they could pull themselves up, just as she had. Not that she was overly stingy; she was selective. Her donations went to causes that fueled her status. The Barrowses chose whatever promoted the family and positioned them in society. There was no check written without Lucinda's approval. What the hell had Samuel been up to?

Once the memorial was over, Caroline longed to avoid her sisters and mother, knowing what was next. Yet she needed to fend off the crowd that was orbiting around Maribelle at the entrance to the Literary Society. Her sister, celebrity widow of the day, would be too overwhelmed by what she had just heard to deal with the onslaught. Too late, Caroline realized this should have been anticipated. The situation practically required a bodyguard. Ryana wisely waved every kind of guest—elegant, old, young, outlandish—in another direction, away from Maribelle.

Aunt Bryant appeared. "You might want to get back to Maribelle's, Caroline. I'll help, don't worry. Look, Stenton Fields and Alex are edging in. Maribelle will be okay."

As soon the girls put on their headphones and opened their iPads in the backseat of Travis's Range Rover, Caroline turned to her husband.

"What's next? Will some Barrows employee from Grand Rapids, Michigan, tell us she's the real wife, the mother of Samuel's child? Was he a polygamist too? Is there some company he was creating to rival Barrows?"

Travis swerved recklessly onto South County Road. He looked like he had been bitten by a shark and drained of blood.

"I swear, Caro, I'm as shocked as you are . . ."

She didn't believe him. He was covering for Samuel, he always had. But why? Were they in it together? Was she going to wake up one Sunday to find Travis gone, having absconded to some island from which no one could be extricated, laden down with buckets of Barrows money, leaving her on the hook for it? Would she have to pack up by night and leave town with Maribelle and her daughters? *Samuel, Travis. Travis, Samuel, pieces of shit.*

"Travis! You were *best friends*. You knew everything about each other since second grade."

"I didn't know what he was up to. Only that he swore it would work out."

"You couldn't tell me that much? Am I your wife or what?"

"That you are."

With each mile that took them farther from the Literary Society, Travis drove more steadily. Wasn't it strange, Caroline thought, how so quickly after the service, Samuel's memory felt sliced into a dozen parts. Slices of him hurled around the stratosphere, beyond their reach. She imagined guests piled into their cars and SUVs, headed to Maribelle's reception.

She and Travis and the girls, they too followed the herd. Caroline closed her eyes and decided to wait for her husband to concede.

CHAPTER SIX

Raleigh

Raleigh's tires crunched against the Belgian block pavers on Maribelle's driveway as she steered toward the garage. The memorial service had been too long, painful really. Speaker after speaker, it was exhausting to sit through, endless to be there. Now she was alone in her car, having decided against bringing Caleb for this portion of the day. There wouldn't be anyone his age at the reception, he would have clung to her. And she needed to be available to Maribelle. Her sister's house, despite the vast square footage, was going to be mobbed.

Located on King's Road, near Mar-a-Lago, Maribelle's house was the dreamiest of their family homes. Dense hedges surrounded the property, hibiscus and petunias were situated along the path. The spare interior and pale hues reminded Raleigh of a cool glass of water. Maribelle was the only one in their family who lived on the ocean side, not the Intracoastal, in spare, feathery rooms. At night, she and Samuel had shone floodlights across the A1A to the beach, and while slightly showy, it was magical to see.

Raleigh angled the rearview mirror, her eyes were bleary from this sad, bizarre day. She began applying eyeliner and undereye concealer to enhance her Palm Beach persona. She had two minutes to spare before the onslaught.

"Over there, that works," Tanya, Maribelle's assistant, pointed to the dining table when Raleigh walked inside.

Rosie and her sister, Denise, Lucinda's housekeepers, were placing trays—smoked salmon, egg salad, and cucumber tea sandwiches—at the far end. While they scurried out through the swinging door and returned with fruit platters, they sniffled. Tears ran down Denise's face.

"Can we try for less emotion," Tanya clapped, directing her to the sideboard. "And the lemon tartlets and brownies from Stephanie's—near the fruit bowl?"

Since Raleigh had arrived ahead of the others, she moved on past the kitchen and into the living room. She admired her sister's art collection, Ashley Andrews, Yasmine Diaz, Frank Moore, Christopher Wool, Caroline Walker. How Maribelle and Samuel had loved spending their Saturday afternoons going to galleries and art shows. Alex and Raleigh, as artists, were asked their thoughts—what art to buy, what was trending. Samuel claimed that art should be chosen with one's gut, not one's head or wallet. For a moment, Raleigh was transported, looking closely at each painting. Until she heard a crunch of bodies. Caroline had arrived and was greeting those who filed in—she held her hand out floppily. Raleigh returned to the foyer.

"I don't know," Caroline whispered. "Maybe we'll start to believe Samuel is gone."

"Why is that?" Raleigh asked.

"Because we're getting through the rituals." Caroline sounded testy.

Lucinda was coming nearer, then Travis and the girls. Raleigh watched how they spun through the living room, Harper in a papaya-colored dress, Violet in mango, as if they believed their uncle might walk in, amused at this colossal layer of woe.

Violet tugged at Caroline's arm. "Mom, what's going on?"

Caroline bent down, toward her daughters. "Your father and I explained—this is the gathering that comes after the service. You heard the eulogies, people talking about how great Uncle Samuel was, and now they'll come to Aunt Maribelle's house to keep her company, for a visit."

Violet eyed the brownies. "And we'll eat a lot of good food? Is it for us?"

"For everyone," Caroline said.

There was a brief break in the weather, a light bounced off the walls. One could easily have mistaken this for a cocktail party for friends and neighbors or a fundraiser. The women were dressed in misty green, shades of blue, and requisite black. No one had approached the food while the crowd at the bar was limitless, guests were three deep.

"What are we waiting for?" Harper asked.

"Aunt Maribelle," Lucinda answered. "She's driving back from the service with Aunt Bryant."

"We're hungry," Violet said.

"Ask Rosie, girls, she'll have some goodies for you," Caroline tried to smile.

The girls floated toward the kitchen while Raleigh remained. Guests were congregating in the middle of the living room. Parts of conversations wafted upward, Trisha Delaney and Ramona Letts were speaking quickly: *Lucinda's daughters, ravishing... the youngest... no, she's the eldest... someplace you never heard of... the father's company... tough road ahead... no, no children...*

More people, mournful, curious, infused the house, including Samuel's tennis partner, Harry Scott, and another group of

Kesgrave relatives. One of them made a beeline for Raleigh, a man probably in his late thirties with a beard and a man bun. He was truly handsome; were he to shave his head, he'd still be that. She noticed that he wore a Pinestream class ring.

"Good to see you again, although for a sad occasion," he said. "I remember you from . . ."

"I'm sorry, you might have me confused with Caroline, the middle sister. We all look alike. I'm the youngest, I was ten when we moved to South Florida," Raleigh felt defensive.

"You live around this place, too? Fancy town," he said.

"Yes, yes. Excuse me . . ." She started to edge away. Lucinda would not approve of their talking.

The room quieted down. Maribelle walked in. Her shoulders were back, yet her chin was tucked. Raleigh wondered how that was doable. Maribelle was in a Jackie O-style sheath, black, sleeveless, a tragic dress. Aunt Bryant steered her to where Raleigh and Caroline stood. Suddenly, Raleigh recalled the film, *Water*, where widows in India in the 1940s were either burned with their dead husbands' bodies or sent to a kind of orphanage for widows. In Palm Beach, there was no such punishment, yet being a widow changed everything. Samuel's death had already rendered Maribelle a survivor, someone other.

Behind her a torrent of people waited to soothe her. Raleigh doubted anyone could absorb Maribelle's sadness or that their gestures made a difference. A few women curved their necks in a questioning position.

"Is there anything I can get you, Maribelle?" Tanya came over to ask.

"I'm fine, Tanya," Maribelle said. But she wasn't.

"You might sit down," Raleigh suggested.

"No, no thanks." Maribelle answered.

Anyway, Raleigh knew whether Maribelle stood or sat, Samuel was dead. No matter who paid their respects, her sister no longer had Samuel. There was no Samuel to open snail mail, trashing solicitations, laughing with his wife and friends. There was no Samuel to choose *Abbey Road* on Spotify. He wasn't ever going to bike again on the Lake Trail or eat dinner at Cucina or Sant Ambroeus. To Raleigh's left, Alex stood with William, who had Lucinda's stole, a Loro Piana fringed number, draped over his arm, anticipating her every need. Beside them were Henry Rochester and Lucas Damon—established Palm Beach husbands.

"Does anyone know exactly what happened that morning?" Henry Rochester asked.

"No, we won't know until the investigation is completed." Alex's voice rose a notch.

"Typically, the person at the wheel, even someone who knows the waterway, speeds, isn't cautious enough," Lucas Damon said.

"You can be certain the Coast Guard will be thorough," William said.

Raleigh watched how Alex nodded. He was working to appear polite. At six foot four, he was too tall for the other men. His eyes skimmed over everyone's heads. He blinked when he saw Raleigh listening and stepped aside to whisper in her ear. "Is there anything special I should do or say?"

"Maybe keep being sociable."

"Sure." He skipped the "r" when he said it.

The wind was starting up, rushing around the house. Raleigh stepped closer to Lucinda. "Ever since Samuel died, the weather has been too blowy."

"You know January can be like that, Raleigh." Lucinda's lips curled, uncurled. "What has happened is a trauma. Poor Maribelle. We must be strong for her."

"What will she do with the nights?" Raleigh asked.

"The nights?"

"Nights without Samuel." Raleigh started to cry.

"The nights are like the days, Maribelle will learn, your sister is popular."

Lucinda looked away, the kindness in her voice rotated into the edginess that Raleigh knew too well. After Reed died, it didn't matter that Raleigh and her sisters were fatherless so much as it was Lucinda's loss. In Palm Beach, there were plenty of widows, but Lucinda ran with it, she became a pro. She had lots of younger men as arm candy for lots of parties. Until she met William. Then she easily traded in widowhood for a second husband.

Tanya switched on some unfamiliar overhead lighting. Raleigh thought each guest looked tinged. Lucinda's cheekbones were too accented, her blush was the wrong shade. Both Maribelle and Caroline looked like they had pulled an all-nighter. Aunt Bryant's roots gleamed for almost an inch, her honey-colored hair followed.

Lucinda handed Raleigh a monogrammed handkerchief, *LBH*, for Lucinda Barrows Harnett. She wiped her eyes and tucked it into her bag.

"Excellent," Lucinda said in a cutting voice. "No more crying, Raleigh."

Like Tanya, Lucinda had begun to hunt the faces of the crowd, an inventory of the guests. Raleigh wondered if it was a diversion or if her mother was simply computing who had come and in what style. There were plenty of looks to choose from—Theory, Prada, Etro, pearls, once again chic—silhouettes that ranged from balloon skirts, to pencil knee-length, to midi dresses, to cropped pants. Those with frizzy hairlines in need of another round of Keratin treatment stood out.

"See how Travis moves around, talking to different clusters, Raleigh," Lucinda frowned. "I'll go off with the ladies from the Literary Society. Caroline is with people from Barrows, a few managers are over in the . . ."

"I worry people are so *curious*, voyeurs, really. Some are

cornering Maribelle," Tanya said. She was pushing her grosgrain headband further back in this quick, repetitive movement.

"They're converging—they want to show up, learn more," Lucinda said.

"Look at the front door." Tanya tipped her forefinger toward the double-vaulted entryway, where a crush of people appeared stuck. A few women had broken the line and emerged. The light fell on the colors they brought into the room. Accents of pale pink, peach, celadon. Raleigh wondered, was it out of kindness that they were paying their respects to Maribelle? Mrs. A materialized, followed by Rita Damon and Patsy Deller. Next was Caroline's group, with Dorey Barnes and Tina Steffen circling in. More mothers with kids at the Academy— Collette Nayers and Katie Casen—had already angled into the living room.

Raleigh saw that Maribelle was paying no attention until her gaze shifted toward Collette. Maribelle eyed her carefully, her narrow arms. How willowy she was. She had red hair in a house filled with blondes.

"Who exactly are these women?" Maribelle put on her sunglasses while she cold stared.

"You know, we've sat at tables with them—at charities. Caroline's group, Mom's friends are coming in, too. Don't think about it." Raleigh tried to be soothing.

"What do you know about Collette?" Maribelle lifted her finger, ready to point. Raleigh wanted to stop her, to say let's not be specific, when Caroline came over.

"Raleigh, didn't you go to Maribelle's reading group a few weeks ago? Will you check whether those women might be outside, huddled together, I suppose, in this weather? Say hello?"

Raleigh wanted to remind Caroline they were in mourning. Instead she walked to the French doors. As she was about to open them, she looked back. Caroline, Collette, and Tina were deep into a chat. Maribelle tapped Raleigh's elbow. "Wait for me, Raleigh, I need to get air."

Outside was a gale force, canisters of anemones were knocking into one another. Raleigh doubted anyone would be there, despite Caroline's plan, and she was right. Maribelle stood next to the infinity pool, water rippled, then slapped onto the flagstones. The two of them huddled toward the sheltered side of the house.

"Let's take a walk in the garden, duck the wind," Raleigh said. "I don't think anyone would care if we're gone a few minutes."

"I'd like that," Maribelle had stopped crying. She seemed distant, as if her husband wasn't the one who had died. If she resisted, this story wouldn't be hers for the rest of her life.

"I think she's one of the ones, you know, Collette Nayers."

Raleigh took her sister's hand. "Are you sure you don't want to come stay with us for a while and not be in this big house alone? Unless Rosie or Denise could stay here with you. Some sort of schedule could be worked out."

Maribelle did an apologetic half smile. "The question is who Samuel really was. Who were those people at the service—what were they talking about? At one point, I thought I was at the wrong funeral, that some other Samuel Walker had died."

"Yeah, well, so much is going on. There's the Coast Guard, there's Mom saying Samuel took money from the company . . ." Raleigh wanted to sound reasonable, confident.

"I want to know if Collette Nayers is someone who had an affair with Samuel. If she's gone out on the *Vertigo* with him." Maribelle's voice was so low, like she could hardly utter the idea.

Raleigh looked east to the ocean side. She wished her sister wasn't fixated on this. "Maribelle, this is overwhelming. It's all too much."

"We can find out about her somehow, right?"

"Maybe you can ask Caroline. She knows everyone," Raleigh offered.

"Maybe. I mean you get it, don't you, Raleigh?

"I do, I get it," she nodded.

Despite how whippy it was, an egret walked around the rim of the property, near the stonewall. Through Maribelle's windows, guests were silhouetted. Fixed objects that filled up her living room and library were brighter, more visible. Raleigh and Maribelle put their arms around each another in what they called a "smoothy hug" when Raleigh was six and Maribelle was sixteen—when Maribelle used to promise, it's the two of us against the world.

CHAPTER SEVEN

Caroline

A fternoon rolled into evening. While it had been ten days since Samuel's accident, no one remembered the last time they had been together—only the three sisters—for drinks and dinner. In the period since Samuel was buried, Caroline and Raleigh had jumped at Maribelle's every ask, including tonight when she decided they should meet at Dada in Delray. When Caroline arrived, the place was buzzing with a crowd that aged her, unlike Palm Beach, where she could count on being younger. At the Leopard Lounge, where she and Travis liked to go dancing on the parquet floor under low lights, there were women who seemed to be ninety, dancing with men who appeared to be sixty. Not that a few hangouts didn't sport younger people, but sixty was youngish in Palm Beach—that was a solace. As Caroline moved toward her sisters, she noticed they were shifting in their chairs, settling in. Were they all going to pretend it was a happy outing? Near the cantaloupe leather bar stools and cognac wood accents, they were seated at a front table, sipping Bianca on the rocks.

"This place seems far away, it's distracting. Almost like we're on vacation," Caroline said.

"*Vacation?*" Maribelle asked. "Any vacation to me would mean getting out of town. I suppose that includes coming here because we know no one, which is fine."

"Yeah, plus it's trending. We don't do that very much," Raleigh said.

The sound system was playing Melanie performing *Candles in the Rain,* a favorite of Lucinda's when they were growing up. Caroline remembered her mother played it over and over on the cassette player. How far from the Panhandle they were.

Harrison, the maître d'—the person Caroline had beseeched to be well located that night—stormed through in search of a client, a guest, someone. He brushed by them, whirling to the check-in desk in his zeal. That would never happen in a Palm Beach restaurant, where subtlety was de riguer. Raleigh turned away to study the menu keenly. Caroline already knew they would favor grilled artichokes, crispy cauliflower, and a mezze board to start.

"Raleigh, are you all right?" Maribelle asked.

She looked up. "I'm fine. Only I can't be gone too long tonight. Caleb has been very resistant to his bedtime, and Alex is taking care of him."

"You need someone to help you on a daily basis," Caroline said. "It's absurd that your plans get interrupted. Isn't tonight an example of why? We need to talk about what's going on."

Maribelle began texting, her thumbs flew across her phone.

"Maribelle, don't you agree? We should be together, the three of us, without being pressed for time," Caroline said.

"Well, I wanted to meet to tell you about Daryl Dexter. I was at his office. He sits behind this mammoth desk with stacks of papers, and at first, I wondered why he was Samuel's lawyer.

Samuel used to describe him as craggy for someone married to the most in-demand dermatologist for miles around." She squinted at her phone. "Anyway, he was very nice, soothing, sort of. I have a few notes . . ."

"He's very well respected. Did you go over everything with him?" Caroline asked.

"I did," Maribelle lowered her voice. "The house is in my name, the stock portfolio in both our names. He left college funds for your three children, paid in full, and . . ."

"Did he? Wow, Raleigh, isn't that generous?" Caroline was surprised, shocked really. It was one thing to be a loving uncle, and another to completely underwrite his nieces' and nephews' undergraduate educations.

"Yes, it's very nice. Very generous." Raleigh seemed preoccupied with the serving station near their table.

"What about his debt?" Caroline asked. "Were you able to sort that out?"

"I'm sorry, what do you imagine could happen? The debt disappears? I'm incredibly worried about it since I've inherited Samuel's financial burdens. Daryl said whatever Samuel owes will be paid by his estate before anything comes to me. It's pro forma unless Mom forgives it somehow on behalf of Barrows and helps me out. If not, it really hurts me. I'm basically responsible for what is missing."

"Mom is hellbent on being paid back," Caroline said. "She's manic about anything to do with Barrows. Nothing could piss her off more than money that's gone, taken by her son-in-law. The one she thought she could trust."

"Well, I'm asking for your help. I'd like you to speak to her about it. Reel her in." Maribelle focused on Caroline.

"As if Mom would listen to us," Raleigh said.

"She might," Maribelle said. "Without her help, it's a question of how to . . ."

"Maribelle, Samuel took money from Barrows. The company has to be paid back somehow. Mom isn't wrong." Caroline said.

"She's her *daughter,* Caroline. Can't that be factored in?" Raleigh turned to Maribelle. "How about we ask her for some scheduled payment, or sell stock, or . . ."

Maribelle smiled pathetically. "I've been reviewing my options."

"We need to know more about what exactly happened," Caroline said.

"Is there anything else for tonight? Because like I said, I have to get back," Raleigh said. "Maribelle, I hope you understand."

Maribelle nodded, her entire being seemed watered down. "If you have to, of course. There isn't that much more to this."

Caroline suspected that her sisters were squeezing each other's hands beneath the table.

"Wait a second, there is more. A lot more. What Mom has found out about the money, how she's viewing Samuel. That was a contention before I knew about his will," Caroline said.

"Remember, I'm not involved with the company, or what I might add." Raleigh's voice was high.

"Raleigh don't be dense," Caroline said. "Samuel was stealing from Barrows—stealing from you by doing that. You might not work there, but you do know where your quarterly dividend comes from, don't you?"

Raleigh, always the one in crisis, be it the responsibilities of working, wifing, or mothering, plunged into her vulnerable act. Although it was dusk, she put on a pair of Ray Ban Wayfarers, the kind she wore in college to go incognito.

"You know, Mom's been searching through files for three days straight," Caroline said. "It's absurd."

"What has she told you? Has she walked into your office and shown you evidence? Something?" Maribelle jumped in.

"To be honest, when I hear her trudging along the halls, I open a compact and practice how to be. My mouth is neither downward nor curled upward. Whatever she tells me, I am not readable," Caroline said.

"See, Caroline, you agree. It's crazy to point to Samuel, that he stole money," Maribelle said. "That he racked up a big debt."

"I don't know," Caroline said. "I keep asking Travis, and he swears he knows nothing." She hesitated, not ready to say that she suspected her husband was covering for Samuel, or for Barrows, or for someone.

Their server, lithe with deep blue tinted contact lenses, appeared. Caroline stared at his tattoo sleeve with a dinosaur theme. He smiled in a wide and open way, like Travis did a long while back when it wasn't rehearsed. Before his chipped front teeth had been laminated.

"Can I get anyone anything? Another round?"

"Yes, another for me." Caroline held up her glass.

"Anyone else?" He kept the smile going as if they were relaxed vacationers, not glum sisters.

"No, thank you." Although Raleigh was in her dark glasses, it was obvious that she was searching the bar and dining room. For what?

Maribelle held up her glass. "I might have another. Why not?"

Once he had left, Raleigh frowned. "Mom's obsessed with— what does she call it?—malfeasance."

"I'm not ready to believe what she suspects about my husband," Maribelle said

"None of it?" Caroline asked. "Because I really don't know what Travis is up to half the time. When he flosses his teeth, he acts sneaky. Who wants to know what her husband is doing?"

Maribelle looked at Raleigh. "What do you think about that?"

"Think?" Raleigh stared past her.

"About insisting Samuel was up to no good." Maribelle said.

"Why would Mom do that? I mean, it seems so unfair," Raleigh said.

Caroline's dress, meant to be crisp, was bunching at her waist. Maribelle's version of chic—a print Altuzarra dress—worked well. People always knew she was stylish. Two tables over were three couples. The women, who looked around Caroline's age, seemed to be eyeing Raleigh, not for her attire but her allure.

"This should go *away*. I mean, Samuel's dead. Isn't that bad *enough* for Maribelle?" Raleigh asked.

"The missing money is a big issue, Raleigh, that's why," Caroline said.

"I don't know. I don't know what to believe." Maribelle squeezed a lime wedge in her hands. "It doesn't make sense to me."

Caroline took a break from the dish of marinated olives and started separating out cashews in the mixed nut bowl.

"I ask myself why my husband, who is dead, is in trouble? Not yours, not anyone's in this restaurant." Maribelle shivered. "How do we know it's Samuel's fault, and why can't the money be absorbed by the business? That's what Dad would have done."

Caroline stuck her chin out in Maribelle's direction. The smallest red spots were forming under her eyes.

"*Absorbed into the business?*" she hissed. "Because of the amount for starters. We're not talking about petty cash, Maribelle. We're talking about seven fucking million dollars."

Raleigh put her right hand over Maribelle's left wrist.

Caroline calmed herself. "Aunt Bryant has found someone who can help," she said.

"Someone for what?" Raleigh asked.

"Aunt Bryant has found a forensic accountant, and Mom hired him."

"I'm sorry, Caroline," Raleigh said. "*Aunt Bryant?*"

"I know, I was surprised. Isn't it Mom who knows the wives of dicey husbands—she'd have access to this sort of person."

For a moment the three of them were perplexed that Aunt

Bryant, their confidante and fierce defender, on their side when Lucinda had been tone-deaf, would do this.

"Not someone local, according to Mom. Except he is rather local. He lives in West Palm," Caroline said.

"She means no one will know him—it's safe," Maribelle rubbed her temples. "Listen, I don't want anything to do with a forensic accountant. You should know that."

Neither Raleigh nor Caroline responded. This time, the two of them traded glances. They stared at Maribelle, as if they knew better, as if she needed to be snapped out of this gnarled dream. "You know this isn't about a choice. We have a situation. You've got to help, Maribelle. Don't you care about the company, *our company*, being okay?"

Caroline was raising her voice; it bordered on shouting. She saw it in Maribelle's face, in how Raleigh folded her head toward the wood planked floor.

"Not as much as I want you to stop blaming Samuel," Maribelle said. "Not as much as I'd like to get away from the whole mess."

"Samuel defrauded Barrows. You must know that. He was your fucking husband," Caroline knew she was still too loud, but the place was getting louder. No one seemed to notice.

"I swear I know nothing about Samuel at his work!" Maribelle shouted back. "What makes you so positive it was my husband? How can you attest to that? It could have been Estelle. Maybe Mom! It could have been your husband, he's the CEO. Travis should know where the money is."

"It couldn't have been Alex," Raleigh was borderline shouting. "My husband never got invited in. Maybe he's lucky. For years, we've been insulted, when now we can be relieved."

"The truth is nobody knows anything." Maribelle paused to glare at Caroline. "It could have been you!"

"Me? Me?" Caroline was furious. "I'm like Mom. I go to bed dreaming of what's best for Barrows. I put my children into

Nicole's hands every morning, and she drives them to the Academy. For me to be at my office early. I'm beyond loyal. Who has missed that?" She was louder than Maribelle, angrier.

"Could you both stop?" Raleigh held up her hands. "It's really obnoxious."

Several feet away, Harrison was eyeing their table. He came forward instantly, as if ready to squelch their loud voices. Perhaps he wanted them to leave.

Raleigh stood up quickly. "I've got to go."

"That is you!" Harrison rushed closer to Raleigh. "How have you been? It's so good to see you!"

Caroline saw how fit he was, bronzed in that South Florida style, meaning self-tanner. Both she and Maribelle, knocked out of their drama by his presence, watched this half hip, half corporate man in Delray greet their little sister.

"I'm sorry, you must have me confused with someone else," Raleigh said.

"I never forget a face. While it's been a few weeks, maybe a few months . . ."

"I've been told I have a familiar face," Raleigh smiled in a deliberate, unfriendly way. "Please forgive us if we were too noisy. My sisters are having a brawl."

"A brawl?" Harrison laughed then stopped. "Well, whatever the topic is, it might be best not to be heard over the din."

"Oh, our conversation is finished," Maribelle said. "We didn't mean to cause any . . ."

"I realize that."

Harrison, who must have seen it all, was facile as he glided backwards. As he faded from their table, he vaguely waved, lifting his cell phone from his pocket and gesturing that he had to take a call. The lighting in the restaurant was suddenly lowered, a second-round cocktail hour kicked in. Raleigh started frantically looking through her bag. "Like I told you, I'm off to Caleb."

"There's more, you should stay, at least a few minutes. We'll talk calmly," Caroline said.

"No, no. I won't do that," Raleigh's eyes were on Harrison. She held up her phone with a screen shot of Caleb gripping a teddy bear. "I'm racing home to him."

Maribelle nodded. "Of course, you must go—at once."

Caroline wondered whether, no matter what, Maribelle believed she had the best view of the map in Raleigh's mind. She noticed the diners watching as Raleigh nimbly zigzagged through the restaurant. "That Aphrodite quality," Aunt Bryant liked to say about her. Before Samuel died, Caroline would have pushed for details, demanded to know why Raleigh was skittish tonight. Instead, she had decided to sit with Maribelle, to learn what she might or might not know about Samuel and the money.

CHAPTER EIGHT

Raleigh

B efore Raleigh had put down her keys, Alex came toward her carrying Caleb. Caleb's toddler eyes whizzed about; his head was nestled beneath her husband's neck and left shoulder. She wanted to pull him out of Alex's arms, to be close to his very small-boy skin. Not just tonight, but any time. Raleigh wanted to be near Caleb for when he teased the long Os out of poodle and toot and favored hard Gs in words like gonk and golly.

"He's had a bedtime snack, and we've read a few books." Alex said. "He's been waiting for you. The storm scared him when it began, the thunder has been loud."

"Mommy! Mommy!" Caleb squealed, holding out his arms.

"I'm drenched—a storm out of nowhere. I ought to change first and not get Caleb wet."

Alex kept him in a tight hug, a quasi-restraint. Raleigh looked around; the house was in shambles. Assorted canvases were scattered about. A portrait she had begun of Charlie Prentiss and her two teenage daughters, in phase one although due in a month, was where Raleigh had left it, leaning against the entrance. Three of Alex's seascapes he had sketched from memory, influenced by Winslow Homer, remained as they were this morning. Although Alex's ambition was to straighten up their work, she knew little progress could be made without someone to help with Caleb.

"I know. Things aren't moved yet." Alex said. He sounded apologetic.

"Don't worry," Raleigh said. "I get it."

An outsider might assume she sounded supportive, but it wasn't how she felt. It was a financial decision. With the Barrows dividends on hold, they couldn't continue to rent their space at the Lotus Studios in West Palm. She hoped it was temporary, that Samuel's "theft," as Lucinda called it, wasn't going to ruin Maribelle, that she wouldn't have to liquidate her life to pay back the company.

"Right, since we're commuting down the hall." Alex attempted humor.

After they cleared out the studios, they had begun painting in their future baby's room, filling it with works in progress. Raleigh knew she should be pregnant again soon; the expectation hung over her. *Collect yourself,* Lucinda whispered to her whenever she found a chance. *Your husband and child need you, try to have a daughter next.*

"Mama!" Caleb shifted to an endearing term, the one he used when he wanted to do what was forbidden.

"I came back as soon as I could, Caleb sweetness," Raleigh said.

Alex smiled at Caleb, not looking in Raleigh's direction. "We're fine, Caleb and I. Aren't we, small Potato?"

"Not a potato," Caleb tried to frown at the one nickname his father and Raleigh both favored. He started crying again.

Raleigh slid out of her sopping cardigan, her T-shirt and skirt were clinging to her. "I can take it from here."

Alex carefully handed Caleb over, placing him into Raleigh's hands so he wasn't against her clothes. Raleigh smelled the baby shampoo as it faded from his hair, his rumpled pajamas brushed against her wrist, his fingers had slight dimples. Who knew for how much longer?

After Raleigh sang *Golden Slumbers* to Caleb, because her mother had sung it to her, and Caroline had followed with her girls, Caleb fell asleep. His eyes were shut peacefully, his hands clenched in two fists. Either he was invested in his dreams or a tense child, Raleigh thought as she smoothed his dark hair, so like his father's, off his forehead. Then she carefully sneaked away, hoping he wouldn't hear her footsteps as she left his room.

"Is Caleb asleep?" Alex was in the bedroom, rearranging their art, moving the watercolor he had painted of their engagement five years ago. The night they decided to get married, they were in Savannah. It was the last year of their MFA program. They were dancing in front of a two-burner stove. Raleigh remembered how they poured pancake batter while swaying to *Uncle John's Band.*

"I hope so," Raleigh said. "He was exhausted."

"Looks good, right?" Alex adjusted the painting and stood back.

"I agree," she said.

He picked up Raleigh's version of their engagement, a pastel that captured the predawn hue, their bodies bent into one another. Recently, Maribelle had the pair reframed by Ursula Hobson on the Avenue as a birthday gift to Alex. Tonight, as Alex hung them, flanking the double window, Raleigh thought they seemed so very weighty. But what sense was there in conveying that?

"Perfect," Alex said.

She glanced at their king bed, the same size as Maribelle's but less adult, less dignified. Raleigh imagined a future where it would shelter a hamster, a kitten, a puppy—whatever Caleb requested. The blinds were still up, the rain kept pounding. She thought of Maribelle, who believed in the moon and tides, blaming the good and bad on their cycles. How her sister was alone, how Samuel was gone.

Raleigh closed her eyes for a minute. "I'm going to get changed."

Alex, looking even taller than most days, followed her.

"Where were you?"

"At Dada in Delray. Not your style, too much a scene."

"Ah, people trying too hard." He placed his hand behind her neck, softly. "And not even in Palm Beach."

"Maribelle's choice. It was fine for a night where we were talking in circles," she said.

"It's a rough time. You could have stayed longer with your sisters." Alex said.

"No, I wanted to leave. I couldn't listen—talk about the will, talk about . . ."

Alex traced her face. "How can I help?" He moved his hands to her waist. Raleigh stiffened, then decided to succumb.

"What's most troubling, Raleigh?"

"This stuff about the missing money. Accusations—my mother's and maybe Caroline's—that Samuel took it," she shuddered. "Maribelle and I don't believe Samuel would have done that. My sisters were screaming at each other at the restaurant, it was sickening."

Alex took her in his arms and rocked her. Most wives with a three-year-old would have been grateful, would have boasted about a husband like Alex. Yet as they lay parallel by night and stood parallel by day, for Raleigh, it was as if she couldn't straighten up or manage the morning to come. Her body was snapping, even her wrists, parts of her secretly snapping.

Beneath his shadow beard, Alex's face was angular. There was a Superman shape to his torso. Raleigh knew she ought to make room for her husband, invite him closer. He put his arms around her, covering her, his tongue was in her mouth. He was familiar, spotless, and steady. If only he knew why she had really left the restaurant, how Dada was a bad idea. That she had been there too many times with North. *North*, that was what she had called him. It hadn't seemed a hazard—that's what they had told one another. Dada was saved for days when they couldn't get far from town and had to see each other. Where tripping over a Palm Beacher in Delray at lunch seemed unlikely, and the risk-reward was factored in.

"Have I ever told you how kind and true you are?" Alex whispered.

Raleigh waited before she answered her unsuspecting husband. Yet instead of feeling comforted that he complimented her, she was jittery.

"You have. You said I'd be a flawless model, inside and out, for your 'Girl in Thin Air' portrait."

"No," Alex said. "What I told you is that you'd be a flawless model, and you said only if I called it, 'Girl in Thin Air.'" You chose the idea and title for my painting-to-be."

When Alex smiled, Raleigh could smell lima beans on his breath. She began to cry in what Lucinda would call an acceptable way. She wasn't squinching her face or weeping loudly.

She knew she should not have gone tonight and sat in that corner of the bar, where she had been with North. His smoothest voice, the fast laugh. How he ate food like it was an adventure. Sitting there, she relived his kisses as he locked the door to the hotel room. She had inhaled his skin, his breath, his wrists, anything she could latch onto that was his. When Raleigh thought of North, it set her back.

Worse, until now, she had been confident that she was a good wife and a good lover. Some days she had dared look into a future where she and Alex could tug apart. She imagined they would divide the pie, bereft at having to juggle a schedule with their beloved son. Without Caleb, Raleigh believed she might have left months ago, walked out with her paints and canvases, a few pairs of leggings, and the dress she had bought last November at Saks. A black sheath that her sisters and mother insisted she had to own; they predicted a hole in her wardrobe without the silhouette. Raleigh knew she hadn't the guts to leave, nor had Alex given her a reason. He wasn't a thug or impatient or dull. None of it was about him. It was about her. She realized that being drawn to a lover makes it hard to love the day-to-day existence of a husband. She knew she was impatient with Alex's ambition; when he turned down portrait commissions and wanted only to be a contemporary artist, she was short with him. Then there was the un-sexiness of sharing a child.

All of it added to the murkiness, to why Raleigh was equivocating. She had awakened on a Tuesday morning, planning to cut out, believing she and North would find a dimension of their own. She was sure they were strong enough to ditch life as they knew it for one another. By Thursday afternoon, she flipped her stance, wracked with remorse. She reminded herself she had signed on for being with her son and husband.

"Raleigh," Alex whispered, "Listen, I promise I'll have more work, I promise I'll be . . ."

"Shh," she whispered back. "Please."

His body enveloped hers, and so they began. While she made herself available to Alex, she remembered her promise. *The only thing I ask for is fidelity, Alex said the day they were married. You have my word, she had sworn to him.*

Afterward, Raleigh held onto Alex for dear life because her favorite sister was a widow, because if her husband chose to be inside her, she wouldn't lose him. She had to convince herself of this, to push the rest away. Wasn't that so?

CHAPTER NINE

Maribelle

E ver since the magazine moved last year to Royal Poinciana
Plaza, a block from the ocean and in the middle of the
island, Maribelle had been happier coming to work.
Although she was slightly hungover from last night at Dada,
walking into her office suite this morning pleased her. She
looked at the *PB Confidential* banner in a lime green script and
felt a sense of achievement and pride. She belonged here, she had
turned *PB Confidential* into a high-end magazine. A must-read
that was displayed in every Palm Beach foyer or living room.
Her office was a refuge, a haven for forgetting about Barrows and
Lucinda's suspicions. It was the safe spot she had created with
her own hard work—a place where she felt protected not only
from Lucinda but from her own misgivings about Samuel.

Maribelle carried her cappuccino from the machine that churned
it out for visitors and staff and headed to her desk. For the moment
all was quiet, the tenor of the morning was only starting up.

Holly Lamm, the publisher, stood outside her door. "The meeting?" she asked. "In the conference room or my office?"

Maribelle checked her out. At the magazine, they dressed for one another, summing up "wardrobe virtue" on a constant basis. Holly was in all white, her shirt was sleeveless, her pants were cropped. Maribelle had taken a different approach in her dreamy, Zimmermann midi dress. Both were trending—clothing as costume—a form of self-expression. What Maribelle liked best was that it wasn't for some luncheon or charity event in Palm Beach, but because she was the editorial director. It was a personal pride. Until Samuel's affair, until he died, she had assumed that if she excelled at work and was a good wife and daughter, things would go well. The reward was within reach.

"Conference room." Maribelle said. Her workspace was not as fresh and uncluttered as she liked it.

"In an hour," Holly turned back.

Maribelle logged into her desktop and read that two full-page advertisers, *Bestcakes,* the dessert caterers, and *Pooch,* a dog spa and boutique, were not renewing their ad schedules. She kept scrolling. Ettin Jewelers on the Avenue had made the same decision. She reread their emails to see if she had misunderstood. In her four years at *PB Confidential,* this had not happened. Merchants, hair salons, interior designers, plastic surgeons, restaurants, they wanted at least a half page per month. Maribelle rushed through a trail of emails for other news, something to counteract this. It was remarkably flat, no feature jumped out at her or was worthy of an assignment. She clicked on her list of potential ideas, created and never sourced.

While she was immersed, a text came in from Tanya, her assistant. *Coffee?* Maribelle texted back. *No need.* Then from Nadia. *Ready?* She tossed her buttery cardigan over her arm and grabbed her iPad.

"I interview the women from the Landmark Society at two today," Nadia said as Maribelle walked in. "Some are fossils."

"Good fossils," Maribelle said. "They have great staying power. I hope that's your angle. It could be multigenerational, you might find a mother, daughter, grandmother, all Palm Beachers, all involved."

"It sounds like something AARP would run, just *not* in Palm Beach," Nadia said.

"Fine," Maribelle said. "AARP has over thirty million readers."

Nadia and Kendall, who wrote up whatever Nadia didn't, flanked Holly. Maribelle was at the opposite end of the teak table. The offices didn't have the patina that Barrows had, yet they had plenty of style. The sun streamed in as they sat on Hans Wegner wishbone chairs. Their exact ages and lifestyles were reflected in the natural light. Holly, in her late forties, had subtle filler, Botox for crow's feet. She was very fit. Her hair was five shades of blonde-brown. Divorced with no children, life was a luxury that pleased her. Nadia, at forty, was impressively fresh looking. She had the air of someone single by choice. Except for her deadlines, nothing stressed her. Kendall, with a young daughter and a husband, was in her early thirties. Some mornings she appeared exhausted, and Maribelle imagined she had been awake too much the night before with a colicky child. She was waif-like. Her voice had a sing-song quality. What Maribelle liked best about Kendall was how she was able find the hook in any story. Maribelle had known from the start that Kendall was a very good writer.

"Multigenerational. I like that." Nadia opened up her leather-bound notebook and wrote briefly.

Toto, Holly's Yorkshire Terrier, woofed from the empty chair by the low bookcases. Holly studied her screen with no attempt to quiet him down.

"Let's talk about layout," Maribelle said. "I've looked at the calendar from the Literary Society. They've got a diverse lineup, poets, memoirists. I thought we'd run a piece on how they've opened up to new talent. They aren't highlighting a stodgy, unidimensional list."

"Sort of juxtaposed with the old guard," Kendall tapped her pencil against the table. "I can see that. Especially if the program is taking off."

"In season it fits and works with our new idea of having more content, not only charity calendars and pictures at events, but more cerebral pieces. Narrative nonfiction, opinion essays, reviews of a Netflix series or two, books, art exhibitions at the Shelteere," Maribelle said.

"Speaking of season," Holly stared at Maribelle. "This South Florida season is concerning for us. We need more subscribers, more ads."

Maribelle's gut clenched. Holly's tone, how Nadia was smirking at her, the disappearance of advertisers. She couldn't have adversity, not when her work mattered so much to her. It was the magazine that got her through the week, armament for dreaded weekends with family and friends at the Harbor Club or Longreens. She showed up, of course, her mother wouldn't have it otherwise. Yet Maribelle had never liked odd numbers and was now the fifth wheel, a young Palm Beach widow. Another reason she welcomed being at *PB Confidential*—there was a mission. They were revamping the magazine, a project that had to pan out.

"Are you aware, Maribelle, we have advertisers who are not renewing?" Holly asked.

Maribelle paused.

"Do we know why?" Nadia reclipped her tortoise barrettes and nimbly moved her hands through her hair.

Holly shrugged "Lots of reasons, generally magazines that endure have trouble enduring. We've been dodging this for the last year or so."

"We've put out great editions this past year," Maribelle said. "I'm confused."

"Funding and revenue," Holly said.

"All the more reason to encourage a larger audience, expand our horizons," Maribelle said.

"I like your plan, Maribelle," Holly said. "I admire your ideas, yet I don't see the point at this stage. Not when there could be a struggle ahead. I don't want to change our sections, our offerings; they're effective. Let's face it, we don't know who among our readers wants an intellectual pursuit. What we do know is that plenty read about galas, cooking classes, local women, couples around town. Do we have enough social events to cover—the usual list?"

"We've got the entire calendar filled," Nadia said.

Maribelle saw that Kendall was waiting. She had promised her a review of a poet or two once things were put into play.

"Kendall?" Holly asked.

"Yes, I'm set, Holly."

Toto jumped onto the conference table where Holly was sitting, wagging his tail. She put her hand on his face, he stuck his tongue out and licked her ring finger. Maribelle couldn't imagine having this exchange with Supy, although she had shared it with Samuel.

How could Holly back out of her commitment? Maribelle thought. She wanted to suggest that the trim size be cut but hesitated.

"The magazine could add depth in any case," Maribelle said.

"Of course, it *could*," Holly agreed.

"Then how about a mix of the two?" Maribelle asked. "Book reviews, interviews with local artists could be added, but no politics, just heightened cultural coverage. Half and half?"

"In theory, Maribelle, it's great, I've told you already," Holly took a deep breath, exhaled. "It's that we need to protect ourselves from what might be coming. We can't be changing our identity.

So, while we keep the content the same, I think we'll have to let go of the form altogether."

Tiny beads of sweat were starting on Maribelle's forehead, which felt clammy.

"Let go of the form? I just don't get it. Holly, how can you renege on the changes?" Maribelle asked. "Do you mean a different layout?"

"Yes, no more distributing copies, delivering to subscribers, selling them locally. We'll be taking *PB Confidential* online."

"I'm sorry?" Kendall asked.

"*Online?*" Maribelle asked.

"Online, most magazines have done it," Holly said. "This is the rundown, if the magazine doesn't fold completely."

"Sort of a more current approach," Nadia said. "*O* has gone this route."

Maribelle knew they were right. Except she needed water, the room was coiling around her. *PB Confidential* was all that she had that was hers alone. No part of it belonged to her mother or sisters. Her friends weren't able to touch it, they had no influence. She alone had built it up, she alone knew it was time for a new framing of content, not an online version of what they had been doing. She thought of Samuel, who at least appeared to care about her work. What would he have advised?

"Holly, why don't we segue?" Maribelle asked. "We'll do hybrid; a paper edition with the option of an online edition. Offered simultaneously. That could be for a few months, at least."

"I am sorry, Maribelle. Our next issue is the last print issue."

Holly sounded so corporate. How could this decision have been made without her knowledge? Maribelle watched as she folded her iPad, indicating the meeting was over. When she glanced at Kendall, she was unreadable, scrolling through her phone.

Nadia walked to the window. "It's crowded out there," she said.

"All these vacationers, probably staying at the Breakers or the Brazilian Court. There are snowbirds, too, I'm sure."

No one answered, it was awkward.

"Right," Maribelle said. "They're unencumbered. Look at them ambling along."

Holly stood up snappily. "You and I, Maribelle, might we have lunch?"

"Yes, we should do that." Maribelle began searching her calendar on her phone.

Holly clapped her hands for Toto to join her. "I meant now, today."

"I'm forfeiting a family lunch at the Breakers," Maribelle said.

She slid into her chair at Swifty's outdoor dining at the Colony Hotel. The hanging gardens created the perfect amount of shade, while guests checked each other out. If Holly wanted to speak privately, why would she have chosen one of the hottest spots, Maribelle wondered. Then it occurred to her, maybe this was a friendly gesture, not a mandated meeting. Holly took off her crystal framed Gucci sunglasses. Up close, Maribelle noticed her elongated eyeliner and how defined the winged outer corners were.

"Do you go anywhere except with your sisters these days?" Holly asked.

"They try to keep me from being lonely," Maribelle said.

In truth, she wasn't certain why they'd been keeping a close watch; they weren't a distraction in any way. When she texted them to announce her change of plans today, Raleigh replied, *Mom will be pissed. You're bold to blow us off.* Maribelle texted back, *This is my business. Mom will understand. She's pure business.* Caroline weighed in.

"It is good to see you outside the office," Holly said.

"It is good to be seen," Maribelle said. She was channeling a remark her father had made decades ago when they'd gone to Teller's in Kesgrave. It was a charmless but popular restaurant with maroon tablecloths and a choice of beets or baked beans as the vegetable of the day. The Barrowses kept a house account, and they went every Thursday night. Every diner would wave happily when Reed led them in. At his end of the table was a large bowl of iceberg lettuce with a few half-dead tomatoes. He would pour chunky Roquefort dressing on top, then dole it out. Maribelle remembered how safe it felt, looped in with Lucinda and Reed and her two younger sisters.

Holly was scanning the crowd. "Whoever fled the Breakers Beach Club is sitting here instead. "To my left are a few celebrities." She was discreet; voices traveled easily over the hardwood floors. Maribelle noticed that Beatrice Moore and her new boyfriend were loudly laughing, locked in the infancy stage of their relationship.

"This is Nadia's type of scene. Every detail suits her column. She's been covering party after party. Restaurant sightings can break it up. Is she on her way, Holly?"

"She isn't joining us because I thought we should talk, the two of us."

Maribelle looked in the other direction, unsure what Holly had in mind. Three tables over, Margot Damon sat alone. Her thumbs were flying as she wildly texted. Her phone was her companion until Celia Nordic swirled in and coasted to the chair beside her. Celia's chin-length hair flipped outward and liquid liner framed her eyes, much like Holly's, circa the early sixties. Maribelle wondered if she had become pedestrian and missed the message on makeup.

Holly tore a roll in two and began buttering it. Maribelle thought of Samuel, how he loved to make a show when they ate out. Slathering butter, ordering the best deserts. Red velvet cake, key lime pie, salted caramel gelato. Not that he devoured it; rather, it was to share with whomever was at the table. In some covert hotel room, did he and Collette raise their spoons and dive into a crème bruleé together?

Waitstaff bustled about, shrimp cocktails were served, oysters, charcuterie and cheese platters were being dispersed. Holly leaned in closer, her bangles clanked together.

"Maribelle, Nadia came to me a few days ago wanting to do a story on Samuel's death and the Barrows family, the company. She said it would be in-depth reportage. The caliber of writing and research you want."

"Did she?"

Maribelle sat on her hands, which had become cold despite the warm afternoon. Nadia, whom she had hired for the magazine. Nadia, who had sought Maribelle's advice about her love life, her wardrobe, Palm Beach rituals, blowouts. Hadn't she become Nadia's personal guide when she first arrived from Miami? Hadn't she detailed why Nadia's position at *PB Confidential* was not like the work she'd left behind at *South Beach Diary*? Maribelle had always approved features or society writing, whatever Nadia preferred. She viewed her as a fine, instinctive writer, always in search of *the story*—a true believer who now proposed to betray Maribelle for the sake of *the news*.

The restaurant was filling up. Maribelle knew that every diner here would read the piece that Nadia yearned to write with curiosity. An intense allegiance to her family welled within her. She had the sensation that she was swallowing air, practically drowning on land. She needed to react thoughtfully.

"I haven't encountered this before, a writer going directly to the publisher without consulting me. I am the editorial director, after all," Maribelle said.

"Oh, she couldn't possibly ask you first," Holly said. "What she's after is a conflict for you this time. She's quite hungry. I'm not asking you to address Nadia's premise. I realize the two of you are close in age, and you've been more than colleagues at the magazine. And I won't judge her for jumping over you, I suppose."

"Of course not, Holly."

Maribelle pushed her fingernails into her thighs. At this very moment she was deciding who had sullied her life the most. Was it Samuel by dying? Or her mother by hiring a forensic accountant to dig around? Or Nadia, who would put a good story before friendship?

"Going online is a must, a financial decision; as for Nadia and her plan, I have turned it down," Holly said.

That Holly of all people was the savior, the one with integrity—Maribelle was stunned.

"I cannot believe you would do that. I know we are in the business of selling magazines," she said.

Holly held up her hand as if she were a crossing guard. "Well, it doesn't mean we are okay. It only means we've stopped Nadia. Money is the hardship. We've lost our benefactor, Maribelle."

"Benefactor? Like Pip had in *Great Expectations*? I didn't know we had one," Maribelle said.

"Oh, yes. Someone charismatic and incredibly generous. For a while, now, at least several years." Holly said.

"What happened?" Maribelle asked. Not that she was paying attention. Instead she was imagining how irate Nadia would be and how to appease her. Maribelle might suggest she write about the history of the charity circuit in Palm Beach. It could be juicier than expected.

Their server came along, platters piled onto his arms. Holly pointed to the center of the table. "I ordered for us when I first sat down. One lobster salad, one crab cake, a side of fries. We can share all this." She reached over for Maribelle's fork, then hers, and began dividing the dishes onto two plates.

"I couldn't have kept the magazine alive without the money,

and now it has stopped," Holly said.

"Stopped?" Maribelle asked. "Was it Stenton Fields? I know he is quite generous, and my mother and William are friendly with him. I could ask . . ."

Holly came so close, it was as if she was about to kiss Maribelle.

"Listen, Maribelle," she said. "It's not Stenton. It was Samuel. He was our anonymous benefactor."

Abruptly, Swifty's started to spin. Sounds moved farther from them, their food smelled like Alpo. Holly was oblivious, she began picking olives out of her salad and sidelining them on the rim of her plate. There was a grainy texture to her, it reminded Maribelle of the print in comic strips. She thought how, when she was in grade school, Lucinda loved those. She called them "the funnies."

"Excuse me, Ms., are you alright?" The host, also grainy, had come over holding a glass of water. "I noticed that you seem rather . . ."

Holly took the glass from him. "She's fine, thank you, Maurice."

When he walked off, she pinched the skin on Maribelle's forearm. "You're dehydrated."

She pinched her again.

"Ouch," Maribelle said. But it helped. Her vision returned to normal.

"Samuel? I don't believe you."

"He came to me a few years after you started at *Confidential,*" Holly said. "He wanted it to be between us, and I was sworn to secrecy. He said he'd underwrite expenses in exchange for you having carte blanche."

Holly handed her the juice. Maribelle took one sip and spit it out. Was it rancid? She knew that was unlikely. What was sickening was Holly's news.

"Before I was editorial director?" Maribelle asked.

Holly nodded. "Samuel wanted you to climb the ladder and have a real say in how *PB Confidential* was run. He cared about your success. So amazing, really. He was eager to help. Your husband wanted you to have a well-compensated, prestigious position."

"That I didn't earn," Maribelle said.

Samuel, seducing Holly with his enthusiasm, his zest for Maribelle's talents. Or his apparent zest. Did he really believe in her? Or was it a ploy to keep her occupied and focused on a career rather than on their marriage?

"That's not exactly it, Maribelle," Holly said. "I hired you on your own merits before Samuel got involved. Your articles, from *Florida Living* to *Elle*, made you ideal for *PB Confidential*. You were climbing up on your own; he made it happen faster."

Maribelle wanted to shout that Samuel had no faith in her—no conviction she had the instinct. Worse, he hadn't any patience. He made the decision to buy her way in while selling her out. It fit his image for her to oversee editorial. Better yet, it kept her busy—a useful foil for whenever Maribelle pleaded to leave Palm Beach.

"Maribelle, *Confidential* thrived," Holly said. "The stress is recent, our monthly revenue is gone. We have to cut back, take the magazine online. We need to turn a profit. That's why I'm not quite ready for the editorial direction to change—we can't lose readers. Let's hope the new format works."

She watched Holly hold up a forkful of lobster and avocado. "Samuel wanted to make sure you had *enough* opportunity."

"Is that what you think?" Maribelle asked.

"Well, put it this way—he was known to be charitable. When it came to the Barrowses, Samuel joined boards, he represented the family, right? I'm stating the obvious to say he charmed everyone. Do you remember two years ago, when he bid on a Buccellati gold cuff at the auction for the Hospital Alliance, and won? His eyes were on you as he held up his paddle, but every woman was watching. He managed to smile at each of us. I felt like he was bidding for me. There isn't a woman in town who wasn't smitten with Samuel's style."

"I remember," Maribelle said,

How she detested that bracelet because of the auction—because of what Holly admired about Samuel. He had not noticed that Maribelle never wore it, or at least he had never asked her why. Clever and instinctive, Samuel was showing off for the crowd. Any and all charitable causes were supported at Lucinda's discretion, and Samuel was fronting. He was good at it.

"The Buccellati, the magazine. Samuel wanted to make you happy with alluring *stuff*," Holly said.

Holly's explanation felt coated in slime. Her take on Samuel's gestures pounded at the center of Maribelle's brain. Holly must not learn the truth that Samuel's investment in the magazine was likely to have been made with company funds. *Part of the stolen money.* A sensation was setting in, somewhere between shortness of breath and someone stomping on her heart.

"I'm going to get some air."

Maribelle almost toppled over when she stood up. Others noticed. The pool area at Swifty's felt infected by Samuel's hijacking of *PB Confidential*, by the irreversible nature of Holly's news. At an off angle, she moved past familiar faces and those she had not seen before. Her presence was a brief interruption to their dramas, but hers was dire. She was winning the *biggest loser husband award.*

In the lobby there was a short line for the women's room. The deep green leafy wallpaper was closing in. Maribelle was grateful that the two women ahead of her were guests at the hotel and unknown. They were too lively; their arms flailed as they chatted about where to have a wedding shower for someone's niece. Their Hermes bucket bags and rock-sized diamond rings looked too heavy.

As Maribelle ran her hands under the sink, she remembered the salt air back in Kesgrave years ago. It had gotten under the hood of their Ford pickup and destroyed the engine. *A good thing ruined . . . no saving it . . . corroded . . .* her father had said.

Where had Samuel been taking his plan?

CHAPTER TEN

Caroline

There was something about being in season that gave hope to Palm Beachers, Caroline thought. Maybe that they'd slogged through the off-season and pre-season until the real season had arrived. Tonight's event, a casino night gala for South Palm Hospital, had always been one of her favorites. And while Caroline loved any fundraiser held at the Flagler Museum—Henry Flagler's Gilded Age mansion, Whitehall—she couldn't be distracted. As guests, mostly couples, twirled around in black tie, she realized it was too soon to feel festive. Her family, having purchased two tables for the fundraiser, was somber. At last year's event, Samuel was one of the honorees. It was too soon, she realized, not to remember.

Travis was leading her onward, past a group lingering on the Lake Terrace that included Lucinda in a metallic dress with a ruffled hemline acting appropriately. Caroline saw her mother mingling, chatting with Rita Damon, Mrs. A, and Allison Rochester while only offering a half smile. The night was rolling in, lamps cast a tangerine light bright enough to see Veronica and Simon Cutler then Priscilla Dole and her ancient husband. When Caroline and Travis passed, conversations came to a halt. She knew it was about Samuel; people were asking what had actually happened.

"Caro?" Travis said. "Did you hear me?"

She tried to declutter. "Say again?"

Above her husband's head she could identify the galaxies. The stars were that bright.

"I asked if you want to find your sisters. They must be nearby. Then I said you look pretty."

She ought to be flattered or at least grateful to have a husband polished enough to convey a compliment, to pull it off. But she wasn't.

"Oh, sure, thank you."

Along the path to the roulette tables, Caroline's four-inch heels snagged the grass. Travis caught her, in a split second, he was guiding her in the direction of the winners. In the light of the flares, everyone's faces, including her sisters', were tipped toward the spinning wheel. Caroline imagined Mary Lily, Flagler's young third wife, on these very grounds at the turn of the century. She and her husband had *created* the season in Palm Beach, entertaining in this palatial home. When the Barrowses first moved to Palm Beach, Lucinda had taken the girls on a tour of the mansion. Caroline remembered passing the bedrooms and Maribelle had laughed when Lucinda commented on Mary Lily's next husband. A cagey guy who swooped in for the prize. She had said that wealthy widows were up for grabs. *Widows.* Something that applied to older ladies at Longreen's and the Harbor Club. Women with craggy skin sitting at the Breakers Beach Club about to play cards. Lucinda, who had married again quickly, and Aunt Bryant, who had never been married, knew them only slightly. Except now her sister was one of those women, and Caroline worried that she'd be alone.

To that point, as she and Travis approached, Raleigh was clutching Maribelle. They were standing so close they looked like a couple, not sisters. Alex was winning, stacking up his fake cash, more animated than Caroline had ever seen him. Surrounding them were other winners. Caroline noticed Amelia and Cecily, mothers from her daughters' classes at the Academy, hovering with their husbands. Everyone was clapping and hooting, clutching their monopoly money as if playing for high stakes in Monte Carlo.

Caroline sensed Travis stepping back a few feet away from the game.

"Let's not bother anyone. He's about to clean up," Travis said.

"Could you imagine if this were real money?" Caroline asked.

Raleigh and Alex began yelping. Caroline looked across at Maribelle. They smiled at each other, at the absurdity of Alex winning even at a fake game of craps.

Out of nowhere, the energy tightened. A scent Caroline had come to loathe was coming toward her. *Fracas.* Lucinda's favorite ever since she arrived in Palm Beach. There she was with William trailing her as he adjusted the lapels of his tux.

Her voice, like the perfume, preceded her. "Let's go straight to the hors d'oeuvres, shall we?" she asked.

They were each balancing a martini glass in one hand, an iPhone as a flashlight in the other. "You know cocktail tables are hard to come by. We'll secure a few, before we visit the casino."

Travis walked over. "That's an idea, Lucinda," he said. "We'll all follow you."

As if Maribelle and Raleigh weren't already in the thick of it with the gambling.

"Lucinda's full of ideas," William said.

He was inscrutable as always. None of the sisters could tell if he was joking, addled, or resigned. Yet they were relieved that he absorbed Lucinda's intentions, at least some of the time.

Caroline dropped her mini handbag onto one of the two tables Lucinda had claimed and began comparing her sisters' styles. Her Gedebe satin bag with crystals was a relatively new flavor, while Maribelle was carrying a black Fendi baguette that had been passed around for years—a classic. Raleigh, per usual, was feigning rebellion with an off-white clutch from the Delray flea market. Caroline had been with her the day she bought it, and she had since hand painted an ocean scene onto the front. Her purse, her long slithery grey dress, a cast off from Maribelle, her hair in a braided knot—all added to the close-to-sublime effect their little sister had.

Lucinda was hellbent on critiquing each woman who breezed by. "What do you think of voluminous silhouettes, Caroline?" she asked. "And what about pastels versus earth tones?"

"I still like streamlined," Caroline answered. "I think it's classic, prevailing . . ."

"You might be right," Lucinda paused, half raising her forefinger, half pointing, "However, if Margot Damon has chosen a print midi, we can all shop in our closets."

"Exactly," Aunt Bryant appeared suddenly, in a lavender dress.

Because Caroline and her sisters loved her so, they did not judge Aunt Bryant's fashion selections no matter how baggy or outdated. Lucinda and Aunt Bryant often clashed in terms of style, along with their values. Lucinda was at Dr. Demi Dexter's every three months for her Botox and fillers while Aunt Bryant claimed there was something to be said for aging gracefully. Caroline agreed when Lucinda claimed Aunt Bryant was the one woman over fifty within a forty-mile radius who hadn't had at least an eye lift or a lower face lift focusing on the neck and jaw line.

"Aunt Bryant!" Raleigh rushed to her. "You made it."

"I did. I've been playing craps and losing," Aunt Bryant said. "While there are plenty of winners tonight."

"I'd like to play a game or two myself." William dared to come closer. This evening, he seemed to be on a mission, intoxicated by the casino. "Would you mind, Lucinda, if I simply walked around the games tables?"

"Of course, William." Lucinda sounded pleased. "Why not take Travis off to the gambling,"

As soon as they left, the double-vaulted doors to the ballroom were opened. Elaborate garlands blew about. She and her sisters lined up beside Aunt Bryant.

"Girls," Aunt Bryant placed one hand around Maribelle's wrist and the other around Caroline's. "Remember that I promised to deliver the forensic accountant?"

"C'mon, Aunt Bryant, not tonight," Caroline said. She needed the night off—no work, no thoughts of Barrows and the missing funds.

"Maybe it is tonight," Raleigh said.

She was staring at their aunt, who was staring at someone. In the dwindling light, Caroline saw him in a shadow. He looked forty or so, tall, lots of dark hair with a rugged, hip quality.

The band ended "Let's Dance," and David Bowie's lyrics—*If you say run, I'll run with you*—were sapped from the air. Some guests left the dance floor. Others waited there for another promise to be conveyed through a song.

"Julian, I was searching for you. It isn't easy to find someone." Aunt Bryant held her hand out to him. "Girls, this is Julian Albert, your forensic accountant—for the family, for Barrows."

Their forensic accountant?

"I know, I know," Aunt Bryant said. "The question being, why is Julian here this evening?"

"We were wondering," Caroline stared at her aunt.

The accountant she conjured up was expected to be a back-room kind of guy with patchy bald spots and a creased forehead, not someone who dazzled. This man stood out against a refined crowd—older men, tired beneath their tans, outwardly genteel, having achieved a certain life; younger men, some semi-buff, somewhat beguiling. There was a Palm Beach pleasantness about this crowd. Aunt Bryant's *pick of a man* wasn't a part of it. Caroline saw that he was more handsome than the others.

Julian nodded. "Your aunt invited me, asked me to stop by. Not my usual scene."

Caroline knew that if she and her sisters had been younger—free of obligations, loss—had he existed when their lives were more random and they were not spoken for—one of them would have landed him, undoubtedly.

"I'm Raleigh. My sisters, Maribelle and Caroline."

"I know," Julian said. "I've seen pictures."

"And read a few articles," Caroline said. "They're easy to find."

He smiled without looking at anyone in particular. Maribelle did not hold out her hand like Raleigh and Caroline.

"What an odd place to be introduced, Mr. Alpert," Maribelle said.

Caroline thought she was bordering on rude.

Aunt Bryant nodded. "I did it intentionally. I thought, what better way to meet someone you'll be working with than at one of the best parties of the season? Business relationships are forged at social events."

"When will we be hiring you, Mr. Alpert?" Raleigh asked.

The wind was whipping up, the lanterns were swinging. Raleigh's hair blew off her face; she seemed wistful.

"Julian, please." He glanced at Maribelle when he said this. "I've been hired. I wouldn't have come tonight had I not already met with Lucinda and Travis."

"I'm sorry, I don't understand," Caroline said. Travis hadn't mentioned anything. She didn't quite understand why. Had Travis *avoided* a conversation with her about Julian being hired?

It smacked of being in cahoots with Lucinda. And being chicken shit. No wonder he'd run off to the roulette table. In her next life, Caroline decided, she would be fully conscious, guided by her own instincts and morals. She wouldn't have Travis as her husband or Lucinda as her mother.

"Your aunt arranged our meeting," Julian said.

"Aunt Bryant, that's not like you." Maribelle stepped back, and Raleigh moved forward a few steps.

"That's enough detail for this evening, isn't it?" Aunt Bryant asked.

In the distance, Celia Norric was gyrating alone to "I Got You Babe." The female vocalist sounded enough like Cher. Caroline watched her, realizing she would want to do the same thing, eyes closed, swaying to the lyrics, if she were apart from her family.

Julian looked at each of them. "A dance perhaps? We *are* at a party."

Raleigh shook her head. "I don't think so, thank you."

Maribelle pretended she didn't hear, gliding toward Holly Lamm's table. "I'm sorry, I spot the *Confidential* cadre . . ." Her words trailed off.

"Caroline, how about you?"

Behind Julian and Aunt Bryant, Raleigh was waving her arms at Caroline, shaking her head no. Maribelle, now a good twenty feet beyond them, was watching her next move. Travis was still at the casino, hiding from her, elbow deep in fake cash. His offer was suddenly appealing. There was this portal that belonged to her.

"Sure, I'll dance."

His hand on her waist, they stepped onto the dance floor, edging toward the center. Voices floated, fresh gossip rose and surged into the night. *Who is he? What is Caroline Sears doing? That Barrows family . . . piles of money . . . they do what they want.* For the rest of the evening Caroline knew her mother would spin the tale. *Julian is just a family friend,* she would say. Better yet, she would call him a second cousin, once removed, on Travis's side who had come to town.

The spotlights turned the night into shades of mauve. There was something about it that invited Caroline in. She decided she might be the best dancer of the Barrows sisters.

CHAPTER ELEVEN

Maribelle

"Why is it that all the young girls are pretty and then you look at them when they're twenty and it isn't the case?" Travis squinted in the sun.

Someone, thought Maribelle, meaning her sister, Caroline, might take him aside to tell him to stop being an ass, be mindful of where he is, and remind him that he is a father to young daughters, not a sexist, social critic. Instead, Caroline did nothing but offer a stony smile before she turned toward her. "Here you are, Maribelle."

Maribelle had just walked into Ocean House at the Breakers, where Caroline was hosting Harper's birthday celebration. She had passed the Vista Palm trees and individual cabanas that overlooked the ocean to reach her nieces, who were dunking their toes in the shallow pool. The sun was haloing around their heads. How could Harper be turning nine and Caroline have given birth that long ago?

"Here I am." Maribelle tried to muster a Palm Beach smile, the kind that blanketed psychic pain. She only wanted to hug the girls, drop off the gold ankle bracelet that had been engraved with *Harper* in a curly font and the Rainbow Surprise doll for younger sister Violet, and excuse herself.

"Good that you are." Caroline waved to Maribelle for a millisecond then switched her focus to Nicole. "Where are the party favors?" she asked.

After last evening's casino night at the Flagler, Maribelle was searching her sister's face for something—fatigue, remorse. There was none of that.

"I'm collating now," Nicole reached into a canvas tote, held up a silver link bracelet, and dropped it into a pastel painted jewelry box. She placed this in a gift bag that read *Harper* and began again.

"Great," Caroline said. "We'll need to check on the pizza and drinks for the girls."

"Scheduled to be served in forty-five minutes," Nicole said.

Her voice sounded like she was a podcaster. Young and acrobatic, she twisted in a relentless motion, keyed up for Harper's party. Maribelle thought how she and Samuel had never passed up one of these birthday celebrations for her nieces. Caroline was so good at it, each year, serving trays of shrimp and California rolls to the mothers and fathers who delivered their daughters, offering a chance to mingle.

This birthday, Caroline had confessed to her sisters, she simply couldn't find a path to something clever and new. Last week, when Maribelle had RSVP'd, Caroline told her she was "stuck."

"Since Samuel's accident, I've opted for tried and true," she said. "That's why it's a repeat party—same place, same theme—water aerobics. Barrows is madness without Samuel. I'm in the office for long stretches, slogging through mud that's four feet deep."

"I know what you mean." Maribelle had said this without really understanding or caring how it was for Caroline. She wasn't the one with a dead husband who was an embezzler. A deceiver who turned his wife's career into a lie. Besides, Caroline was a charter member of the Samuel Fan Club and, among family, a true believer. He had been her supporter at work. Together, they had launched the Stop In & Stay Barrows concept that included tables and comfortable chairs for laptops, an espresso bar, inventive food stands.

Maribelle couldn't stop eyeing Travis at the bar, chatting with the men, laughing, at ease with their Palm Beach youngish fathers' lives. Money, wives, kids, golf, cars, attitude. She wondered if Travis knew about Samuel's deal with Holly. He might very well know. The brothers-in-law were confidants. She imagined Samuel justifying his actions, boasting about how he had secured his wife a place in this world by funneling cash to *PB Confidential*. The idea bothered her. The fact that Travis and Samuel had such a long history together made it intolerable. They had been inseparable pranksters in high school—painting the water tower, breaking into the principal's barn, raiding Pinestream's cafeteria. Travis always got caught; Samuel never did. Travis always refused to reveal that Samuel was the ringleader. Once they were married to two of the three Barrows sisters and set up in Palm Beach, Travis was still protective of Samuel—she knew it.

Raleigh appeared, gossamer and dreamy, carrying a squirming Caleb on her hip. Maribelle stood taller, waving at them. When Raleigh put Caleb down, he ran the length of the room and back, teetering at the far end. He raced back, clinging to her calves. Raleigh didn't pry him free, and together they hobbled toward Maribelle. When the sisters air-kissed, Maribelle thought that up close, Raleigh seemed spent.

When mimosas were passed, Maribelle almost snatched one, while Raleigh wrinkled her nose.

"Orange juice," Raleigh sighed. "Maribelle, do you remember when I was eight, a year younger than Harper, you came home late from a date with Samuel? I was waiting up for you in your bed, really sick. Mom had insisted I drink orange juice."

"I knew what was wrong. You were allergic to it," Maribelle said.

"Mom forgot, she was busy, Loraine Dorse and Aunt Bryant were over," Raleigh pulled her hands through her hair, which was more tangled than usual.

Maribelle watched her. "Raleigh, are you okay?"

She nodded. "I am. I know, I shouldn't be doing this, reminiscing. Especially with you, I mean you're . . ."

"You threw up on my favorite coverlet, the one with pink rosebuds. Mom had ordered it from Bloomingdales. I grabbed a wastebasket from under my desk," Maribelle said.

"Yeah, and you began to vomit too. Such a good big sister. Empathetic."

Why was Raleigh acting so wistful? Maribelle didn't like it. Caleb had gotten back in her arms somehow. Raleigh and he were looking at the ocean view, waves were glinting in the afternoon sun. The palm trees started swaying like they'd been staged. The water had a pearly sheen.

"That's when Dad—Mom and Dad—were building the business," Maribelle said. "Mom couldn't believe money kept blowing their way. It was my senior year at Pinestream. People in town gossiped about how we were changing."

"We were," Raleigh said. "Mom was busy devising a plan for our decampment. She couldn't get us out of Kesgrave fast enough."

Maribelle shrugged. "Good riddance. You sound like you miss it. You were too young to know what a dead end it was."

Raleigh pointed toward the windows, the room. "Maybe being at Harper's birthday isn't right for you, it's too soon. Some events . . . more than others."

Maribelle wanted to agree. Instead, she smiled. "I wanted to see the girls, before they get too busy, and the party is in full swing."

A few nine-year-old girls had arrived and were winging

around in their cool attire, some in Lily Pulitzer shifts, others in yoga pants. They sized each other up, unaware of Maribelle and Raleigh, even Caleb.

Three more girls arrived. The first had her hair in a long braid and wore a fitted cheetah print T-shirt. The next wore leggings and a leotard in an iridescent purple. The third was what Lucinda called a tomboy. She was robust, very athletic. All the girls were wearing nail polish—bottle green, dark blue, and neon yellow respectively.

"Why, hello!" Nicole, springier than before, greeted them. "Let's see, you are Sydney, Sophie, and Annaleigh, right?"

"I'm Sophie." The blondest of the three walked over to Harper to hand her a gift. "This is from CrazyKids. My mom said it can be exchanged if you want."

"Sophie, thank you!" Harper said. The girls embraced for a moment, air-kissing.

Caleb wrenched his body for a better view.

"Want to be with the older kids?" Raleigh asked.

Maribelle put her hand on his head and patted it lightly. She raised her eyebrows at Raleigh.

"You can do that, cutest Caleb," she said. But she wasn't so sure.

More girls were filing in. Caleb instinctively began to look away.

"Wow, I'd love to sketch these girls," Raleigh said. "They're like Lululemon models. Or like their mothers."

"Maybe both," Maribelle agreed.

The chances of escape were diminishing, but she really needed to get out. She decided to focus on the far side of the room where Travis was being as cordial as the father of a very girly party could be. His blondish hair was thinning in that predictable pattern—how had she missed it? His shoulders still belonged to the football star he was at Pinestream but were mutating into those of a man close to forty. Today, as always, he and Caroline presented as the couple they hoped to be. Maribelle decided to leave Raleigh to walk over to them.

"I'll be back," Maribelle said to Raleigh. "I need to talk to Caroline."

As she walked through the room, she expected to see Samuel, drinking a Boozy tea, charming the mothers while playing the role of delighted uber-uncle. Instead, he was dead, drowned in the Intracoastal, not far from where he had docked the *Vertigo*. A single drowning, a short story compared to one of Samuel's favorite ship-wrecks, weirdly. That was the *Vasa*, a 17th century Swedish warship, destroyed on its maiden voyage to the Stockholm Archipelago. It was less than a thousand feet from the harbor when it went under.

"A tragedy," Samuel had told Maribelle when they were in Stockholm two summers ago. The Vasa was the first site Samuel had wanted to see. The two of them walked through the vessel that had become a maritime museum. Maribelle remembered how he described it that day.

"Those in charge must have misunderstood the current, the wind, maybe the mechanics of the ship. An incredible loss for so many families."

The memory begs the truth about Samuel's accident. Samuel aspired to own a yacht, he knew what it took to navigate a speed-boat *or* a warship in tricky waters. He understood the weather that morning on the Intracoastal. Samuel was capable, someone who kept her safe. That the water filled his mouth, his lungs, that his body was *brought in*. None of this should ever have happened.

"Maribelle?" Caroline was tipping her chin toward the food table.

A cheese tray was there for the parents who usually lingered. Maribelle knew, without looking, that Caroline had chosen triple crème cheeses—Saint André, Brillat-Savarin, a wheel of Délice de Bourgogne, water crackers. "The Breakers was opened by Henry Flagler at the turn of the century for travelers on his railway," Reed had told her when he first signed up for a family mem-bership at the Breakers Beach Club. It was the early 2000s, and

Barrows was *flourishing*, as Lucinda loved to say. They had moved to Palm Beach, where Maribelle knew her parents felt remarkably welcome. Their net worth was a magic key, they eagerly joined everywhere—Longreens, Harbor Club, Justine's. Private membership was captivating to them and extremely seductive after life in Kesgrave. They were drawn to the idea. They sought it out, and were surprised at how easy the ladder was to climb. If there was any speculation about their origin story, it disappeared after Reed wrote a few checks to the plum charities.

Ariana Grande's "Stuck with U" was winding down. Maribelle wondered for a fleeting second what the playlist might be. She knew little about trending music. Nicole whistled through her fingers. Caroline stood at the doors facing the pool and did a half turn of her head.

"Okay, girls, let's get started," she said. "Please follow Harper outside for our water aerobics fest!"

Maribelle watched as Harper stopped fidgeting, her face brightening. Her party was about to begin. Then Raleigh was pressing Maribelle's upper arm, her fingers digging in.

"Maribelle? Let's stand outside, check it out," she said.

To their left, the girls were dancing in the water, splashing, springing up and down to "Another Night" by the Real McCoy. As Raleigh led Maribelle past the California rolls, they heard the women, Caroline's guests, speaking in that rushed, gossipy way. Maribelle listened to their excited voices, their exclusive chatter . . . *French, no Spanish lessons . . . Mandarin . . . a tutor for math only . . . filler and micro needling . . . after the lecture, Penn, weekend coverage, divorced with two boys under eight, dinner with the Fords, every last cent . . .*

Caroline clapped her hands. "Would anyone like something more to drink?"

That's when Maribelle noticed two mothers breezing toward the group. *Collette! Tina! You're here. Collette, great earrings. Tina, that bag!* With their hands on the crackers and their drinks, the mothers made room for the latecomers. Something about this pair made Maribelle remember what Samuel used to say—that there was no one as pretty as the Barrows sisters. Yet looking at these two women, she was not so sure.

It came back to Maribelle who these women were. They had been seated together at last season's Arts and Media ball. Tina Steffen, the first mother, had worn a medium blue Lela Rose print, and Collette Nayers, the second, was in a black Jenny Packham. Maribelle remembered how Collette had spoken to both Samuel and Travis that night. How she sat between both men, twitching from one to the other. She was so pale with flowing auburn hair, like a Dante Gabriel Rossetti painting. Toward the end, when the band played "Bette Davis Eyes," she had lifted her hand near Samuel's heart. When Maribelle and Samuel got home, she asked what they had talked about. "Not much," Samuel had said as he untied his bow tie and hung up his tuxedo.

"Nothing in particular?" Maribelle remembered how she had pressed her husband.

"I don't know, Maribelle. She's not that scintillating, she's just pretty. Another superficial woman at the table you and your family put together," Samuel had said.

"Barrows took the table, Samuel. You front run the charity choices," Maribelle was defensive. "She must have had something to say for all your conversing."

Samuel was frowning. His mean side was simmering.

"Her daughter, a friend of Harper's, what sports she plays, that's what she talked about."

There was a pang. Maribelle thought *if I had a daughter, I'd call her Lila.*

She had looked at her husband, weighing how she wanted their night to end.

"Fine," Maribelle said. She knew she had to let it go.

"What else would there be?" he asked.

He started to kiss the back of her neck, guiding her toward the bed. Why wasn't she appeased? She so wanted to believe him. It was merely a conversation at a charity dinner. Whatever the trigger, after that, she searched for Collette at every black-tie fundraiser. Maribelle sensed she was scouting the room for him, hoping to trade glances. Except Samuel was discreet, cautious. There was no proof, he made certain of that.

"Ladies," Caroline said, bringing Maribelle back to the present.

No one stopped their prattle. Didn't her sister see how they were—how their mouths worked, the sheen of their hair? Judgmental, nosy, their voices glided along. Only a few feet from where she stood, the ebb and flow continued . . . *widow . . . so sad . . . she's alone . . . has to be brave . . . PB Confidential, no, the editor, chicest of the sisters, he was very philanthropic, at every event together, very attractive, no, no kids.* Except Caroline would not have their talk spoil her daughter's birthday. Instead, she barged into the center of the klatch, slightly sweaty, after she passed Maribelle.

"Ladies, my sisters are here," Caroline announced. "They're the most wonderful aunts to my girls."

Some nodded, including Cecile Griff and Dorey Barnes. With Caleb back in her arms, Raleigh jutted her upper torso out and started shaking everyone's hands. Maribelle stood still, wondering why Raleigh needed to act like a candidate.

Tina Steffen came close to Collette, their necks were the exact same length, their jawlines were aligned.

"Maribelle," she said. "I was telling Caroline that we ought to do a luncheon. Our group —the mothers from Harper's class— we'd like to host you, to be supportive."

"Thank you, Tina. And what a nice time of year for a luncheon," Maribelle said. She sounded like Lucinda, it was that pseudo-calm pretense, the one she despised.

"Can I come too?" Raleigh put her arm around Maribelle's waist.

"Of course," Dorey Barnes said. Maribelle saw how gummy her smile was. "We would love that."

"Let's look at a calendar," Collette said. "Maribelle, we'll work with your schedule. You'll let us know what's best."

"That sounds great." *Truly, why do I live here?* Maribelle asked herself.

At the same time, she was computing Collette's age. Her lips seemed naturally plump, meaning she was under thirty-five. Maribelle couldn't place where she had seen her recently. Was it at Vintage Tales or the Harbor Club, in the locker room? Suddenly, she had an urge to amplify her position at *PB Confidential*, boast that it was glamorous, read by everyone in town. As if her achievement was a tool in staving off the truth—that her husband had been with this woman when he lied about his plans. *PB Confidential* was a façade, a consolation prize while Samuel sneaked around with other women. Had Collette known that—had she and Samuel talked about it while she was in his arms? Maribelle had this vivid image of parts of her body against Samuel's. Had Collette doubled over at Samuel's paltry jokes, had she smiled at his obsession with the *Vertigo*? Maribelle knew she despised this woman.

As she stepped backwards. Raleigh, behind her, whispered, "Who is Collette? She's too . . ."

Maribelle put her fingers to her lips. They needed to be quiet, not rude. Although it was comforting that Raleigh too had an aversion toward her, for whatever her reason.

Nicole came over wrapped in a Breakers Beach Club towel. "Caroline, it's time to cut the cake."

"Shall we go to the table?" Caroline raised her voice. She was inviting in that Palm Beach mother-of-young-children style.

"Everyone, please sit down," she said.

A birthday cake in the shape of an oval swimming pool was on a sidebar. Harper's friends collided toward it, admiring the glitter and sparkles. On the miniature diving board, there was a figure of a swimmer. She was poised, ready to do a flip. Scripted in orange icing was *Happy Birthday, Harper.*

"Hey, Mom!" one of the girls shouted. "Mom, look! Harper says the decorations are edible. Like that time when it was a red velvet cake. Remember? And Harper's Uncle Samuel brought her over before my party started, and we . . ."

Collette went flying toward her. "Kylie." She was attempting a message through eye contact.

"Mom, remember?"

"Kylie," Collette said. Maribelle noticed how outwardly gentle while quietly firm her voice was. What was with these mothers?

"Let's be seated," Nicole sounded like a schoolteacher.

Harper, in her pineapple print two-piece bathing suit, slid into her seat at the head. Within seconds, she was flanked by four girls on either side. Violet, essential little sister, sat at the other end. "Boss," by Fifth Harmony, was blasting from an iPad. Two girls jumped up and started swaying to it, then realized Caroline was carrying the cake to the table, and sat back down.

Nicole switched off the music, and an off-key rendition of *Happy Birthday* began. The minute Harper finished blowing out the candles, Maribelle moved her gaze back to Collette. She was kneeling, whispering to her daughter. Kylie was frowning, shaking her head. When Collette stood up and twisted to see who might have caught their exchange, Maribelle was the one staring at her.

CHAPTER TWELVE

Raleigh

Why was Caroline carrying two mallard duck decoys to the middle of Maribelle and Samuel's vast bed—larger than a California king—Raleigh wondered.

"Is this part of the agenda?" she asked.

"I know we're sorting through clothes today," Caroline said. "But I found five of these in Samuel's closet on the top shelf. They were his dad's, right, Maribelle?"

"His dad's or our dad's," Maribelle said. "Samuel cherished them."

"Maybe you could do a row of them in the library," Raleigh said. "The carvings—look at how they're embellished."

She suggested this knowing it might be the wrong angle. Caroline scowled while Maribelle looked away.

"Mom won't be happy. She won't find them very Palm Beach," Caroline said.

"You mean duck hunting isn't as popular as golf?" Maribelle asked.

Raleigh glanced at Caroline. Was this a joke, was Maribelle emerging slightly from her overwhelming gloom? Were they allowed to laugh?

"Hey, it's okay," Maribelle laughed. It was a new sound, squinched, woodpecker-like.

Both Caroline and Raleigh forced their own laughter, for a second. Next, Caroline edged over to the fuchsia Finn Juhl Pelican chair—something Raleigh had loved since the day Maribelle and Samuel bought it. Mounds of Samuel's sweaters, an infusion of colors, were stacked there. From where Raleigh stood, half the floor was covered, too. Through the alcove, on a settee, were Samuel's Lacoste polo shirts. Color-coded, shades of blue, greens, pinks, yellows, an entire group of whites. Caroline began flipping through like she was at the men's shop at Saks on the Avenue.

"The colors are luscious," Raleigh said. "It's a little like the shirt scene in *The Great Gatsby*, isn't it? There's that whole idea of an abundance of stuff."

Maribelle shrugged, eyeing the sweaters and polos as if she didn't know there were so many. "I thought in Gatsby it was about lost opportunity."

"Let's not do symbolism," Caroline said. "Let's stick with our plan."

"These shirts, they have meaning," Raleigh insisted. She wanted to make a point. "They have a history, where Samuel wore them, what happened while he wore them. Maribelle, you think so, don't you?"

"Some of them." Maribelle touched a few. "He said the pinks were for lobster night at Banyan or grill night at the Harbor Club. He liked the yellows for early tee times."

"Well, maybe these could be divided," Caroline said. "Travis is about Samuel's height and weight, Alex is a few inches taller, still the polo shirts should fit. Raleigh, you take some, Alex might like that. Travis would do well with the darker blues."

Raleigh tried to imagine Alex in the kitchen one morning, wearing a white Lacoste polo shirt that had belonged to Samuel. While she would be begging Caleb to stop throwing oatmeal, Alex would be avoiding them both to preserve his shirt. She looked to Maribelle for approval of Caroline's idea. Maribelle was unreadable, running her hands over the shirts that Caroline was ready to divide. As if the same truth hit her over and over, Samuel won't be wearing these ever again.

"Thanks. I don't know. Probably not. What about a not-for-profit?"

Maribelle sighed. "Yes, we'll give them to Housing Works in West Palm. Samuel was on the board."

"Samuel was generous, as every speaker said at the memorial," Caroline said. "He was the most altruistic of our husbands."

"He was known for it," Maribelle said.

"There's not a person who didn't admire his altruism," Caroline waited for Maribelle to now praise him. Like a game of ping pong.

Maribelle cleared her throat without saying more. Raleigh knew it was her turn "He was, I agree. Very giving."

"Everyone loved him," Caroline kept going. "He glided into this life like it belonged to him. Travis wasn't like that, he was awkward, he lacked Samuel's charm. He's kind of grown into it, but truthfully, he's still kind of a bumpkin."

Raleigh and Maribelle laughed.

"It's true," Caroline continued. "Mom and Samuel became instant Palm Beachers . . ."

"Please," Maribelle said. She had stopped laughing. "We realize that."

Raleigh counted to ten. How long could her sisters do this, what was she meant to contribute?

"Well, Alex is a good husband and a really sweet father," she said. "Except that the level of shopping, parties, and club life baffles him, you know. He doesn't like to show up. It isn't that hard to figure out. He calls it a reality TV show."

"He wishes he could be a great American artist of the 21st century," Caroline sounded snarky.

"That's a goal, Caroline," Maribelle said.

Raleigh appreciated Maribelle's defense but knew not to thank her. Caroline wouldn't like it, she never did.

"Alex is all about his art. He wants a patron," Raleigh said.

"He might consider Mrs. A. If he paints her looking twenty-five years younger, it's a sealed deal," Maribelle said.

This time, all three sisters laughed. Raleigh and Caroline watched Maribelle, remembering how she was before Samuel died.

"Okay, to continue . . ." Caroline held up a melon-colored shirt and examined the label. "Trillion—on the Avenue. Didn't Lucinda buy this for Samuel for his last birthday?"

As if it was precious, she smoothed, then folded the sweater and headed for the closet.

"Look at this—look at Samuel's uniforms for Palm Beach." Caroline started carrying sport jackets on large wooden hangers. Two classic blazers, a pale grey sport jacket, a soft taupe one that looked like a silk and cashmere blend. One black number, the hipper side of Samuel. Beyond that, some patterns and checks that Raleigh thought were awfully old-man.

Maribelle ran her hands across the lapels. "Samuel was great in every one of them."

"That he was." Caroline flattened out a wrinkle in the first jacket.

She began arranging the jackets onto the mid-century rosewood desk. They slipped around, she steadied them. They slipped again. She moved them to the floor, dropping all of them.

Raleigh wanted to scream at Caroline, *stop it, let's put this off, another day will be better.* She began to cry.

"I can't stop thinking of what was," she said. "How Maribelle and Samuel were back in Kesgrave. Remember when Samuel came to our family picnic at Henderson Beach? We had that red-checkered cloth spread out on the dune. Maribelle, both you and Caroline wore cuts offs and bikini tops. Mom was in a floppy straw hat and a thigh-high shift. Afterward, Maribelle and Samuel drove off in his GMC Sierra."

Caroline made a noise with her tongue. "What good does it do to sit around remembering Samuel and how we lived in Bumblefuck."

"I liked it there," Raleigh said. "It felt milder."

The way that Caroline and Maribelle stared at Raleigh, she knew she had made a stir. Her sisters were too Lucinda-like; too many of their mother's preferences came first. They were sliding into Lucinda's vision of how they should be.

"What makes you say that?" Caroline asked. "Mom was miserable, pushing Dad to make gobs of money. She'd be reading catalogs from civilization. You know, Bloomingdales, Saks. She subscribed to *The New Yorker* one year. She kept planning our exit."

Raleigh stopped crying. "Now you think our hometown was the culprit?" she asked. "Because that's wrong. Kesgrave gave us some dimension, something beyond being privileged and going shopping on the Avenue."

"Maybe," Maribelle said quietly. "Maybe not."

Caroline shook her head, there was nothing more to say. She walked to the dresser and lifted a carved wood box. "Wow, Raleigh, did you see this? Look at the cufflinks."

"Cufflinks? Who wears those?" Raleigh asked. "I remember Dad did when I was little, but not very much."

"Dad liked to wear them when he dressed up," Caroline said.

"Dad," Raleigh shook her head. Their father; Samuel. The men they thought would be around.

Raleigh felt her sadness mix with the weight of the room. Despite the cool furniture, she thought it screamed married life, somewhere between uninspired and sheltered. She had certainly been there enough, having spent hours in Maribelle's walk-in closet. About four times a season, she would borrow something vogue for an event. A black tie at the Norton or the Children's Zoo or Educational Life. Barrows had taken a table at each fundraiser, and Maribelle considered dressing properly as work related—for both Barrows and *PB Confidential*. She told Raleigh that *PB Confidential* had an audience, and she was the avatar. After Raleigh borrowed a dress, Maribelle told her to keep it, saying she couldn't pull off that Oscar or that Jason Wu anymore. "It's too good on you, Raleigh. It can't come back to me," she told her. "That dress should be yours."

"Raleigh, are you with us?" Caroline asked. She was onto her next task.

"Wait, a few watches too. A Rolex, one Cartier Tank. Wow." She picked up a Patek Philippe. "Isn't this Dad's?"

Maribelle came over. "Samuel didn't wear that. I guess Dad gave it to him, and he thought it was too old-guard or something."

"Patek Philippe is pretty elegant," Caroline said. She turned it over. "It has Dad's initials. Look *REB*, Reed Edward Barrows."

Maribelle moved to the window. Raleigh wanted to ask if she were imagining Samuel at this moment. Had they stood there together? Did they make love on Saturday mornings in this bed, once uncluttered with Samuel's clothes?

"Do you have any idea why Dad's watch would be with Samuel's things? And look at this!" Caroline unwrapped two miniature statues. "Aren't these the Edo figurines Dad bought for Mom in Japan. They're part of her . . ."

Maribelle wasn't turning around; Caroline was hissing a low-level hiss.

"So what? Who cares?" Raleigh asked. She wanted to protect Maribelle, wherever Caroline wanted to take things.

"Well, I care," Caroline said. "Seriously, why are Mom and Dad's treasured belongings in some box of Samuel's? Maribelle?"

"I can't answer that, Caroline," Maribelle said. "But when I met with Daryl Dexter, he told me nothing can be taken out of the house except the clothes. We shouldn't be going through watches or anything else you've just started to go through."

"I suppose later, after probate, whatever is here for some inexplicable reason that belongs to . . ." Caroline said.

"Please, stop it," Raleigh said. "Stop."

She saw her sisters freeze, then shallow lines began in both their foreheads. They seemed distracted, looped together without her. Like when she was little and in one of their bedrooms in Kesgrave, early on a Saturday evening. Raleigh would twirl around in one of their outfits that was too large and too sophisticated for her while they got ready for to go out. Maribelle braided her hair and called her Rapunzel. If she had time, Caroline would put liquid eyeliner on her upper lids.

Raleigh sucked in the air. "Can we move on?"

Caroline put the figurines down. Maribelle lifted them, with the watch. "I'll put these back for now. Let's concentrate on what can be sorted and tossed since Caroline is on a purge."

A midday breeze was kicking up along the ocean. Seagulls swooped through cumulus clouds. They were missing it all, thought Raleigh. She inched closer to the terrace.

"We could go outside, take a walk on the beach, put this off for another day," she said.

"Excuse me, Raleigh?" Caroline eyed a collection of Samuel's belts and ties on the desk chair. "With a mess everywhere?"

"Ms. Walker?" Rosie knocked at the French doors. She came into the bedroom with a tray of Saratoga water and a platter of ginger cookies and, eyeing their lack of progress, backed out.

Raleigh grabbed two at once on the off chance that, if she ate enough, she would stop feeling empty inside.

There was the sound of Caroline's ring tone—the Kinks, singing "You Really Got Me." She snatched her phone from her pocket, studying it. "Harper, hi, honey," she said too cheerily. "What did Nicole say?"

Caroline stepped across the pale wood floor. "You might check with your father. He'll be able to—I don't know," Caroline paused. "A while, at least an hour, I'm at Aunt Maribelle's. Of course, the minute I get home."

"We need more to eat," Maribelle said. "I'll go into the kitchen and hunt around. I have yogurt, peanut butter, mini pretzels . . ."

As soon as Maribelle was gone, Caroline was off her call.

"Listen," she said. "Maribelle's a mess. What's going on with Mom and this missing money is irrational, it's adding to Maribelle's anxiety. And Julian's working on it, we do not need our mother digging around."

"Lucinda seems remarkably pissed," Raleigh said.

"I know," Caroline said. "She's convinced that Dad's largesse kept Travis and Samuel from the slagheap, and they weren't grateful enough. Especially Samuel. You know how she disdained his family. Anyway, Mom's in a punishing mode."

Raleigh turned her hands out toward Samuel's clothing collection. "Okay, I get it. But look at what Maribelle's going through that has nothing to do with money. Look at this."

"Yes, it's troubling how alone she is and how much she's lost," Caroline said. "And a separate issue from what Samuel has . . . had done. I only hope that you and she understand the ramifications of the funds that are gone."

"Why is it always about the company for you, Caroline?" Raleigh asked.

"Raleigh, please, listen to me. Julian believes the money is off-shore, so does Travis. We'll find out."

"Travis? What does he know?" Raleigh asked.

A baneful layer that had fallen over every family member, thought Raleigh. Like noxious fumes where there had been light currents of sea air. Before that, before Palm Beach, there had been the tides along the river, back in Kesgrave. Now she wasn't sure who to believe. For the first time ever, she was pleased that Alex wasn't popular with the Barrowses, that she had been placed off center too.

Caroline shook her head. "Travis swears he *doesn't* know. He suspected something was off about Riptide, and he confronted Samuel. Samuel persuaded him Riptide was legit. You know how Samuel was. He could sell ice in winter. Travis worships . . . worshipped the ground he walked on." She folded another polo shirt for the pile. The Travis pile. "In any case, we have Julian. No stone unturned there."

"I'm thinking of Maribelle, not the money," Raleigh said. "She's *our* sister."

"You feel sorry for Maribelle, we all do," Caroline sighed.

"We shouldn't be doing this now. It's not . . ."

"Not right," Maribelle said. She was at the archway, holding a box of cheese straws in one hand and a bowl of grapes in the other. Her eyes were jumpy, the irises were dark. "I heard what you said, how you pity me."

"No, we don't, Maribelle!" Raleigh said. She jumped up to put her arms around her. "We're waiting for the days to move on, for you to be less upset."

Raleigh was lying, because Maribelle's silhouette reminded her of characters to weep for—Miss Havisham, Emma Bovary, Bertha, the first wife in *Jane Eyre*. She was lying because she revered Maribelle when she was eight years old. Caroline too, maybe more so, since she had been the cheerleading captain at Pinestream with her highest jumps, her sparkly smile, her buckets of hair. Over twenty years ago. What an awakening it was to realize that what she thought in third grade about her big sisters didn't cut it today. She had been so young, longing to mirror them, to catch up.

"Yeah, *not* pity," Caroline said. "I'm channeling Mom, how she views being without a husband. You know, men need to be good *enough*, nothing more. Every Tuesday morning on the Lake Trail, Tina and I have this conversation about who is ready to divorce, or who is having an affair. I lean toward not bothering to swap out one for another. The lover could turn out to be worse."

Maribelle nodded. "You haven't been married long enough to know, Raleigh. There's this theory Lucinda has about husbands. When I was engaged to Samuel, she sat me down for it."

"Wait, she told me too. Mom's take on husbands, right?" Caroline asked.

"Number one: public is not private," Maribelle said. "I've been thinking about it a lot since Samuel died. You know he'd charm everyone in the room, and on the car ride home, he'd be mocking people while in a snit."

Caroline snickered. "Well, number two is what I couldn't get right. That tall is not strong. In my dreams Travis takes charge. He's tall enough."

No one laughed, it was too true. Raleigh thought she'd throw up, or at least cry.

"Number three is that handsome is rarely kind," Maribelle spoke quietly.

They were all stumped, sorry. Raleigh felt their regret, like an illness, had invaded them. How did someone weed out regret? After a bit she said, "Lucinda did not have that conversation with me. I've never heard her theory before."

"Really?" Both sisters said this together, only mildly surprised their mother had not shared the same information with each of her daughters. In the moment, Raleigh determined if she ever had another child, he or she would be given everything that Caleb had. Equal parts, always.

"I was a lost cause, could that be it?" Raleigh asked. "She only said that smart is not everything when I wanted to marry Alex."

"Ah, yes, her fourth precept," Caroline said.

"It might have helped to tell me," Raleigh said. "I could have used guidance."

But her sisters were staring at her as if she were too separate, too apart to have benefitted from such strict, practical points.

They had no idea what she was capable of, Raleigh realized. Or that she defied their expectations. They had no idea she was the sister who had stopped being loyal to her husband. That all day, she was imagining North, their secluded afternoons along the coast, whatever town was unrecognizable, for their manifest love. Afterward, Raleigh remembered, the rides home alone in her car, swerving back to her role as wife and mother. Rarely had she asked herself if anyone was worse off for what she and North had done.

Raleigh got up, swinging her arms, waiting for the other side of the conversation. Maribelle was twisting the wedding band on her left hand. An Etoile design from Tiffany with five rows of pavé diamonds. Something she and Samuel had chosen several years ago—an upgrade. Was she going to file it away, store it in a drawer with other gifts, buckets of jewelry, from Samuel?

"Besides, you and Travis are a team, Caroline," Maribelle said.

"And Raleigh and Alex aren't?" Caroline asked.

Raleigh waited a few seconds before answering. "A team, sure. Except do you ever wonder why nothing is what you believe it will be? Every right thing with the wrong person?" she asked.

Caroline did a twitching downturn of her mouth. "That's how it is. I try not to let it cross my mind."

"You used to say that Samuel looked like Bradley Cooper, Raleigh." Maribelle sounded defeated.

"Well, he did." Raleigh said.

The three sisters looked at each other, because never before had anything like this happened. For once, Raleigh thought, neither Maribelle nor Caroline knew what was expected. They were huddled together sorting through a dead man's possessions, one of their own.

The daylight was veering away, yet nothing had become softer. The large, slanted mirror over the dresser was tilted, they saw themselves. Three sisters, skeletal, as if the skin was missing over their bones.

PART TWO

CHAPTER THIRTEEN

Maribelle

"Are you too cold?" Nadia asked.

Maribelle noticed how she sported a hot pink pashmina, circa 2000. Wasn't it borderline between brave, chic, and trying too hard? But Nadia was good at that.

"I'm fine," Maribelle said. She zipped her cropped pleather jacket. After today, she ought to give it to Raleigh, she thought. It would suit her well.

She and Nadia stood in front of Sant Ambroeus and peered at the gelato flavors in their outdoor Sorbetto trolley.

"How about two salted caramel gelatos?" Nadia pointed. The server started scooping. She smiled at Maribelle. "Maybe this will cheer you up. Let's sit outdoors, even if it's only sixty-eight degrees."

"That's fine," Maribelle said. "We'll be uninterrupted."

Nadia raised her eyebrows. Voices were swinging along the sidewalk, and Maribelle realized they were among late lunchers; it was shopping weather. Women over forty were in their palest cashmere sweaters or wore featherweight scarves looped around their necks. Younger women wore jeans and patent leather booties or Gucci sneakers. Mrs. A and Allison Rochester, deep in conversation, waved as they headed inside. Ina Coles and Veronica Cutler were leaving the restaurant, both on their cell phones. Everyone smiled brightly when they saw Maribelle and Nadia—especially Nadia. Even the slightest mention in her *Trends and Spottings* column was coveted.

The women seemed to not have a care. Their hopefulness reminded Maribelle of Lucinda's belief that there is ownership in being happy. Yet not everyone was part of the glee—was it that facile?

She and Nadia sat at a table below an umbrella. Nadia crossed her long legs and leaned closer.

"How about that feature on the Barrows family, a rags to riches piece?"

"Nadia, why would you pursue it?" Maribelle asked. "Holly already vetoed the idea."

Nadia exhaled. "It's a natural; it's what I do."

"You can't write about my family," Maribelle said. "You can't do this where I work."

"Why not? Before *PB Confidential* goes online—for our last hard copy of the magazine—we should do this," Nadia said. "Remember the piece on the Harrisons and *Vintage Tales*? That was a hit."

Maribelle was floored, imagining not only the ire of Lucinda, but Nadia's entire approach. As self-aggrandizing as her mother could be, she had never allowed any journalist to excavate their past in Kesgrave. When the family first moved to Palm Beach, Lucinda worried when people whispered about their money. Drug money was the rumor—that Reed had built the Barrows chain from it. He had hired Lee Clefort, famed publicist, to put out the flames.

"It isn't determined that you can control this, Maribelle," Nadia took a big spoonful of her gelato. It's a big story. Young handsome rich Palm Beach businessman dies in a boating 'accident.' People are already talking . . ."

Panic and fury slammed together. Maribelle decided to channel her mother. "Talking about what?" she asked icily.

Nadia waved her spoon in the air. "Oh, you know, the usual. Was Samuel Walker drinking that morning, was he hiding something, did he have depressive tendencies? People love to speculate. They assume everyone has a secret. It's human nature. Glorified gossip, right?"

Maribelle sank deeper into the wicker chair. "It's obvious that any story about my husband's death or my family . . . the company . . . isn't suitable while I'm the editorial director,"

She smiled a mentor to mentee smile. "How about another direction. I've got a poem by Jean Valentine in mind called 'Trust Me,' with that line about the river frozen beneath the snow. Or that update on climate change you were pitching?"

Nadia scowled. "Right, less slick. But also, less *PB Confidential.* I mean we're not *The New Yorker.* We're not *Harpers.* Isn't a juicy story best for our readership?"

There was something about the set of Nadia's mouth and her chin. Maribelle resisted telling her that disloyalty came at a price.

"You might write up stepmothers and their stepdaughters, interviewing prominent local duos about the ups and downs of their relationships, if that resonates with you," she said.

Maritza Abrams, divorce lawyer, and Demi Dexter, dermatologist, were circling around the gelato trolley and waved to them. When Maribelle waved back, this memory of Samuel swept in. One of their last conversations, where he couldn't grasp why she wanted to leave Palm Beach.

"A production company in LA?" he had repeated when she said she wanted to be in California. "Look at what you have right in Palm Beach at the magazine, it's *your* magazine."

How could Maribelle have known how profoundly untrue that was? Samuel's overarching power grab through this investment only proved he wasn't confident that she could do it on her own. It was tempting to despise him for it, except he was dead.

Nadia put on her Krewe Collins Nylon sunglasses and stared past Maribelle to the corners of the patio.

"I've been working to keep any of the other papers, especially *The Daily Sheet,* quiet, while they're fishing," she said.

"Fishing, digging. I'm sure," Maribelle said. "There's not much of a story. It was an awful accident but flat news."

"Maybe, maybe not," Nadia sighed. "It's all good until people become nosy. If we run it, *if I write it,* it can be filtered, and not only about Samuel. If not, other writers will go to the Coast Guard or at least to the marina. It's exactly what I would do if I didn't work for you."

A sickening sensation overcame Maribelle, like she had missed the last plane out, as if she had been ambushed.

"Whatever there is to it, I'm vetoing the story, Nadia," she said.

She was using her calm, media-trained voice, yet her panic was rising. She had to get to the dock where Samuel kept his Riva Rivamare.

"Got it," Nadia says.

Holding out her arm, Maribelle tapped on her Chopard sport watch, the one Samuel bought for her thirty-fifth birthday. Before he had met Collette, before he had started dabbling in money at Barrows. It was the year they had sailed a Hobie Cat together, flown to New York to run the Marathon, and driven along the Amalfi Coast. He had called them a team. When had he stopped saying that?

"Not to be rude, but I didn't realize how late it is. I'm off to the tailor before I go back to the office," Maribelle said.

"What tailor?" Nadia took off her sunglasses to stare. "Doesn't your mother's seamstress, what is her name, Janice, visit each Barrows sister's house for fittings?

"I have two Lily shifts from C. Orrico, they only need to be hemmed. It's easier to stop by . . ." Maribelle made up this excuse since the dresses had been in her trunk since before Samuel died. Proof that her plan was real. She needed to go.

She stood up and smiled slightly. "Again, sorry to be rushing off."

Her gelato was melting slowly into soup in the dusty rose cardboard bowl, the color of the restaurant's awning. She decided to leave it there.

She raced toward her car before Nadia offered to come along.

Not ten minutes later, Maribelle headed west. When she made a right on Flagler, Bob Dylan came on, singing "Like a Rolling Stone." She raised the volume, lowered it, shut it off. She was too uneasy to admire the Intracoastal. She started speeding. If stopped, she knew she'd get out of it. She and her sisters had charmed the Palm Beach police before.

She parked and walked along the wide wooden planks to the manager's office at the Yacht Club marina. Again, a dull sunlight reflected off the water, the temperature hadn't risen, salty air blew about. Enough boats were docked that it didn't feel like the season, the place was too quiet. An afternoon wind whipped the water across the pilings and bulkhead. Maribelle was relieved, it meant fewer people to greet or avoid.

"Can I help you?" A thin, bearded thirty-something man asked. His tone and tan reminded her of how Travis and Samuel would have been had the Barrowses stayed in Kesgrave. Had her father believed in his two sons-in-law? Surely both rose to the occasion when they were carefully guided into becoming sophisticated men. Might this one behind the desk be worth it to someone—a similar kind of aspiring family, Maribelle thought, determined to make a sea change?

"I've come to collect my husband's possessions, whatever was onboard his Riva Rivamare, the *Vertigo,*" Maribelle said. "I had called about it yesterday."

"Your husband's things. Ah, yes . . . you are?"

"Maribelle Barrows Walker. His name is—his name was Samuel Walker." Samuel at this pier, at the bar and restaurant, the Yacht Club, she wanted to shout.

"Our condolences," the thin man said. "Your husband was popular, friendly. He offered to help my stepmother one day when she had a flat tire in the parking lot."

Maribelle was certain his stepmother was attractive. "That's nice," she said.

The young man suddenly pinned his nametag onto his polo shirt and stared at his desktop. *Roger.* There was light around him from a slim window, the walls were a dark wood. He bent down to produce a large white plastic bag, one that would have depressed Maribelle in any event. She almost started to cry, she wanted to leave. Why hadn't she asked Tanya to arrange a DocuSign, followed by a pick-up? Samuel's things could have been sent to her office. Short of that, she wished that Raleigh had come along, that would have helped. Maribelle invoked Lucinda 101: *Never display your feelings in public, regardless of the occasion.* She knew that included retrieving one's dead husband's gear from a marina.

"I'll need to go through this with you, Miss." He pulled a paper bag out, spilled what was inside onto the counter. A pair of black framed Ray Bans without a case; a tablet that read *Barrows* on the top; two pens, also from Barrows; a set of keys that looked unfamiliar; several charts; three flashlights. Maribelle lifted the keys and slid her hand across the ridges. Whose were they? Collette's? No, too risky. Were they to a hideaway, their hideaway?

"Miss?"

He was patient, waiting for her.

"Here you go." She placed them with Samuel's other things.

"That was in a drawer, and here's the rest." From the larger bag, Roger took out a set of emergency flares; a baseball cap that had Longreen's across the brim in script; a spray can of Coppertone sunblock; a short dog leash; and two bright blue life vests.

"Nothing else." He began to arrange Samuel's possessions back into the bags. "You know, I was with my boss that morning after it happened. The cops and the Coast Guard came and asked questions about your husband. Then nothing until an officer brought this back yesterday, said it was okay. All wrapped up, a bad accident on the waterway, nothing else to it."

Maribelle didn't emote. Nor was she incredibly relieved the investigation was over. Instead, as if she were Nancy Drew, she was trying to imagine what Nadia or other journalists might glean if they came into the marina and asked Roger some questions, delving for details. If they were to question the Coast Guard.

"Right, of course." Maribelle's mouth was mealy.

"Is there anything else I can do for you, Miss?" Roger folded the top of the plastic bag and walked around to give it to her. He smelled of open waterways.

"Do you remember the officers?" she asked. She hoped to seem conversational.

"I dunno. Some big guy seemed to be in charge."

Breeley—it had to be. Maribelle opened her mouth, closed it. The oversized nautical wall clock ticked too loudly.

"I'm sorry for your loss," Roger said. He was very sincere.

Maribelle considered whether she should press on, explain that someone might come snooping around and she was counting on his discretion. She felt like screaming *loss? It's hell on earth.*

The wall clock was ticking more, out of nowhere its speed and decibel level were louder. She imagined slamming it, breaking the glass. Instead she silently recited a hasty mantra—ersatz mindfulness that remarkably worked. Maribelle thanked Roger, sounding rushed. She began the walk from the manager's office to her car, farther from the boat slip where her husband had docked his precious speedboat. Where, one morning, Samuel had dashed out of her car while Supy barked maniacally.

"Ms. Walker? Maribelle, wait up. Wait where you are."

She stopped sharply. It reminded her of playing statues with Harper and Violet. *Freeze, Aunt Maribelle, Uncle Samuel,* they instructed as they ran along the beach. When it was the girls' turn to freeze, Samuel invoked Wonder Woman. *Freeze, girls, be bold!* They ended up contorting themselves into young female warriors. Samuel was fantastic, wasn't he?

"Hey," Julian Albert said, "It is you."

The wind blew at his face. He seemed less rugged today. Still, his coloring was vivid enough that the rest of the scene—the boats, the pilings, a few others walking around the pier—was pallid.

"Julian, hello," Maribelle held the bag closer.

"Are you meeting someone?" he asked.

"No, no. I came to pick up what was on Samuel's boat and returned by the Coast Guard. Why are you at the Yacht Club?"

Julian stared at what Maribelle was carrying. "I might move to this dock from Palm Harbor. I'm checking it out."

"I didn't know you had a boat," Maribelle said. Then, why would she know—or care.

"Ah, I do, a Sea Ray, Cobalt series. I wanted one for a long while and finally bought it."

"I'm sorry, I should know the model," Maribelle said.

"It's fast enough, I like it. One day, I'll have a houseboat and live on it. Not in this area, not in Monte Carlo, someplace easier. That's my goal," he said.

Maribelle wanted to leave. She cared little about Julian's dreams but knew to be polite. He was their forensic. She tilted her face toward him. "A houseboat?"

"Not your style, right?" He seemed amused.

"I liked the one in *Sleepless in Seattle*, although it looked a little worn," she said. The bag with Samuel's things was heavy.

"Well, Seattle sounds eye-catching, but even I would prefer a fresher, newer kind of houseboat," Julian said.

"I've never really seen one up close," Maribelle said. "It depends on where the boat is docked, I think."

He laughed. "How about the 79th Street boat basin, New York City? Is that more like it?"

"Yes, more like it."

He pointed to the Yacht Club. "Let's go have a drink at what floats before our eyes. I'll carry that to your car first."

Maribelle was about to hand over Samuel's things and go with him, briefly forgetting that she wanted nothing to do with the investigation.

"Wait, are you following me?" Maribelle asked. "Why are you really at this pier, right when I am?"

"Following you! Whose side do you think I'm on? I'm hired by your mother. I'm prioritizing the case. I was going to reach out anyway. I'm planning to speak to each family member. Caroline and I have met already. She was very helpful," Julian said.

Caroline. Of course, she was helpful, thought Maribelle. An image of her sister filled her head—a honed Palm Beach wife and mother, tilting her upper torso toward him, her green-tinted lenses, her hair precisely blown out. Flirting with him, despite her thoughtfully curated life and family.

There was more to it, Maribelle knew. Julian had access to Samuel's cell phone records and credit card bills. He was about to learn, or maybe already had, that her husband was unfaithful. Worse, soon enough Julian would figure out that Samuel had funded *PB Confidential*. A cold fear ran through her, could she be implicated?

"C'mon, Maribelle, we'll have sparkling water. We'll talk about the case. We'll have a business drink."

At most, Maribelle and Julian stood only a foot apart. With the sun setting early at this time of year, she thought they both seemed almost airbrushed. If only she were able to forget how she had met Julian. And skip the widow part.

Maribelle shook her head. "It's better if we make a plan. We can meet at my office."

She said this although she wanted nothing to do with the investigation. Her rather rusty come-on was about Julian and a chance to see him. She figured if Caroline, married with children, was in play, she might be as well.

CHAPTER FOURTEEN

Caroline

After a late afternoon appointment with Demi Dexter for Botox and filler, Caroline decided not to go back to her desk at Barrows. Instead, she walked through her house on Tangier Avenue, a place she knew better on weekends than weekdays. The rooms were preternaturally calm because her girls had gone to the Finley sisters for tie-dyeing T-shirts and working with macramé kits. Noel Finley, an activity-driven mother, was one of few Caroline could count on. Harper and Violet were guests there more than it worked in reverse. Nicole was at Publix, food shopping.

It had been a day—every day was like that since Samuel's accident. Caroline was delighted to kick off her semi-practical, palest beige Manolos and pad into the library, straight to the wet bar. She surveyed the selection as if she were at someone else's bar. Anything she might pour, from Prosecco to whiskey, seemed like a fine idea. Whatever had the capacity to blunt

Lucinda's interference, her insistence that she check every revenue report from every location and that Julian wanted files, hard copies, and any email trail. Her mother had been so vile that Travis had put his hand on Caroline's wrist and lowered the volume on the speaker phone—her method of delivery—as she droned on.

A sympathetic side to Travis. As Caroline contemplated this, she trailed past the bookcases to find her husband sprawled on the couch, reading his Kindle Fire. Clearly, he hadn't expected to see her. He held a bottle of Michelob Ultra in one hand and a bag of tortilla chips in the other—a quiet rebellion, since Travis knew Caroline poured beer into a tall glass and served chips in a bowl.

He seemed surprised but also fidgety. "Why are you home so early, Caroline?"

"Dermatologist appointment. I thought I told you. I decided to head straight here for the rest of today—what's left of it." Besides, she was a bit bruised from Demi's poking and filling, not that Travis would get that.

"Yeah. Well, our Peloton was just delivered, so I came back too. I mentioned that. Anyway, I'm taking last calls in about an hour."

Travis went back to his Kindle, a thriller no doubt. The ambient light in the room on a Thursday at four o'clock was unnatural. The paint, Farrow & Ball's Light Gray, had an odd tinge.

"Funny that we're both on this schedule," Caroline said.

Travis nodded, slid his hand inside the tortilla bag, and jammed a fistful into his mouth. Caroline thought it was gross; besides, if he were to unexpectedly sneeze or cough, everything would fly out. What was it that some wives were known to say—they would do anything but watch their husbands eat? How had this happened so soon—she was only thirty-six.

"Caroline." He suddenly got up. "Maybe it's a good time to talk."

"I've got a few minutes. Then Nicole picks up the girls. Is it something specific?"

"About your mother's mission when it comes to Barrows," Travis said.

"Ah that," Caroline said.

She glanced at her mini backpack on the coffee table, wondering whether she should go on the Avenue for another color, say a honey shade, same version. *No holes in your wardrobes,* Lucinda liked to remind her daughters. Usually after she bemoaned for the millionth time how she had so few clothes in Kesgrave growing up. How her parents were destitute, how far she had come. Caroline and her sisters hadn't decided what their mother told William, however. Their stepfather, a title they refuted, was either uninformed or rattled about her past—the time before Lucinda, as Mrs. Reed Barrows, arrived in Palm Beach. They doubted she confessed to having created her destiny after reading Wayne Dyer and *Redbook* magazine in the mid-eighties. *Run, don't walk away from these woods,* she used to say when Maribelle and Caroline were in grade school. Had William learned yet that Lucinda was the brains behind Barrows?

"Caroline?" Travis asked.

"Oh, I know, utter chaos. What good is my mother doing? We have Julian, whatever he finds, he reports to us," she said.

Julian had been at the office all week searching for clues. Because he was one of those people whose presence washed everyone else out, Caroline and the entire staff had been drained. When he spoke to Caroline in the smaller conference room, he was so vivid the Anne Norwich paintings seemed bleached, the primary colors faded.

"Well, that's the thing, Caro. You don't need to come to be on every call, at every meeting. I know how busy you are with the opening in Orlando."

"Excuse me?" Caroline asked. She walked toward their Regency desk. How traditional it was, she thought, compared to Samuel's, the one in Maribelle's bedroom.

"Plus, the girls, of course. There's plenty going on for you already." Travis said. His voice had changed in the last half hour, like it had been run over.

Caroline paused, counted. "In truth," she said, "I'm considering the opposite, Travis. Not only should I be at those meetings, I should take Samuel's position at Barrows. When I think about his plans, what he did, and what he was about to do for the company, I really get it."

Her husband opened his mouth to speak, sputtered, closed it, and backed up a few steps. She saw his astonishment. He cleared his throat in the annoying way he did before a board meeting. She knew his hands were clammy, like he had held a wad of silly putty for too long.

"I'm sorry, Caroline?" he asked.

"I can repeat it. I said I should have Samuel's position at Barrows," she said.

"I'm not sure what you mean. You can't be asking for Samuel's job. He was the *CFO*. He was a businessman. He had an MBA," Travis said.

"Asking? It's more that I'm stating it," Caroline said. "I deserve the position. I am educated, primed for it. I have a BA in finance. My MA is in marketing. I've been taught by my father. You remember my summer jobs at Barrows starting in ninth grade? I always wanted this. For the past seven years, I've been the CMO without the exact title, and I'm not sure why. I don't need a man to front for me while I secretly run a company. Lucinda did—it was a different time. It was wretched."

Caroline looked at her phone and began scrolling through pictures. She found one of her parents in front of the first Barrows in Kesgrave. Lucinda, in a complacent pose, was pregnant with Maribelle. She held it up.

"I know that photo," Travis smiled for a millisecond. He fidgeted, walked back to the side table, and lifted his bottle of beer, swigging it.

"If this were ever worth considering, it isn't the time," he said. "There's the company to run, the investigation, there's the family. We're doing a search for the position."

"Let me ponder that, Travis. You and Samuel, who never seemed exactly keen on my parents, got to run their company— and today you are running it solo. Neither you nor Samuel started it, you didn't invent it." Caroline said.

She felt as if someone had burst her open. Who believed she had the guts for this?

"Hey, listen. Samuel and I made it more profitable," Travis said. "We expanded, we created the new template, where customers come in and want to stay."

"Oh, I know," Caroline said. "Not just to pick up food, lunch, soup. People like a destination, they like fast food that tastes homemade. The seating areas work, the big screens—what we say at every pitch. I've been the one marketing the themes, right?"

She walked back to the wet bar, to get her shoes and slide them on. She pulled herself up to the best height possible, then moved to the windows that faced the pool. For her, their pool was an oasis. She was lucid because she swam laps every morning at six thirty. At the office, Samuel used to ask her, *how was the swim, did you clock it?* They had laughed because her answer was always the same: *A mile in thirty minutes. It was the best.* Not a significant joke, still it had been their joke.

"I'm aware, I know what Samuel and you did for Barrows," Caroline said. "I want to be a bigger part of it, I care about it. I care about it like my mother cares."

"Lucinda won't like this, she won't approve," Travis said. "If anything, she's too vital, without a title herself. Emeritus, I suppose. Isn't her hope that you'll be more of a Palm Beach wife and mother with fewer work hours?"

"She might not agree. Still, my mother wants what's best for the company, what's profitable. Lucinda might have to forfeit her fantasy of me as an uber-mom princess. But I'm okay with that. You and I, the girls, we've done plenty that's right for her. We're pleasing, living close by, showing up. No one misses her command, especially us."

"I'm sorry, Caroline, it isn't a good idea," Travis said. "Lucinda's already talking about using a headhunter. This has to be someone with business credentials, experience as a CFO. Besides, we need you where you are, heading up marketing."

"How about we move me to CFO and find a new marketing executive—someone who works for us already. How about Amy? She's polished, she's been with the company for as long as I have. I can help with the training."

Travis gulped down the beer. "I don't think so."

"If I didn't know better, I'd say you're sexist. Except we both believe in parity," Caroline said.

"In this family?" he laughed and started counting on his hand. "I'm raising two daughters, we've got your two sisters, your mother, Aunt Bryant. How could I be a chauvinist?"

He stopped himself, as if an idea had landed. As if this could be the very cover-up he needed.

"Hey, I don't *mean* to be, if I come across that way." Travis sounded weary. He reminded Caroline of how her father had sounded when the stock market was tanking, or his golf game wasn't up to par.

That's when she realized how serious it was, what she was up against. Travis didn't want her at Samuel's desk, near Samuel's files.

"What is it, Travis?" Caroline asked. "What's really going on—what was Samuel doing? How much do you know?"

"I've no clue, I know nothing," he said. "Caro, let's table it for a while. Let's not let this get between us."

"I don't understand you," Caroline said. "I brought up sexism, and you grabbed it because it helps you out. You need any masquerade you can find. That you'd stoop so low."

"You are misunderstanding me, Caro."

There was a waxen quality to Travis that reminded her of how some wives described their husbands in the changing room at Longreens. Including Tina and Dorey, from one row over, when their voices traveled over the mahogany lockers and through the filtered air. *You never really know whom you are married to . . . once buff . . . paunchy, bunchy . . . servicing my husband . . . as long as the money is coming in . . . who cares if he plays thirty-six holes a day . . .*

She had never been one of those wives, or had she?

"Travis, I don't misunderstand you. You're the one missing the point."

He came close and tried to take her hand. She remembered how his hands felt when he played quarterback at Pinestream and came off the field. How it mattered that they touched.

"Caroline, listen to me. Do you want a big raise, is that it? Do you want more staff?"

"A big raise when money has been stolen?" she asked. "Is that something you can arrange? You think we're talking about the paint color on the latest model Bentley? You think you'll coax me?"

"I'm asking what you want."

"No, you're not. You're telling me what I might have."

Caroline wended her way through the dining room. Orchids were placed on the sidebar. A lacy pattern, cast by the sunlight, traced over the tables and chairs. Outside were her four acres that backed up against a neighbor's four acres, creating an illusion of eight. Her trees were like heads of broccoli, her hedges were like walls. Hadn't she aced Lucinda's creed: *location, land, and layout.* Yet, Caroline doubted it was safe or private or worth it if she couldn't trust her husband anymore.

He was up, then right behind her. Spotify was playing Faith Hill and Tim McGraw's rendition of "Tougher Than the Rest."

The music stopped; the room became very quiet. When Travis attempted a smile, his features were realigned. He had a twisted mouth. The deep blue was missing from his eyes. Gone for good, Caroline imagined, replaced with a watery shade. In Palm Beach, people were always surprised by how early on she and Travis had become a couple. Dorey once said she imagined them as children when they had started out. Until now, Caroline too believed that being young together was some sort of guarantee. An imprimatur for what was to come.

She thought of what both her parents, particularly her father, had shown her about assembling one's life. I am Reed Barrows's daughter, she told herself, a newly realized mantra.

"We'll figure it out, Caro," Travis said.

"I don't know. Will we, Travis? Because I deserve to be CFO, and I'll need the truth about Samuel."

As she said it, she couldn't fathom what Samuel told to whom.

CHAPTER FIFTEEN

Raleigh

A Lucinda mother/daughter lunch, five weeks since Samuel was buried. Raleigh dreaded it yet had to show up. Besides, these gatherings meant a lot to Lucinda. She loved showcasing her mini Versailles gardens. The idea for the gardens began when Raleigh was ten and the family was in France for the first time. On their tour of the palace and the grounds, her mother and sisters admired the fountains, parterres, and the two bronze sphinxes. Lucinda declared she would replicate the manicured gardens in Palm Beach. Raleigh, fixated on how Marie Antoinette was separated from her children, then executed, begged her to reconsider. "Have some imagination," Lucinda had said to Raleigh when she cried over her mother's idea, "be adventurous."

Reed, guided by Lucinda's whim, found a landscaper for her scaled-down version of Versailles. Every time since, Raleigh was expected to sit on replica stone benches and pretend it was comfortable. There was nothing else to do.

Today, since she was early, Raleigh stood at the edge of the lawn, facing the Intracoastal. She had taken off her sneakers to walk on grass so tight and short it brushed at her toes. She wanted to appreciate the sky—the few clouds, the dense blue—but that often ended up in dicey conversation in Palm Beach. Depending on her mother's or Aunt Bryant's mood, talk of humidity was loaded. There were concerns about the level of air quality. When it rained, people went into a decline. Raleigh never understood. She loved rainy days.

"You're first!" Lucinda said. She glided toward Raleigh in a diva-type caftan, her hair was flat. Raleigh assumed she had a blowout planned for later in the afternoon.

"I am."

They kissed both sides of their faces. Raleigh remembered again that trip to France, watching the French greet one another. Except she and Lucinda were tepid, less enthusiastic.

"Ah, I wanted to speak with you, Raleigh," Lucinda adjusted her sunglasses. "Before the others arrive."

Raleigh nodded, already on edge. She had no idea what her mother's angle was, but it was usually tricky. Lucinda led her toward the birdbaths made of stone. Water was falling from a fountain into a delicate hand-painted ceramic bowl.

"Is everything alright, Mom?" Raleigh asked.

They stopped walking. Lucinda was biting on her lower lip. Raleigh folded her arms under her ribcage. This was going to be an ask of her.

"Are you aware that Collette Nayers wants you to do a portrait?" Lucinda began. "Not the usual family notion, but one of herself, her mother, and her daughter."

"I'm not aware of anything," Raleigh said. "How did you hear?"

"Caroline mentioned it," Lucinda said. "Collette's daughter and

Harper are at the Academy together. The mothers are friends with daughters in the same class. Like that?"

"Right."

"What's chancy is Maribelle," Lucinda said. "When I casually praised Caroline and her circle a few days ago, she said to keep her away from Collette. When I mentioned that Collette's recent divorce was painful—Caroline described the custody battle, the finances to me—Maribelle wasn't sympathetic. That isn't like her. Caroline is baffled too."

"Right." Raleigh said.

She wished her mother would stop, yet she wasn't going to. She faced Raleigh straight on, ready to present her request.

"However, it puts Caroline in a spot." Lucinda said. "If I didn't believe she would be upset, I wouldn't bother speaking with you, Raleigh."

"I won't paint a portrait if Maribelle has some sort of antipathy for the person who wants to hire me, if Maribelle feels so strongly," Raleigh said.

"I understand your allegiance," Lucinda said.

In the outdoor light, Raleigh thought her mother looked pretty. Without make-up on, she was refreshed. Like when Raleigh was little, before they came to Palm Beach. A few times on Saturday mornings, Lucinda took Raleigh fishing for bass and stripers on the lower Apalachicola. If they weighed too little or too much, they threw them back. Raleigh remembered Lucinda was beautiful then, with no place for her to go. There they were, stuck holding their poles, while Reed was busy loading up on the catch. She and Lucinda were a pair back then. Raleigh thought if she stayed beside her mother, no matter that the fish smelled, she had her attention. She was safe.

"Do you know why Maribelle feels this way?" Lucinda asked.

A Glass stream whirred by, perhaps breaking the speed limit. Raleigh didn't have to answer until the boat passed by. She paused.

"Of course not, you are too faithful to her." Lucinda said. She pulled her hair back into that low-lying knot of hers. Her lips got thinner.

Raleigh stared at the waterfront, where boats moved at different speeds. A Baja Marine was followed by a Mercedes Cigarette. If any of the husbands were around, they would have commented. That's how Raleigh knew the boats, how she and her sisters had learned to identify them. The water traveled in tiny swells. Raleigh didn't understand why it wasn't always like that, how the morning that Samuel drowned, a storm had kicked up. Then the accident changed everything.

"Raleigh, you must have a sense of what it's about," Lucinda said.

"I'm not sure," Raleigh needed to pretend.

"Well, since I want both Caroline and Maribelle to be okay with a plan, what if Alex does the portrait?" Lucinda asked. "You might be in demand, but he does fine portraits, he has talent. Let him paint the Nayerses."

"Mom, he's trying to get the Leit Gallery to rep him," Raleigh said. "He doesn't relish portrait work. I do. Alex is busy creating a portfolio. He's leaning more toward big canvases, abstracts now. I respect that. It's about his work. It's about my family."

When Raleigh said this, she realized how little her mother and sisters considered her marriage and child. Almost as if she came upon Alex and Caleb when she was out doing errands one day. After an hour at Publix, she had returned with the goods—a husband and small son along with pineapples and papayas. What Alex said about people was true, including her family, especially her family. There were plenty of ulterior motives and a shortage of empathy.

Lucinda waited a beat.

"This mother, Collette . . . I don't really know her, the family is from New Haven originally," Lucinda said. "I suspect she wants you for the work, Raleigh, because other mothers at the Academy do. For these purposes, since you and Alex are a team when it is germane, you might somehow convey that Alex will do it, the two of you work together."

"Which we don't, really. We don't work together," Raleigh said.

North crossed her mind, popped inside, somewhere between a midnight lover and an interloper. Weren't Alex and Raleigh the team that Lucinda described, were it not for North crushing those chances? Raleigh began to invisibly swat him away. She craned to see the hedges and topiaries, the jasmine, and roses. She wanted the conversation to shut down.

Caroline was walking toward them. "Raleigh! Mom! I've just come from speaking with Julian."

Wasn't it was puzzling how Caroline had become the conduit to their forensic accountant, Raleigh wanted to say. Instead, she waited while Lucinda came one step closer, wedging them all together in her vast, luxurious garden.

"What's his news?" she asked.

Raleigh flashed back to casino night. Julian, his hand territorially on Caroline's waist as they danced together. Radiance mixed with defiance on her part. Raleigh didn't quite divine her deliberate, practical sister starting up with their forensic accountant, no matter how enticing he was. If there's anyone who avoided complication, it was Caroline. Raleigh had long wanted to be more like that instead of unreliable, the treacherous one.

"He's asking around, interviewing people," Caroline said. "He'll know something soon. I'll tell Maribelle how vigilant he is . . ."

"No one cares how vigilant he is. We only care about what he uncovers," Lucinda said.

"There's Maribelle now." Raleigh said.

Maribelle was standing at the top tier of the terrace, her arms crossed.

"I'll go to her," Raleigh offered. A perfect excuse. Besides, she couldn't listen to anything more.

If they were not going to be out and about—La Goulue, Longreens, or La Bilboquet—it wasn't worth swirling around. Still, Raleigh watched her sisters swish into Lucinda's garden like they were at a dress rehearsal. She studied their faces, wishing she could sketch them in this moment. Maribelle's hair was messier, longer, her jawline was finer, her shoulder blades were wings. While Lucinda kept commenting that Maribelle was too thin, Raleigh liked it. She also liked that her dress was a chic beige midi. Caroline and Lucinda believed that Maribelle's work made her a fashionista—she needed to be chic to steer *PB Confidential.* Raleigh didn't quite buy it. Her whole childhood, Maribelle had been hip and stylish. It had little to do with the magazine.

A few years ago, Maribelle told Raleigh that she was still pegged the plainest sister by Lucinda, but it was over. "Besides, every time she does that, Samuel says I'm the smartest and prettiest." Not only did Raleigh agree with Maribelle, she wondered whether these incessant comparisons would ever stop. Would their mother ever let them go?

She was relieved when Lucinda headed into the kitchen to tell Rosie what to do. She and her sisters sat on the terrace beneath an awning, sipping Voss water.

"Hey," Caroline said. "Isn't the menu from Bricktops today? I love their grilled artichokes. "

"She is not still mimicking menus, is she?" Maribelle asked.

"Totally, she is," Raleigh said. "And Bricktops is a favorite, you know, the kale and quinoa salad, fish tacos, Ahi tuna burgers."

"Why can't we just go to the restaurants?" Caroline asked. "Order the food there?"

"We know why," Raleigh said. "There can't be any serious conversations, we know too many people."

"I used to wonder why Lucinda asks us to meet in the middle of a workday," Maribelle said.

"She expects us to be available because she wants us to be available," Caroline said. "She's expert at working wherever she is. Her cell phone is a desktop; she barely misses anything. She figures if she can adapt a work schedule to her whim, we can too."

Her sisters had no idea that Raleigh had been singled out, that Lucinda had an agenda that only applied to her. She was about to confess, not out of a moral high ground but in despair, when Lucinda's voice moved ahead of her.

"The air quality is ideal, today is a ten," Lucinda said. "This is the first impeccable weather we've had in days—perfect for a family lunch."

Raleigh and her sisters looked at one another. Rosie was following with a tray, her affect flavorless. She began placing the Bricktops, favorites on the wrought-iron table. Each sister jumped up to help unload the plates onto the sidebar. The food was stunning, yet Raleigh felt ill, thanks to what Lucinda was asking of her.

"Girls, let's praise Maribelle who manages a great magazine," Lucinda held up a Bloody Mary.

"Popular topics: cutlery for picnics, cheeriest bedding, un-put-downable books, exotic travel, can't-live-without jewelry." Caroline spoke with a mouthful of food, which surprised Raleigh.

Although she was beginning to eat her Little Gem salad, Maribelle filed her knife and fork to the side of her plate politely. "Soon, hopefully, the magazine will go online with a literary bent," she said. "We'll publish Adrienne Rich, Anne Sexton. One of my writers will do a fiction roundup, including a few poignant novels."

Lucinda frowned. "Is that what readers in Palm Beach want?"

"I say Maribelle has fine ideas," Raleigh said.

"Raleigh, aren't you eating?" Lucinda held the grilled artichokes toward her.

Maribelle's eyes were dry sockets. "How amazing that we forge onward," she said. "My staff is terrific. Someone, maybe it was Kendall, said to me that I'm the poster widow for how the train leaves the station whether your husband's on it or not."

No one responded. As if they were modern dancers and this was part of the choreography, they kept eating. Except Maribelle was only pretending. Had her wrists become more tapered too? Raleigh wanted to measure them with a cloth measuring tape, the kind Aunt Bryant used in Kesgrave, when Raleigh was in grade school.

Then thoughts of North littered her mind. How a year ago this very day, they had met at The Sands in Highland Beach. Raleigh had arranged it so easily, telling Alex she was hired for a portrait. Two sons and their father in Delray. Her intention was to take photos, maybe a few sketches of them. It was going to take longer than a few hours. Never had she asked what North's fiction was to spend the afternoon with her, she hadn't wanted to know. There was a restaurant at the hotel called Latitudes, where they dared to have a very late lunch. They weren't about to run into anyone, he had said. Still, Raleigh remembered how nervous it made her, she couldn't touch her vegetable soup. She watched him eat a crab cake.

"Let's try for a pleasant lunch, shall we?" Lucinda's voice was tight.

Raleigh dropped her fork on the patio. Rosie, out of nowhere, appeared to pick it up.

"I'm sorry," Raleigh said.

"Never mind, it's okay," Rosie said. When she smiled, Raleigh saw that her front teeth were separated. How had she forgotten that?

Rosie held up a Nikon in her free hand, the kind people used to have.

"Would you like a picture?" She gestured for them to strike a family pose.

"Rosie, thank you, but we're not camera-ready. Look at us, we're . . . this is a private gathering," Lucinda said.

"How about a candid shot, a cell phone kind of picture?" Rosie asked.

"No, no." Caroline waved her arms around.

Rosie shrugged and headed toward the house.

"Excuse me, Rosie, may I see that camera?" Lucinda asked.

Rosie handed it over. "Maribelle gave it to me. It was Samuel's. I'm developing the photos myself. I made a kind of dark room."

Lucinda turned the camera over in her hands.

"This Nikon is mine," she said. "Reed bought it for me during my nature walk phase. It was somewhere in my desk at Barrows. I don't remember when I last saw it."

"This was in Samuel's drawer in the library at our house," Maribelle said. She made no eye contact with anyone. Her shoulders were scrunched.

Maribelle faced Lucinda. "It was Samuel's. I wouldn't give anyone else's Nikon away. I wanted Rosie to have something of Samuel's."

"Whatever has happened," Lucinda said. "Rosie, you have a good camera now."

Raleigh knew, and her sisters did as well, how suspicious Lucinda was. Still, she handed the camera back.

After Rosie walked off, Lucinda said, "I don't recall lending Samuel my camera."

"Maybe he borrowed it for some charity shots," Raleigh said.

"From my desk?" Lucinda asked. "Without a conversation?"

Maribelle looked stricken. "Mom, you can't be suggesting he stole it!"

Raleigh shuddered. Crossing their mother was not acceptable, whatever the excuse—a grieving widow, temporary insanity, sleep walking.

"I did not say that, Maribelle," Lucinda said. Her voice had this rusty, mineral sheen.

"I wish Samuel were alive to explain," Maribelle said.

"That would be useful," Caroline said. "But he's not. How about there's no more talk of it, not another minute."

She clapped her hands three times like she was breaking up ill-behaved preteens. There was a brief interlude before Maribelle spoke, "Being together like this makes me very sad. I shouldn't have come today."

"I'm glad you did," Raleigh said. She meant it.

Brown pelicans flew along the waterway. Maribelle began to weep. She put her hand beneath Raleigh's and whispered, "The dead. They're very dead, aren't they?"

Although she ought to have been the first to leave, Raleigh was the last. Her sisters explained they had "two o'clocks" and rushed off, somehow excused by Lucinda. Afterward, in the vast kitchen with two Wolf ranges and two Sub-Zeros, more restaurant grade than home life, Raleigh poured herself another Voss water. Lucinda's Jack Rogers sandals tapped hard on the bleached wood planks.

"I'm sorry, I'm leaving too," Raleigh said.

Rosie was placing leftover butter cookies from Stephanie's in a tin. She looked at Raleigh with a sympathetic smile, bordering on soapy.

"Raleigh?" Lucinda held her forefinger up in the air.

Raleigh followed her into the grand entryway. The interior light was too artificial for daytime, why had her parents not cared about that?

"How tragic it is for Maribelle," Lucinda said. "We must see to it she doesn't unravel."

The "we" meant Raleigh.

"It's horrible," Raleigh agreed. "I've invited her to stay with us for a few weeks, at least. Or maybe we could do a sisters getaway. Whatever she wants, whatever might help."

Lucinda pressed her lips together, a sign she was sticking to a script.

"So, you'll convince Alex about the Nayers portrait," she paused. "While I'll see what I can do for him. He's a graphic designer, too. It is feasible that he could work at Barrows. There are women, friends from cards, the clubs, too. If he'll paint grandchildren, siblings, punctuating occasions, there's a demand."

"Mom, like I said, Alex is —above all—an abstract artist."

When Lucinda nodded, Raleigh checked out her hairline. When Raleigh was younger, Lucinda had a widow's peak.

"I realize that Alex has wanted his own show for some time. I'll take it into consideration. Perhaps we could start with a portrait of William and me. It would hang in our front gallery," Lucinda said.

Raleigh tallied up the amount of work and cash this would provide for her husband. She was grateful. What her mother was mapping out could make a difference. "Please, listen . . ."

She inched nearer. "I'm confident you'll do the right thing— you always do, in your own time, Raleigh—and ask Alex."

Without a yes or a no, Raleigh did a fake smile, as if it had been a nice lunch. Her mother always had tentacles to draw her daughters in—slippery tentacles that had grazed the bottom of the river in Kesgrave. In Palm Beach, they had been soaked in the Intracoastal.

CHAPTER SIXTEEN

Caroline

According to Caroline's measure, Maribelle had been in the Barrows offices more these past weeks than in the last five years. How unpleasant the meetings were for her, it was obvious in how she walked along the corridors, passing Samuel's office. Sometimes, she paused in front of the glass floor-to-ceiling doors, staring at Samuel's desk. On the bookshelf were a few tennis trophies, scattered pictures from their travels to Florence, Vienna, Vancouver. The two of them faced a holiday sun and sky per locale, entranced to be there.

Today, Maribelle was turned out for work. Her eye makeup was both flattering and indiscernible. She had traced her arched eyebrows perfectly. Her leopard-print dress and mules made her a candidate for almost any Palm Beach lunch. Yet, Caroline knew that spending time with Maribelle was no longer the reward it had been. Her sister was pure grief, regardless of the venue.

Still, Caroline chased Maribelle through the doorway to the commissary, a meeting room that wasn't as formal as the conference room. Two white-leather, mid-century couches flanked a coffee table. Usually, they served English water crackers with Stilton cheese and sparkling water but today there was nothing out.

"Hey," Caroline said. They air-kissed and separated in a matter of seconds.

"Travis is on a call. He'll be out in a minute. Caleb has a stomachache, so Raleigh isn't coming." Caroline announced.

"I got a text about that. What about Lucinda?" Maribelle asked.

She was focused on her wrist, admiring her link bracelet in multi-wood and gold, from Seaman Schepps. Caroline remembered the day that Samuel bought it for her on the Avenue. She had been behind the scenes and had choreographed the surprise.

"She's here. She's gone to fix her hair," Caroline said.

Maribelle lifted one perfect eyebrow. She used to be so much fun. Caroline smiled. Laughing was probably an overreaction. These days, everyone was guarded and restless.

Estelle, flustered, led Julian into the room, huffing slightly at what Caroline called "the Julian jolt." Caroline and Maribelle shared a glance. Did the man disarm everyone?

"Hello, Caroline, Maribelle," Julian said.

He was in khakis and a white polo shirt with a blazer over his right arm. He was spot on for the Worth Avenue effect, but not for the quality of his clothes. There was no Ralph Lauren insignia anywhere. His briefcase was overloaded and scuffed. At least he wore loafers without socks. So, in theory, he had finessed it. Yet, Caroline and Raleigh computed it all, meaning they had become the snobs their parents endeavored to be.

In contrast to Julian was her husband, Caroline thought. While Travis's shirt and trousers were from Trillion on the Avenue, his presence faded beside Julian. His hairline had receded in the past month, his nose wasn't as enviable and straight. How had this happened? Wasn't he a noticeable man by most standards?

"Are we all accounted for?" Travis asked.

Travis delivered this line in his best business voice. Estelle began, rushing toward the windows to open the blinds, hesitating when the light was too intense.

"It's fine, Estelle," Caroline said.

She squinted and left. Caroline opened her notebook at the same moment Maribelle opened hers. They were from Lucinda's stash at her house, a leftover item from when Reed was alive. *Barrows* was written on the front in a forest green Times New Roman font.

Julian unloaded his papers, glancing at Maribelle and Caroline. "Do people tell you how similar you look?"

Maribelle tapped her pen and sighed a new kind of sigh, like a short moan.

"We hear it from time to time," Caroline offered.

Lucinda was in the doorway, coiffed, as if she had come from a salon. "Oh, yes, they are quite the sisters. Raleigh too. A trio."

"Raleigh's much younger than we are," Caroline said. She needed to clarify this rather than be compared to Raleigh.

"I'm the youngest in my family," Julian said. "Three brothers."

"We should begin," Maribelle did this running-the-meeting tone. "I've got to get back by . . ."

"We're ready, aren't we?" Caroline asked no one in particular.

Stiffly, they determined on their places on the two couches. Lucinda, Maribelle, and Caroline faced Julian and Travis. Julian opened a file, everything he had been working on appeared to be sorted and printed. He shuffled papers in fast motion. Caroline imagined he could be a stand-up magician.

"In the past two weeks, I've been able to uncover what happened to some of the money. It seems it's gone to fictitious vendors for at least a year. Travis, did you notice anything during this period?"

As the question for the CEO rocketed toward him, Caroline stood up and headed to the windows. She began adjusting the shades nervously. The sunlight was shifting, she was anxious. Whatever Estelle had done, there was too much glare. Maribelle put on Chanel cat eye sunglasses. Caroline hadn't seen her wear them before.

"I did not." Travis stared at the space beside Julian, where Samuel liked to sit.

"Truly, Travis, nothing whatsoever?" Lucinda asked.

"I don't understand. How could this have happened?" Maribelle said.

"Barrows is a private company, which makes it easier to pull off," Julian said. "Underreported sales, a second set of books, that's what was going on."

Julian seemed so confident, like he was the only real person in the room. It was revolting to Caroline.

"I don't believe it," Maribelle clasped her hands.

"I can't either," Caroline said. She imagined Samuel in the office, whistling, cheery, dedicated to the company.

"Does anyone know what Samuel's motive was?" Julian asked. Travis shook his head.

"I have a feeling Samuel confided in you, Travis. It's critical that you tell us." Lucinda said. She was using a semi-soft voice.

Travis jumped up. "You come into this office, Lucinda, nearly accusing me. Samuel and I worked together, we traveled to the sites, we were like brothers. The locations were packed, Barrows was—is—thriving. That's what we did."

"When money is stolen by an insider, the person can sometimes rationalize the actions by convincing himself—or herself—that it's a loan eventually to be repaid. Perhaps that's how Samuel contemplated his actions. Many people who steal money do," Julian said.

"This is not a company that makes loans to insiders." Lucinda asked. "Who needs over seven and a half million dollars?" She was inhaling, exhaling.

"What our father believed in was honesty. He taught both Samuel and Travis how to do business. Samuel wouldn't have done this. He was an athlete from the Panhandle. His family was . . . they were plain," Maribelle said.

"This discovery must be arduous for you, Maribelle," Julian said.

Caroline watched Julian watching Maribelle.

"It is difficult for the entire family." Maribelle spoke in a fake style. She looked surprisingly shiny, she needed to take out a compact and blot her nose and forehead. Her deliberate elegance was missing.

"There must have been the realization of what was being earned, telltale signs while you were expanding," Julian said. "If revenues were increasing, who was grabbing the money—why were margins thinner?"

Julian was a pro, Caroline realized. How many meetings had he gone to where a family member was a perpetrator?

"Travis, please, tell us. Please," Caroline said.

The minute she asked this of her husband, the room was cut into triangles of freakish light. As if she were on a psychedelic drug or on Mars. Was this man, Travis, not the boy she ate Carvel with when they were in grade school and biked with on the back roads? The two of them had lied to their parents to be together. By their junior year, they had started to have sex in his father's Wrangler. Caroline brought him along on her parents' ride to riches because she wanted him there. What had Travis done?

"If you know something, don't make us find out later, it will only make it worse for you," Lucinda said. Again, a pseudo-soft voice.

"We just need to know," Caroline said. "That's how it is."

She was mimicking her mother's inflection, but she was furious. He was her goddamn husband. They shared two daughters, they had a life.

"I'm not lying, I'm telling the truth," Travis said.

He was almost hugging himself. But he was not stroking that place where the mustache belonged. They were beyond that level of stress. Travis seemed hollow, more a tin man who hadn't been oiled. He wasn't answering anyone. Julian condensed his folders on the coffee table.

"Well, we'll move on," he said. "There are only a few more questions for this afternoon."

"Of course, Julian," Lucinda sounded stronger. "Go ahead."

"Did Samuel have enemies? Did he owe someone money for some reason?" Julian asked.

"I'd say no," Caroline said. "Travis, what do you think?"

"Everyone loved Samuel," Travis said. "He took the time to listen, to pay attention to what people were saying. He had that . . . charisma, I guess. He always had it, even back in Kesgrave. Even in second grade." He stood up and stretched his arms.

"Maribelle? What are your thoughts?" Julian asked.

Lucinda's razor vision seared in her direction. She and Caroline both knew Officer Breeley had asked her the same question before the case was closed.

"Enemies? No, he didn't," Maribelle said. "I mean, I'm not sure. I mean I have no idea."

Why was she being so weird, Caroline wondered.

"Maribelle," she said, "You are aware of what your husband would do or not do."

The minute she said it, she was sorry. None of them knew what Samuel's intentions were.

Maribelle's eyes were glassy. "I'm *not* aware of what Samuel would or wouldn't do. I was *not* aware he was pilfering money from the company. I was *not* aware he was bankrolling causes down the coast, around the country, funding daycare centers for employees I didn't know he had."

They were dumbstruck. Twice in two days Maribelle had spoken up—been "cheeky" as Lucinda used to say when they were kids and she was tempted to strike them, back in the Panhandle.

Maribelle shrugged. "I'm sorry," she said without an ounce of regret, "this is getting to be too much for me."

Although Lucinda was on a warpath, she accepted the apology. "It's hard for us all, Maribelle."

Maribelle darted her head, like an injured creature. Caroline couldn't stand that she was so not herself.

Lucinda sighed. "Unfortunately, we've got several versions of Samuel. He was the devoted CFO, the kind uncle, dedicated in-law. There's also the flipside—Samuel out for Samuel, too amiable, unreadable."

Caroline was doubly regretful she had grilled her sister. Maribelle crossed her legs, uncrossed them, eyed her wedding ring.

"I wish I could be more helpful. I wish I had more to offer. I've told you that I don't want to be part of some kind of trial," Maribelle said.

"I'm sorry, it isn't a trial, but none of this is easy." Julian started clearing his papers off the coffee table.

Through the shades, Caroline saw a silhouette of two gulls swooping toward the window. Their shadows distorted their size; they loomed over them, perilous.

Caroline tried to signal Maribelle—waving her right hand with her wrist on the table. She didn't notice.

"There's one more question before I go," Julian glanced at a document. "I am assuming that MBW stands for Maribelle Barrows Walker, is that correct?"

"They're my initials," Maribelle said. "Why?"

"I've been reading through emails, and MBW has come up quite often," Julian said. "What about Lara, can anyone tell me who she is?"

"Lara? I can't imagine any Lara. Who is it?" Maribelle straightened up.

"Didn't you hire a Lara some time ago, Caroline? An intern from Palm Beach Atlantic?" Lucinda asked.

"No, I don't recall a Lara. I always remember a name, including when the person doesn't stay in the job long. That intern was Lisa," Caroline said.

With her arms crossed, Maribelle was tapping her upper arms, like someone who had just learned a new method for dealing with PTSD. If she weren't able to comprehend Samuel's trail of chaos, how could anyone else?

"Maribelle?" Lucinda said. But she was staring at Caroline. The burden was shifting, it seemed, like a bad game of musical chairs.

Julian was at the door. "These are my findings for the moment. If anything comes to mind, you have my cell and my email. We'll get to the bottom of it."

Afterward, Caroline rushed to her office and began trying to break into Samuel's emails, to track down Lara. Lara, who held the key to Samuel's plans. The afternoon light had drifted once more, Travis walked in.

"What time are you going home?" she asked. "We have the Friends of the Literary Society tonight—one table. Mom filled it, including Aunt Bryant. A Barrows jubilee."

"Is it black tie?" Travis asked.

"Not sure, maybe festive attire. I'll check," she said.

"I'll leave at five o'clock," Travis said. He was shopworn. Caroline wished it was about the extra workload without Samuel to share it—not something beyond that.

"So, who is Lara, Travis? Because you might fool Julian and the others for a brief time. Not me," Caroline said. "Who the fuck is she?"

"I've no idea. I swear it." This man, the one she had married, must be weighed down by hundreds of pounds of lies.

"You swear it?" Caroline asked.

"I do, Caro," he said.

"Just leave, just get out of here." She was slamming her hands on the keyboard, still searching for a password into Samuel's files.

When they both turned, Lucinda was there, listening. There was this timbre to her—rage disguised as exhaustion.

"I expected more from you, Travis," she said. "I'll wait. See what comes to mind."

CHAPTER SEVENTEEN

Raleigh

Although Alex had recommended five ways for Lucinda to pose outdoors in natural light, Raleigh knew they would be in the library with the shades drawn. For her portrait with William, Lucinda wanted a muted, golden tone. It was a shame since their grounds on Jungle Road in the Estate Section were lush and colorful. Every house on the street was stately. The Intracoastal remained ultra-calm, as if a sumptuous setting had power over the tides.

"One day you'll be my age, and you'll understand," Lucinda said while Alex was setting up.

He was taking pictures of Lucinda and William to enlarge, a template for their portrait. Except Lucinda wanted them Photoshopped. A shame, really, Raleigh thought, since the light in what she still called her "parents' house"—despite that Lucinda had been married to William for six years—was nuanced. Lovely, really. As for William, a man who slotted himself into Lucinda's life, he deferred to Lucinda. He was in line like the rest of them.

Now Lucinda and William were in the pull up chairs facing one another, perfectly clad. Lucinda had chosen a pale blue cashmere sweater and triple strand of pearls. Her smile was subdued; she was getting into character. William, a quintessential Palm Beach husband, was in a fresh, maybe brand new, coral polo shirt. His comb over was subtle. They exuded the pedigree for which Lucinda aimed.

On a tripod, Alex positioned a vintage Hasselblad that his grandfather had given him. He loved that this piece of equipment was historic. Raleigh watched Alex as he flitted about, measuring the light with his meter. He was the fittest, leanest of them all—exactly the kind of husband her friends wished they had. North was a contender, too, but she wasn't with him because Alex wasn't handsome or buff, she was with North because she couldn't be without him. From the day they were too near one another at a tennis party at Mrs. A's, Raleigh knew. Mrs. A had called it a multigenerational gathering; everyone in the Barrows family was invited. Caleb seemed too young at the time, Raleigh had left him at home with a sitter while Caroline brought her girls.

"Tennis whites only at Mrs. A's," Lucinda had warned. "Mrs. A is traditional, an old-time Palm Beacher."

Eighty guests, dressed in sparkly whites, were glistening in the sun that afternoon. North and Raleigh were paired for mixed doubles and won. Everyone was surprised, and while she played well, North carried the game. She simply didn't make too many mistakes. Reed had taught the girls to play and had arranged for lessons. As the Barrows sisters, they were schooled in what flies in Palm Beach, including how to be at a tennis party. North and Raleigh didn't speak much that afternoon; it felt like he was there in some dream sequence.

Afterward, Raleigh knew there was someone she would risk

her contained life to walk beside. That *enough* had no meaning, since she already had a child, a husband, her art, a home. Wasn't that ample? She and North existed in an extra cordon of time.

Alex adjusted his camera and began a series of shots.

"Alex, how long will this take?" Lucinda asked.

"What's the difference, Lucinda?" William said cheerily. "We've decided. We'll see it through."

In the quietly lit room, their faces were in repose. Alex was in motion. He lifted a double white orchid plant from the coffee table and placed it on the floor.

"Raleigh?" Alex turned to see her in the doorway. "Let's unload a few more things, make it less cluttered."

"Oh, sure," Raleigh said. It was a relief to help, to be lost in Alex's work for once. A reprieve from thoughts of North. Raleigh came closer to help, but the scent of Fracas pushed her away. When would her mother believe that she and Violet were allergic to perfume? Never, thought Raleigh. Her rituals ran deep. William took Lucinda's hand; Raleigh imagined her father's ghost giving him tacit consent.

"Alex, you are kind and patient," Lucinda said. She seemed uncommonly nervous, therefore not bossy. Raleigh knew it wouldn't last.

Alex straightened up. "Lucinda, if you and William sit down, we'll start."

Lucinda curled her forefinger to lure Raleigh over. "I have false eyelashes on."

Raleigh already knew. The lashes were fringy, too dense and dark in contrast to her caramel-shaded hair. She had a comb with picks on her lap and started fussing around for more volume at the crown. Raleigh counted years, maybe decades since Lucinda had that tousled, young mother-by-the-river style.

"Mom, you look pretty. Remember, you're the youngest mother around who has daughters our ages," Raleigh said.

"A child bride. A beauty." William beamed at her.

"Please be forgiving, Alex, with your camera, your pencils, and those brushes." Lucinda said. She was over-focused. Raleigh disliked her mother like that. Too intense, like at Barrows right after Samuel died, when she told them about the missing money. For the first time.

"I won't disappoint you. Today I'll take photos first, maybe sketch after. Might you and William face me?" Alex was like a doctor with a fine bedside manner.

Invisible, Raleigh walked to the window. Warblers tossed about then righted themselves to keep flying in the direction of Miami. Then a memory of North again. What he had said to her the first time they dared meet.

"I love my wife," he said.

He had told her on a Tuesday afternoon two weeks after their tennis match at Mrs. A's. They were at an outdoor café in Palm City. He was heading back to Palm Beach from Vero Beach for his work. Raleigh had been in Port St. Lucie at a potential client's. The portrait was to be of four children under the age of ten. Had it not coincided with North's schedule, Raleigh would have blown off the hire.

"I love my wife," he said again.

"I understand. I don't want her to be hurt. We mustn't ever do that. I don't want to hurt Alex either," Raleigh had said.

The other part—what she didn't say—was that she and North belonged together, beyond time and purpose. There was an uncanny sense in being together. He obscured the scenery, a space that didn't exist. They were like Chagall figures floating above the earth.

Already, as they sat there, sipping iced lattes, she believed she could pull it off. She would separate out the good wife and good mother from being a good lover. That morning, after she had carefully dressed in a midi-dress with a drawstring waist, what her sisters called 'cheap and cheery,' she had kissed Alex well. In anticipation of stolen space with North, she had made sure of it.

"Lucinda, can you look in this direction? And next at one another? Straight ahead?" Alex asked.

They had fine posture, their bodies were fit—Pilates for Lucinda while William still bench pressed at the age of sixty-five. Raleigh watched her husband move jaggedly to get the best angles, to grab them in an unstudied moment. The better he searched, the better he saw. So unlike Raleigh's method of setting up her subjects. If she scrutinized her subjects, their faces became tired. Her simple rule was to be kind, if not completely realistic. For anyone who needed to be brighter, less tired, Raleigh lessened the lines. This was fine in Palm Beach, where everyone wanted a soft-pedaled rendering of their children or themselves. Alex was a more original painter than she was; his work belonged elsewhere.

Lucinda was exquisite, Raleigh noticed, because she wasn't speaking. Only her face, that set of her chin, gave a message. Alex clicked and loaded, clicked, and loaded. The three of them blended into a common goal.

"You're a pro, Alex," William said. "You could be the Gilbert Stuart of Palm Beach."

"You will be after our portrait is completed and we throw a cocktail party to exhibit your work," Lucinda said.

Alex and Raleigh looked at each other, surprised at Lucinda's sweeping gesture.

"That would be terrific, Lucinda," Alex said.

Raleigh was delighted. How long had she waited for Alex to be invited into her mother's inner circle? Always it had been Samuel and Travis, with Alex an outsider. Yet this chance for her husband coincided with impermeable images of North. Raleigh was practically swatting them away, forcing herself to focus on Alex. There was a battle between a memory of North's hand on her thigh under the table at the café, versus her husband contemplating the palate for her mother in real time. Suddenly, Raleigh was losing hold of the present, Lucinda and William faded, while North surfaced. Like a time traveler, she was roaming through hotel suites with private terraces facing the ocean, where she and North had hijacked the afternoons. His touch had tattooed her skin, leaving marks only she could see.

Alex was winding down the shots. "Hey, Raleigh, what would you think of a double canvas? One indoors sitting like they are. The other in their garden, standing, faces in profile? Or I could do a montage."

Her husband's idea was so smart she was yanked from her thoughts. In the seesaw in her brain, North was down, Alex was up.

"I love it," Raleigh said. "Are you guys sold on it?"

"We'll give it a go," William said. Lucinda gave a covert nod, reminding Raleigh of people who keep their voices low and everyone has to lean closer to hear.

"Great!" Alex started folding for the next leg of the photo shoot. "Raleigh, want to come? We're going to the rose beds."

"I will come," she said. "I'll follow you—I'm going into my old bedroom for a minute, getting my Winnie-the-Pooh for Caleb."

Lucinda smiled the smile she reserved for when she felt benevolent. Meaning few ever saw this side to her.

"Your frayed and weary Winnie-the-Pooh," she said.

"I know, but I promised Caleb," Raleigh said.

She craved a short break. That Lucinda was paying attention to Alex and to her was mystifying—it made her suspicious. Raleigh walked into her teenage bedroom, which was a shrine to being fifteen. CDs were piled up, Avril Lavigne and Fergie, a cut out picture of Orlando Bloom was still on her bulletin board. A book about impressionists and one about Mary Cassatt lay on her desk. An earring tree was empty, like it had been looted. Only a pair of pearl studs that Lucinda had given Raleigh when she was sixteen and a pair of chandelier earrings remained. She had gotten the dangling earrings at a flea market, and her mother had warned her earlobes would be infected.

Raleigh passed her bookshelves where Winnie was still crammed in, alongside her favorite titles, *Anne of Green Gables, Rebecca of Sunnybrook Farm, Harry Potter.* On the wall to the left were two of her early paintings. One was from eleventh grade of the clocktower at the end of Worth Avenue. The other was of Maribelle, Samuel, and Raleigh at Raleigh's graduation from the Academy. It had been a warm Florida morning, they were standing in front of the school. Raleigh wore a cap and gown, and they flanked her, like parents would do. She had painted this from the photograph that Reed had taken that day. In the painting they have these open smiles, welcoming what was to come. Maribelle's smile was widest; she appeared to be thrilled.

She lifted the painting and placed it on her desk. After that, she curled up in the center of her girly pastel duvet and wept.

Alex was so pleased as they drove home along the A1A, it was as if they were lottery winners. The ocean was the deep turquoise it became some days in the winter, the mansions were almost welcoming. Raleigh knew they were both exhausted yet happy with the portrait session.

"After I finish with this for Lucinda and William, maybe my new canvases—my abstracts—can be shown . . . if it works for your mother. She told me she knows the owner of a gallery in Lauderdale."

Raleigh saw he was earnest, proud of a plan that was bold for him. She leaned toward him to kiss his mouth and moved away. He didn't notice or decided not to react—a relief.

"That's the goal, isn't it?" she asked.

She resisted pointing out that Lucinda might not be reliable, that she was only helping Alex because it was a trade. Raleigh wasn't going to paint Collette Nayers and upset Maribelle; in exchange, his work and talents would be promoted by Lucinda and her contacts. Except Raleigh felt fishy for cutting a deal. When Alex reached out for her hand, it was like a lobster claw, a tentacle. Oblivious, he put his palm over hers as if they were an upstanding couple, dedicated to one another.

"Alex, it works even if it's only about money. If your art sells, we're better off," she said.

"I suppose," Alex said. "Especially with distributions from Barrows diminished, until the Samuel mess is figured out. Though I'm hoping it's about my art, Raleigh. That a gallery, with an introduction from your mother or not, would take me on for the work. That my art stands for itself."

Raleigh stared at his face, his hands on the steering wheel. *He's my husband, my husband*, she began twisting it around, as if it were a slogan.

"Of course," she said.

She tilted her head toward the ocean as they whirred by. Although the conversation was going well enough, she wished she could open the window and evaporate.

"Don't get me wrong, Raleigh, I'm grateful," Alex said. "And it's competitive out there or I wouldn't . . ."

"Do what everyone else does to get ahead?" Raleigh asked.

"I suppose," he said. "I'm excited about getting an opportunity, but while you were in the house, Lucinda and William were talking. I think they forgot I was there or thought I couldn't hear."

Before he told Raleigh what was said, she was repelled. If Alex was offended, she would be too. Plus, she was expected to apologize for Lucinda. She had spent her life apologizing for what she had done or would do in the future.

She took a breath and asked, "What did they say?"

"Did you know Caroline and Travis are making their house bigger—much bigger?"

"No, I didn't know," Raleigh said. "Why are they doing that? It's pretty big now."

"Well, your mom's giving Caroline two million dollars to fix up her house, so she's sort of in the game, I guess. William was surprised too."

Raleigh was stunned. "What about Maribelle, who's, like, hysterical about money, and Samuel's debt, and the findings, and . . ."

"Right. That your mother would do this when Maribelle is struggling and is responsible," he paused.

They drove along, closer to home.

"Look Raleigh, I'd like your mom's help," Alex said. "She can open doors and, quite frankly, I'm willing to walk through them, but these people are tough to stomach. They've not a clue about real life, there's this endless quest to have the most, best, newest. I'm trying to understand your mother and why Caroline would have agreed. What do they believe in?"

She nodded. Here she was with Alex, who had never veered toward opportunity versus principles.

"I'd like to defend my mother, except I can't," Raleigh said. "I don't know what to say about Caroline. Or anyone else. They're just doing what everyone does."

She closed her eyes, and there was North. He knew how to calm her down. He might have helped with this, explained away her doubts.

"You don't have to like them," Raleigh said. "You just need to paint their portraits and take their money. There's no gallery show by wishing for it, Alex, or by talent alone. Everything we have comes from "these people." Do you want to give up the Barrows dividends or our house?"

She leaned over and kissed him. His mouth was ultra-soft, his lips unchapped. "Be happy. If you always felt like you were on the outside of the Barrows cartel, now you're in."

When Alex swung into their driveway, Maribelle's Tesla was there. A car Samuel had ordered last spring after convincing her that she'd be happy with it.

"My sister's here? That's odd for a weekday—she's always describing back-to-back meetings at the magazine," Raleigh said.

Maribelle, in biker shorts, came out with Caleb in her arms, goo on his fingers. Her sister wasn't the type to take a wet wipe out or lead Caleb to the sink. Not that she didn't want the result of clean hands. What was Maribelle doing there? What had happened? Raleigh rushed toward them.

"Mommy! Mommy! Aunt Mabbie brought me a dragon book!"

"That is so nice, my sweet boy."

Gabriella, Nicole's cousin, their sometimes sitter, came to the front door. "Hi, your sister stopped by a few minutes ago. Something about a surprise for you."

"For me?" Perhaps it explained why Maribelle was not in her fashionista best. What was the surprise? Was she taking Raleigh up on her invitation, moving in with them for a few weeks?

Alex stepped springily to the front steps. Gabriella was behind him.

"Caleb, you go inside with Gabriella," Alex said. "Mommy and I will be there in a minute."

Maribelle and Alex waited a beat. Raleigh didn't like their weird, shared smile, directed at her.

"Is everything okay?" Raleigh asked.

"Yes, of course," Maribelle said. "I wanted to tell you . . . to say, you've been available, you've been supportive. Alex and I thought of something you might like."

Without knowing anything, Raleigh bristled.

"Maribelle thought of it. Aunt Bryant too," Alex said.

Aunt Bryant needed to be sent for? Raleigh felt suffocated.

"I'm not flexible, not good with a surprise," she said.

She regretted her remark immediately—after what Maribelle had been through, it was self-centered, shallow. Based on Alex's news, Maribelle about to be screwed by Lucinda, who, at the moment, favored Caroline and her unneeded renovation.

"Well, try it out?" Alex seemed tense. "I know you've been wanting to get to Kesgrave. The plan is to pack up right now, for two nights. We'll paint, sketch by the Apalachicola. We can explore, go to your old house—take pictures for landscape paintings, backdrops for portraits. I'll set up our canvases. It's arranged already. Your sister and Gabriella will stay with Caleb."

Raleigh held up her hands, as a shield. "No, no, no!"

Alex stopped breathing, while Maribelle watched her curiously. The good will, the "in sync" of earlier today at Lucinda's was gone in a flash. Raleigh felt it draining out of her.

"I can't, Alex. I'm sorry," she said.

"Why not?" He was crushed, clueless. "You say you *long* for Kesgrave, to be there again. Your sister and I strategized. Caleb will be fine. Your aunt will check in. She can sleep here, too, if it helps. We can leave Caleb with three adults."

"I won't leave Caleb. Not with anyone. I'm not ready to go."

"Caleb will be fine," Maribelle's voice was measured.

"I checked. The calendar is clear for you. We're booked at the Pearl Hotel. I took a suite for us." Alex's eyes were pulling down in the corners.

"I am sorry. I'm not able . . ."

"Excuse us, Alex." Maribelle gave Raleigh the kind of stare Lucinda used in the worst situations. "Raleigh, a word?"

"Okay." Raleigh followed her sister into the front hall, then the powder room. Maribelle closed the door. They stood at the oyster-colored sink that Raleigh had always wanted to replace. An early still life of pineapples and apples with a robin red breast that

Raleigh had painted her senior in college was on the wall behind her. What a strange combination, Lucinda had said when she gave it to her that Mother's Day. Somehow it was returned to Raleigh.

"What are you doing?" Maribelle's tone was low and cautious. "Alex made these arrangements to please you. You always want to go to the Panhandle. "

Raleigh started shaking her head. "The plan isn't right."

"How would you suggest it be fixed? You haven't been back in *years*. No one has," Maribelle said.

Years. Not exactly, since she had been there with North in November. On the road to Kesgrave, they had admired each other's profiles and listened to John Mellencamp singing "Jack and Diane," Bono singing "One." They had driven past the house where the Barrows sisters grew up, their grade school, the meadows. When they had gotten to the last landmark, Lucinda's childhood home, it had turned dark out, there was a film over the moon. Lucinda was sixteen when she did what every local girl swore to do—she married her boyfriend. Yet she was ambitious, she pulled him up, out of the Panhandle.

North paid attention when Raleigh talked about her parents, how people whispered in Palm Beach that it was drug money that gave Reed's business a start. That her sisters and mother had always denied it. *What do you believe happened?* North had asked. He cared what Raleigh thought. She liked that their mother had convinced their father when he was still behind the cash register to save up to buy the General Store. Next, they bought another old-time store on the outer rim of town and made it modern— and so it began.

North and Raleigh had their own alternate universe, she never felt alone with him. Of their many inventions to be together, the escape for two days to Kesgrave and the Emerald Coast was the whopper and the jewel.

Maribelle sighed. "Raleigh? What is it?"

"Caleb doesn't know you or Gabriella well enough. I'm with him most days, it won't work, Maribelle," she said. Lame to her own ears.

"What about your husband, doesn't he deserve the trip? He did it for you, for your marriage."

Vaguely, Raleigh wondered why Maribelle was cheering intensely for Alex.

"I'm sorry, it was thoughtful of Alex," Raleigh said. Fair enough. And she liked being appropriate, giving Alex credit. Yet she wasn't persuaded.

Very little air was left to breathe, more of that seesaw jounce overwhelmed Raleigh. While earlier today had seemed safe with Alex—they shared a point of view, they agreed about her mother—nothing was ever certain. Nor was anything secure. Raleigh knew it too well. She was capable of fading, switching allegiances on a dime. This round, Alex was down, and North was up.

North's face was all that she could see.

CHAPTER EIGHTEEN

Caroline

While Caroline had avoided coming to the Yacht Club marina since Samuel's accident, she knew Harper and Violet were entitled to be on the open water in a fabulous speedboat. There they were this morning, racing down the plank toward Dorey and Gavin Barnes's Donzi 41 GT. Dorey's daughter, Isabelle, in class at the Academy with Harper, was fine with Violet tagging along as a family friend. Caroline followed her daughters, blotting out her last visit to the docks back in December with Travis, Maribelle, and Samuel on the *Vertigo*. They skirted the waterway with Maribelle complaining about Raleigh and Alex—they had bailed at the last minute. For Caroline, no matter who came, it had been a mini escape. They were "off-land," it was like being high.

"Mom! Hurry!" Harper said. She ran ahead to the Barnes's boat slip.

Violet tapped Caroline's arm. "Mom, hurry, they're leaving!"

Caroline took her hand. Since Violet was only six, she was what was holding the family together. A serious schism with Travis would have to wait. She had to endure him until Violet was at least ten, a better age to break up a family and destroy a child's life. Depending on which expert on divorce one followed.

"Mom!"

Violet was practically screeching. They half-ran down the dock. Boaters were organizing themselves for their weekend outings. Assorted boats graced the pier, glistening in an unusually warm sun. Dorey, in an Eres short, black-and-white dress over a red, tank-style one piece, waved at them. She had a visor on and darkest sunglasses. She was slathering on sunblock and scowling at how bright the day had become.

"Can I convince you to join us?" Dorey asked.

Gavin was behind her, handing out the L.L.Bean life vests to the girls. The entire scene was eerily similar to the day Samuel invited the girls on his boat. *Samuel.* How empty the harbor must have been so early that morning, Caroline thought, the weather swiftly changing from light rain to an intense storm.

"No, thank you, Dorey," Caroline said. "I wish that I could. I've got tennis in twenty at Longreens, lunch at the Breakers." She stopped herself. She sounded so like her mother, her friends, tourists—as prosaic as they come. Worse, it was true, she was en route to meet Aunt Bryant and Lucinda.

"I know this must be upsetting," Dorey said. "Harper told Isabelle you haven't been on a boat since your brother-in-law died. I want to assure you, Caroline, we'll be careful. Gavin is very familiar with the water."

"My girls are happy to be back," Caroline said. "They're thrilled."

She saw Violet trying on baseball caps, laughing, and squealing with the older girls. Isabelle and Harper were thrusting their hips, loosening their ponytails. Caroline reached into her bag to offer more sunblock. Dorey waved her away.

"We're set!" she said.

Caroline lingered for a few minutes as if she could protect her daughters by her mere presence.

"Caroline? We're heading out," Gavin raised his voice as the engine revved.

The sun was showing off her daughters. She saw what a blend they were, a milkshake of the three Barrows sisters with nothing from Travis's side, which was fine with Caroline. Her husband didn't deserve any claim, not since they had words over Samuel's replacement. After that, Caroline had been arriving late for everything in her life. At the Letts's last night, drinks were ending when she and Travis arrived. During dinner, while filet of sole and haricots verts were served, Caroline smiled at her husband from the other end of the table and referenced him in conversation. Neither spoke on the ride home. They wound around the A1A with the moon over the ocean while Caroline tried to remember why she had to date and marry Travis. Some days she loathed him more than she had ever loved him.

Most days now she wanted to shout, *What did Samuel tell you? Who was he?*

"Great!" Caroline waved as they pulled away, heading south. The slips were emptying out fast, gulls and warblers flapped around the marina. As the Donzi receded, the sound of the Intracoastal lapped against the docks. Caroline couldn't keep her eyes on the water—there was too much sadness. She wanted her daughters to experience it, a place to go boating in Palm Beach. Yet for her, and for her sisters, there was only the same revolting fact—people drown, including those who had proved adept at saving themselves on land.

Before Caroline left, she decided to walk by Samuel's boat slip, which was not six boats down on the other side of the docks. When she got there, she stared at the emptiness. In two days, according to what Maribelle reported, the boat was to be returned, and the new buyer would be lined up. Parts of life that were crucial to Samuel continued beyond him. Caroline needed to stop being the family pusher—pushing optimism, flexibility, togetherness. She felt as miserable and heartsick as her sisters. She was exhausted from skirting the pain.

Halfway to the parking lot, she heard her name being called. "Ms. Barrows? Ms. Barrows?"

When she turned, a young man in a nautical blue polo shirt that read *Roger/Yacht Club* was behind her.

"Yes?" she asked.

"I wanted to give this to you," Roger said. "You came the other day to collect your husband's things. After you left, I opened my locker and remembered I'd found something on the pier that morning, the day of the accident. I forgot to leave it with the belongings for the Coast Guard."

Caroline was about to explain that he had mistaken her for Maribelle Barrows Walker. That they were often called by their maiden names, although she wasn't sure why. She knew to offer her sister's number for him to call or text her—it was the proper thing to do. Except what this man, Roger was pressing into Caroline's hand was in an envelope that appeared slightly bumpy. Instinctively, nosily, she accepted it. She quickly zipped it into the backpack Violet had decided against bringing on the Donzi. Caroline smiled at Roger.

Caroline had to confess. "I'm sorry, I'm not Maribelle. I'm her sister, Caroline Barrows Sears. We're confused for one another at times."

"I didn't know," Roger said. "You're in sunglasses and a hat, I thought . . . I didn't realize . . ."

He held out his hand for her to return the envelope. She ignored his gesture.

"I'll be seeing my sister, and I'll give this to her and tell her what happened," Caroline said.

Roger hesitated—he seemed to be an ethical man.

"Roger, please don't worry," Caroline said. "I'll take care of it."

"I thought it was in the bag I gave to her . . . your sister," Roger said. "I found it after we cleared out the boat that morning. I was alone, walking around. I found it between the planks on the dock. A locket or something on a chain."

The instant Caroline was back in her SUV, she opened the envelope. In the daylight, the aquamarine, pear-shaped pendant that each sister had gotten from Lucinda, glistened. It was the only gift their mother had given them that wasn't a name brand, perhaps in their entire lives. Growing up in Kesgrave, Caroline had loved Lucinda's tradition of the same jewelry for her three daughters. She had begun with gold-plated charm bracelets from Macy's. When Barrows started taking off, Lucinda moved on to Elsa Peretti silver hearts from Tiffany. By the time the family had gotten to Palm Beach, they had graduated to Vhernier, Verdura, and Seaman Schepps. The pendant Caroline held in her hand was an anomaly in style and name recognition. Lucinda had found a jeweler called Indigo on her travels abroad with Reed. Possibly, Caroline recalled, it was a boutique in the south of France, a local jeweler. Or was it when her parents were in London? The necklaces were each signed.

"Unique, aren't they?" Lucinda had said ten years ago when she handed them out—the color of water, a symbol of hope and youth.

The aquamarine dazzled in Caroline's hand. Although agonizing to sort out, she now understood. Maribelle hadn't merely dropped Samuel off at the marina early that morning, racing to Yoga Sunrise, as she had sworn. She and Samuel had been together on the pier.

CHAPTER NINETEEN

Maribelle

Maribelle supposed whatever gossip wafted around the five tables of eight at Tina Steffen's luncheon was considered news. The women were seated beneath the pergola, rose bushes and wisterias, their conversations bounced into the air. *Vicious stepmother . . . out at Wellington, Westport, no, Greenwich . . . scratch golfer . . . holistic approach . . . bookfair at the Academy . . . date stacking . . . poorer than we guessed . . . vile wardrobe . . .*

Katie Casen, Allison Rochester, and Noel Finley, whom Maribelle had come to know through Caroline, were seated together and waved her over. With her place card in hand, she joined them. Their bags, Bottega, Chanel, and Valentino, were compact enough this season to be draped over the backs of their chairs. Tina deserved plenty of psychic rewards for her efforts. Maribelle gave her credit for that. Her luncheon was insurance against the unknown, wasn't it? Aunt Bryant liked to call it "good deeds with a return." To ward off misfortune, wasn't that why everyone had shown up? Maribelle realized what the women were thinking: if I do this, I won't suffer similarly. I won't be the one whose husband drops dead at a Polo match or leaves me. No wonder everyone was in attendance.

The flowers were too pungent and close. Maribelle disliked that. The soundtrack from *Pretty Woman* was playing, Roxette's "It Must Have Been Love." A film she had watched with Caroline on Sunday nights in Kesgrave when they were in grade school. They had pegged it Lucinda's primer on how to land a man and get a wardrobe makeover. Maribelle doubted Raleigh had received the same instruction. Lucinda's plans for Palm Beach were in place by the time her youngest sister was ready for such a lesson. Today, the song saddened Maribelle. Who had chosen the playlist, seriously, since anyone would recognize why a young widow might reject it. Maribelle excused herself and headed indoors, through the kitchen.

"Hello, Ms. Walker!" Lacey, the best caterer around, said.

She looked at Maribelle a second too long, then added. "Bathroom? Down the hall, to the right."

Maribelle stepped away from Lacey's brief pity. When she looked back, the wait staff was positioning platters of mini crab cakes and endive filled with brie and pecans. Lacey was leading them, her arms poised in the position of the conductor of a visiting orchestra at the Kravis Center.

After she locked the door to the guest bathroom, Maribelle noticed in the muted light that she looked better and kinder than she was. She assumed Tina must stand in the same place to preen and primp before she raced to the Academy for pick-up or to the Harbor Club for a tennis game. Is that why the light was so welcoming? In truth, Maribelle had disappointed herself by being the focal point of a Tina Steffens's event, no matter that

Lucinda and Caroline were enthused about it. "You must show up," Caroline had beseeched her. "She's doing it as a gesture for *you.*"

So, why not to take a tour through Tina's Sims Wyeth house, Maribelle decided. Caroline had spoken of the contemporary art—in contrast to the Mediterranean design of the house. The living room was whitewashed, as so many were in Palm Beach—white couches, chairs, window treatments alike. There was the art—a Claire Tabouret, a Rita Ackerman, and a Cindy Sherman. Raleigh had to come see it, thought Maribelle. How delighted she would be with the collection. Maribelle was scouting out more art when she noticed a woman beside the piano.

"Well, I thought we would get a chance to chat today, and then we meet like this!" Mrs. A said. She was majestic in an older Palm Beach lady style. Her hair was sprayed stiffly, Margaret Thatcher-like, while her dress was timeless. Akris, no doubt, a colorblock shirtdress.

"Hello, Mrs. A," Maribelle said.

"Hello, Maribelle." Mrs. A sat on the piano, patted it, inviting Maribelle to sit beside her—an honor.

"Your mother speaks of you often," Mrs. A smiled.

"Does she?" Maribelle never quite trusted what her mother said to anyone, ever. This was true long before the accident.

"She is so proud of your work at *PB Confidential.* And now, so concerned, a daughter who is a premature widow. I am sorry for your loss."

"Thank you, Mrs. A."

"I'll give you some advice," Mrs. A said. Up close, Maribelle could see the caked powder streaked across her forehead and beneath her eyes. "Sound advice."

Maribelle wasn't in market for an old socialite's wisdom. What could Mrs. A know of Maribelle's pain, the crazy machinations of the Barrows family?

Still, she had manners. "Of course, I'd like to hear it," she said, mustering Lucinda's phony baloney best.

"I have been a widow a very long time. I hardly recall having had a husband beside me most mornings and nights. What I suggest you do is find another man. Look at your mother, look at Liz Lotts, look at Danielle Jensie."

Maribelle began, "Well, Samuel's accident is recent, and I'm adjusting, trying to . . ."

There was a tapping of heels on the hardwood floor. Tina, the actual host, had come to find Maribelle.

"Maribelle, is everything alright? Should I get you something?" Tina asked. She was the blondest, blandest version of herself— including her headband in the palest blue.

"Tina, apologies. I'm heading back outside right now," Maribelle said.

"As am I," Mrs. A said. "We've had a talk that fortunately covers the territory."

The woman was compelling, anyone would believe her.

Across from Maribelle's seat at the table, Lucinda was subtly head-bobbing in every direction, taking count of the guests. She seemed pleased. There were plenty of mothers and mothers-in-law included in Tina's gesture. Since it wasn't often that there was a gathering for a young Palm Beach widow, Tina was hosting as if it were a fundraising luncheon or a wedding shower. In fairness, Maribelle thought, what other template did she have?

The younger women, closer to Raleigh's age or less, appeared, smiling skittishly. Their dresses were printed pastels, some were mini, others flowing midis, like they were advertising Saks, Eye of the Needle, or Lily Pulitzer. The older women wore McLaughlin green or coral prints and offered sympathetic nods. Everyone was collected, socially polished, slowing down their gossip as Maribelle passed by their tables on her return to table number one.

They knew one another, Caroline's and Tina's friends. Together they made an uneven chorus.

"Maribelle! Lovely!" Tina walked toward her as if they hadn't spoken a moment ago inside. Her stilettos made a strange tapping on the outdoor slate. They weren't as popular as in seasons past, now women favored kitten heels, booties, and wedges. Some women were taking their no-longer-favored pumps to Andre, shoemaker of choice. He replaced the thinnest, tallest heels with chunky versions. Lucinda had hauled twelve pairs over to him right before Samuel's accident and was only getting started.

Maribelle met Tina halfway. "Thank you. What a turnout," she said.

She fuzzily half-smiled at the guests. Caroline waved from the table farthest back, facing the gardens.

Allison Rochester cheered, "Maribelle, you are so brave!"

It was like being on a rocket ship, without gravity, Maribelle thought. A reminder that before Samuel died, she was firmly planted on earth. Had she been invited to a luncheon such as Tina's, it would have been about her work at *PB Confidential.* Her presence had added something beyond pity and curiosity.

Maribelle was about to sit down when Raleigh arrived, late, of course, but somewhere between a breath of fresh air and a show-stopper. She placed her hand on Maribelle's forearm.

"Well, someone went all out for you," she whispered as they air-kissed.

"That's the PB way,"

"Is it?" Raleigh looked around. "Is Collette part of the party?"

"Totally. See her? She's two tables over," Maribelle pointed. "With Caroline."

Both sisters watched her. Collette appeared pleased to be part of the sympathy luncheon. She, Caroline, and Tina were huddled together, locked in conversation. Most likely about their daughters, as if motherhood were the supreme bubble, a special club.

Maribelle shifted her gaze to Raleigh as she slid into the only empty seat. She lifted a fluted glass and took too big a sip of a Bellini while eyeing the crisp, off-white linens, folded napkins, the blue hydrangea/white rose centerpieces. Next, Maribelle watched Raleigh hold up the empty plate in front of her, with a Roman God in the center, and flip it over. Was she a deciphering Limoges from Royal Copenhagen? Three tables to the right, Lucinda, with a superhero's razor vision, caught her and glared fiercely. The Barrows sisters knew better than to overtly check out a host's porcelain set. Raleigh put it down, shrugged.

"I had to do it, these are so interesting!" she said. "And Ginori! Love it." A short silence fell over the table before everyone returned to their chatter. Collette was beelining toward their table, though Maribelle wasn't sure why. She had this insipid expression, one of her front teeth was longer, maybe wider than the other—something one might not notice in the first few times around. Her look had changed, her long auburn hair was now in a blunt cut below her chin, bordering on corporate. Unpredictably, Lucinda favored this tamped-down look and wished her daughters would wear it. Maribelle saw that Caroline and Dorey were following, as if Collette had been let loose and was not on solid ground. Everyone knew, not only Maribelle, that their table wasn't the right destination for her.

"Maribelle, Raleigh." Collette clasped her hands, feigning she had met them no more than once and had polished manners. "So good to see you."

Her body language indicated she was about to go into a faux hug mode, yet she stopped herself, realizing neither sister would come near it.

Caroline materialized. "You know, we thought long and hard about where to seat you both and decided this is such a special group," she said. She made a sweeping gesture that encompassed the entire terrace.

"We like our table and the appointments, the flowers and place settings are so pretty," Raleigh said.

She was staring, waiting for Maribelle, known to be more socially acrobatic than she, to say something smarter, pithier.

"We're fine," Maribelle said.

That was all because she knew so few of the women at the gathering, which was uncommon. Many were Academy mothers, she supposed, where would any clever comment take her? She began counting down to when the luncheon would end.

Collette put her hand on Caroline's forearm, her long fingers too visible for Maribelle. Suddenly she was sickened by the idea of how her touch felt to Samuel.

"Caroline," Collette smiled an overripe smile. "Such exciting news about the addition on your house! I hear it's going to have panoramic views of the Intracoastal and, with your grounds, it will be stunning."

"Are you set with your contractor? I know that Travis spoke with my brother-in-law, who is delighted with his GC," Dorey asked.

"Addition?" Maribelle asked. "What addition?"

Raleigh edged closer to Collette, contrasting their styles. A tendril of Raleigh's hair fell across her forehead, her eyelashes had mascara at the outer corners, like she had been prepped by a stylist for a photo shoot.

"Your sister's expansion of her house. It's going to be wonderful." Collette said. She was staring at Maribelle, waiting for her response. "Once it gets started. We know how these things get delayed."

Maribelle was stupefied. Caroline wasn't doing this when their mother was obsessed over the missing money and Samuel was under suspicion, was she? How had she managed this?

"We're titillated, Caroline," she said. "Especially when the house is ample already."

Caroline twisted her upper body away from her sisters. She wished she could rewind her walk to their table, vanquish the last few minutes.

"We're not buying a new home, we're making changes," Caroline said. "Purchasing some new art, fixing up the pool house, maybe it will be bigger—what people do. Recently, we started considering the guest room might become more of a guest wing,"

"And isn't there sketch for the sitting room that will lead into the guest rooms? The space will be striking," Dorey said. "You have a double lot. What an advantage—lucky you."

"Why, Dorey, you have a fabulous set-up too," Collette said. "Your house is enviable—especially the mini spa and screening room."

Fracas. Per usual, the scent wafted ahead of Lucinda's presence. She had come up behind Caroline, her annoyance was visible, palpable.

"Excuse me, ladies," she said. She took off her sunglasses to make eye contact. "Perhaps we should sit down and not delay Tina's plans."

"Of course, Mrs. Barrows," Collette and Dorey recited together like schoolgirls and fluttered off.

The three sisters were alone with Lucinda. She offered a taut, public nod. "No one should be broadcasting construction plans at this moment. Particularly when it's about a family member."

Maribelle wondered if their mother meant it or was pleased to broadcast that Caroline had gotten into the game of home expansions, second only to home purchases.

"We didn't bring it up," Raleigh defended "Caroline's friends started talking . . ."

"Always, there is a script to stick to," Lucinda said. "One that covers benign topics. You know—women's doubles at the Harbor Club, the fundraiser for the Family Health Care Center."

Her eyes were flashing—code for conversation closed. "Let's have a glass of chardonnay, shall we?"

While Raleigh and Maribelle stayed quite still, Caroline followed Lucinda. They glided toward the trellised wet bar, where guests were three deep in their print, papery dresses, billowing in the breeze. Maribelle thought how obvious it had become where she and Raleigh fit into Lucinda's ordered world. Clearly, she and Caroline were the twisted mother-daughter duo of the moment.

"We have a few minutes alone," Raleigh said. "We should talk."

The wind was from the west, and the Intracoastal slapped against the bulkhead when they headed to the Steffens's waterfront. From this angle, Tina's sympathy lunch in Maribelle's honor mirrored any party for any cause. There's was an overt festiveness about it.

Raleigh slanted her chin down, eyes up. Maribelle suspected she had used a fruit-based shampoo, this morning, cherry or papaya, something that attracted bees. She was wearing tinted sunscreen for that sunless, ersatz tan on her arms and legs.

"I've been meaning to tell you about Caroline's house. I heard about it through Alex," she said.

"You heard about Caroline and Travis making their house bigger and better from Alex?" Maribelle asked.

"I know. When Alex was working on the portrait, Lucinda and William were talking like he wasn't there, or he couldn't hear them. He was offended, sort of repelled."

Maribelle crossed her arms. "What about the house, Raleigh?"

"Well, what he heard is that she's giving Caroline two million dollars to fix up it up, although it doesn't need fixing," Raleigh said.

"Two million dollars for a home makeover? To keep up with Tiffany and Dorey, whoever. She's *giving* Caroline that kind of money? Meanwhile, I'm gutting Samuel's estate for millions that Barrows could easily have absorbed. Lucinda could have given *me* two million to pay the company since she's so intent on settling."

Raleigh began hand signaling for Maribelle to lower her voice.

"What about you?" Maribelle whispered. "I don't remember our mother ever offering you a financial break until the portrait, a meager compensation."

Raleigh shrugged. "I suppose it's her way of punishing me for not being in the Palm Beach life. She knows I'm a lost cause. I don't have a husband who co-runs Barrows."

Even if Raleigh wasn't bothered about not being favored or rewarded, it bothered Maribelle. Beyond that, she found Caroline's latest windfall intolerable.

"No one stands up to Lucinda," Maribelle said. She was deliberately calm, secretly seething.

"But Caroline seems to walk the tight rope voluntarily. So, we have to hear her out, we owe her that."

"Sure," Raleigh agreed.

She pressed her mouth together and frowned like she'd just come upon an ant hill. Maribelle waited, certain Raleigh was about to cry. She always did, whatever the situation. Instead, she blew her nose.

"Look, Lucinda's directing us," Raleigh said.

Lucinda and Caroline were lined up, doing a false mother-daughter wave for the sake of the guests. Despite that it was a sunny Florida day, there was a thin, grey rim around them. Maribelle wondered who else could see it—if it really existed.

Instinctively both sisters ran their hands over their hair and straightened up to return.

"And pretend that nothing was discovered," Maribelle said. "Or changed."

Except they both knew that wasn't possible.

CHAPTER TWENTY

Raleigh

R arely did Raleigh ask her sisters to meet for a specific reason; rather she was the one expected to show up when summoned. Yet, two hours after the luncheon at Tina's, Raleigh was on the Lake Trail, waiting for Maribelle and Caroline, at her behest. The late afternoon light along the path flickered, above the gulls circled and cawed. She had chosen the trail, not anyone's home or office, because it was neutral territory. Although Caleb loved to come along this path with her in his jogging stroller, he was at home for dinner with Alex on duty. Caroline had made noise about her solidly booked daughters, who had gymnastics or riding after school, but Raleigh insisted. Since she rarely did, Caroline knew she meant it. No Supy either, she told Maribelle. Raleigh shocked herself, she was in charge, she was running the sister meeting. A breeze from the east blew at her, her breath felt sharp with anxiety.

Caroline, her ponytail swaying like they were at a pep rally at Pinestream, came toward her. She was staring at one couple, early twenties, running at a clip, checking their Fitbits.

"We can move away from everyone," she said.

"When Maribelle comes," Raleigh said.

Caroline opened her miniature backpack and applied sunscreen on her face despite the hour. "She's late."

"She's a widow," Raleigh said.

Maribelle arrived. "I'm here!"

Raleigh hoped she hadn't heard her. In yoga pants with a grey sweatshirt tied around her waist, she looked forlorn, worn out. She needed three days at Eau Spa, that was obvious—a short respite, only to be spat back into the melee.

"Let's start," Raleigh said

Maribelle ducked her head in both directions, satisfied that no one familiar was about. They began in a clipped, rushed way although Raleigh wasn't sure why. She didn't remember when they were last together for this walk. Definitely before Samuel's accident. They moved forward as if in a line surge.

Out of nowhere, North cluttered Raleigh's thoughts. He viewed the Lake Trail as open theatre for mothers and daughters, friends and rivals to compete or complain to one another. He was right—as Raleigh and her sisters proved this very moment. Yet, North seemed more real than her sisters, as if she could put her hands against the base of his neck, and promise. Her sisters became foggy. Raleigh shut her eyes while North ricocheted through her brain.

"Raleigh," Caroline said, "there's a reason we're doing this, right? I mean you've pulled me away from the girls—they have homework. I've been away from my desk today for hours after that long, if gracious, lunch for Maribelle. Barrows is constantly busy—I have a *family*."

Raleigh tossed her head, North receded. She stared at both sisters.

"This won't take long, Caroline," she said. "I only wanted to ask how you had time to work with architect's plans and approvals. For your extension? Maribelle, you agree, don't you, with my question? Don't you agree it's obscene when we're trying to save our company, the company that you, of the three of us, adore and would die for?"

"Obscene? I don't know. It feels inappropriate." Maribelle said. "I'd like to know why it's happening."

"Look," Caroline said. "This wasn't my idea, it was Mom's. She suggested it, she contends it's compulsory." Caroline opened her hands toward the houses they were passing, exquisite waterfront properties. "Mom understands what it's like to be in the game with children."

"Wait a second," Raleigh said. "I need to say this. Caroline, you could have refused. Maribelle? Aren't you as pissed as I am about Caroline doing an expensive renovation, whatever? She didn't want us to learn about it, although we would have if we had driven past her house during construction."

"I'm a new widow," Maribelle said. "There's a private investigation into what my husband did. I might lose everything. I don't even know why I'm included at this powwow."

"Because it affects you, because you're suffering," Raleigh said. "Caroline, we need to help Maribelle, not fix your fucking mini-mansion."

"And why shouldn't I add on to my home? Am *I* supposed to be punished for what *Samuel* did to the company? Is *my* family supposed to miss an opportunity because Samuel was a thief?" Caroline asked.

Maribelle twisted in the other direction, toward the palm trees. "Please don't say that."

"What should I say?" Caroline raised her voice. "How do we know where Samuel got the money for his toys—the Tesla, the *Vertigo*? His order for another Tesla, the latest model. Can you beat that? Julian uncovered the order and the receipts."

Raleigh looked at Maribelle. "Caroline, no matter what we find out about Samuel, you don't have to do a house extension."

"It's okay, Raleigh," Maribelle said quietly.

"Do you think so?" Raleigh asked. Why was Maribelle compliant? It was infuriating. "Aren't you angry about it?"

"Angry, maybe, and worried," Maribelle said. "Julian's investigating what Samuel did. I might lose everything. It's hellish."

Caroline turned to Maribelle. "If you would tell me what you know about Samuel and the money, that might help."

"You're making this a conversation about Samuel when it's about you, Caroline," Raleigh said.

They were at the North Bridge and came to a halt. Raleigh kept her eyes on her sisters. They look so much alike, a warped set of almost twins.

"Whatever you're covering up, I don't like that you're lying to me. Stop protecting Samuel, who ruined everything," Caroline shouted. "Including my plans for my house—everything winds back to his . . . his shit."

"I'm not protecting him, I'm trying to understand what he did—why he did it," Maribelle began to scream.

"I am too, Maribelle," Caroline kept shouting, wagging her right hand at Maribelle. "Remember, before you get a penny from the estate, you'll have to cover Samuel's debt at Barrows. At least I'm not the one with a husband who stole."

"No, you're the one with the husband with information about my husband," Maribelle said. "Yet he says nothing and gets rewarded with a fucking bigger house."

"Oh my God, stop!" Raleigh raised her voice. "This isn't supposed to be an argument, yet again, about the money? Maribelle isn't going to skin our family business. Just stop!"

Caroline and Maribelle stopped, surprised, as if they'd forgotten Raleigh was there. She began sobbing.

"Why is *Raleigh* crying?" Caroline lowered her voice.

"She cries on a dime," Maribelle also spoke softly.

Her older sisters watched while Raleigh became inconsolable. How could they know she was the one, the perpetrator? She was the one who slept with her husband the same day as her lover, the one who knew how it felt to cheat, to lie, to steal. While she didn't understand exactly why Samuel took money or Travis stayed silent, she understood deception.

Caroline grimaced at Raleigh and reached for Maribelle, shaking her.

"Tell me what you know for Chrissake. Because whatever Samuel has done, he's dead and left an enormous mess behind."

"Caroline, no more!" Now Raleigh was shouting too. Two bikers were to the north of them, heading in their direction. "People are coming."

Her sisters kept at it. Maribelle yanked away and started smacking Caroline's upper arms. *"He was my husband. I loved him!"*

Raleigh pried her sisters free, wishing she had never begun this walk to clear the air.

"You loved him?" Caroline asked. "Are you certain? You loved a ghost, a pariah."

"Go ask Travis! Ask him what he knows." Raleigh said.

"Do you think I haven't tried? "Caroline was shouting again. "Travis is slippery. He slinks around, looks past me when I try. Ever since Samuel's accident, he's . . ."

"Ask your friend Julian, Caroline," Maribelle was loud too. "You see him enough, alone. He'll confide in you."

"Julian, ah, there's a thought." Caroline said. Her voice faded, she faced away. "You're both wrong—about everything."

She started down the path, her walk purposeful and exaggerated. Raleigh remembered how Lucinda used to have each daughter practice with a book on her head.

"Caroline, wait," she shouted after her.

"I won't wait," Caroline kept going, like leaving was the best idea of the day.

Maribelle and Raleigh looked out at the Intracoastal as an eighty-foot Bertram and a smaller yacht, a Viking, passed by. No matter where they were, there was a reminder of Samuel, Raleigh realized. This knowledge they now owned, that boats were not merely joy rides.

"Not a lot, but sometimes, Samuel and I walked the Lake Trail with Supy," Maribelle said. "It doesn't seem real, it's like it never happened. Any of it. I'm waiting. I'm ready for the day when this will be over."

"Over, sure," Raleigh said. "Today I wish you guys hadn't been in a fight."

Maribelle bent down, retied her running shoes. When she straightened, she was taller than a moment ago, tallest of the three. "What fight? We're sisters."

Raleigh laughed sympathetically in agreement. Except it was too heavy, it was unending. She kept waiting for the gloom of it to end, for the long shadows to not eclipse them. The air felt putrid.

PART THREE

CHAPTER TWENTY-ONE

Caroline

"Caroline and Travis are peerless hosts. Look at their lavish party!" Lucinda said. "You know how it goes in Palm Beach—you need money *and* style."

Because her mother was louder than the banter, even though Caroline was busy, she heard her at once. Lucinda was speaking to Aunt Bryant, the one person in the party tent who did not care what sort of hosts they were. She had never, as far as Caroline understood it, subscribed to the idea that outsiders might be more relevant than insiders. She was not out to impress anyone. Unlike Lucinda and William and the rest of Caroline and Travis's guests, she was not at a party or a dinner or a charity event per night. Aunt Bryant managed to be on every roster in Palm Beach and still, on chosen evenings, she stayed home to series surf on Netflix or reread *The Handmaid's Tale*.

"Truly, Caroline," Lucinda approached her. "Absolutely, you have outdone yourself. The place settings, the flower arrangements. I'm admiring the color scheme. I *adore* gold tones, a rich palette."

Based on her mother's oozy tone and glazed presence, Caroline figured she had put away two martinis already. She decided to not comment, where would it get her?

"Why is she speaking in these phrases?" Maribelle asked. She was off to the side with Raleigh and Alex.

"It's the dialect," Alex said. "While I've been working on Lucinda's portrait, she's on her cell phone, on speaker, chatting to her friends. They speak in hyperbole."

Caroline decided Alex was not meant to be the arbiter, it was a huge mistake. And so, she passed by with a silky, phony wave, enroute to other guests, who thankfully were not her family. This was the night to take wardrobe inventory quickly, it told the story. Her friends sported *the uniform*, meaning flowy dresses by Zimmermann or Love Shack, balancing themselves on three-inch wedges. Lucinda's crowd and beyond wore Prada, Roland Mouret, and Dolce, depending on low kitten heels to not slip or fall.

Conversations ambled along, benign bordering on a yawn was her goal. *Low humidity ... only a tummy tuck ... lost the money ... wicked mother-in-law ... golf camp, Keto diet, Positano ... no longer a trustee ... frenemies ...* She began to relax, almost able to put the sisters' scene at the Lake Trail three days ago out of her head. And so she focused briefly on her girls, young PB daughters in training. They happily moved among their friends, relishing the hors d'oeuvres—trays of miniature crab cakes, a dollop of caviar on new potato, baby lobster rolls.

"Include everyone rather than forget someone and make an error, it's best to not offend a soul. The grander the bash, the better one's status," was Lucinda's new motto. A few years ago, during her ornate sit-down dinner party period, she had excluded a few couples, claiming there wasn't room at the table. Lucinda managed to offend several women, although she was following their very motif. Now she and any daughter who might be entertaining erred on the other side—they included everyone.

Tonight, Caroline invited everyone who had invited her the past year. One hundred seventy-five closest and dearest were present. Travis and Caroline were choreographers, concerned with every detail. The deejay had begun cocktail hour with Concrete Blonde singing "Everybody Knows" while Dirk O, with her favorite lead singer Saige, was setting up in the tent. Tables for guests were by category: those who rode at Wellington; Academy parents; club life—Longreens, the Harbor Club; Barrows (a work table); and a *PB Confidential* table for Maribelle. Lucinda had curated her two tables and appeared satisfied. Among her crowd was Mrs. A, Bettina Gilles, Faith Harrison, and Veronica Cutler, who looked incredibly chic and face lifted.

Her sisters were somewhere between wallflowers and quiet hawks, watching, judging. Travis gravitated toward his golf buddies, other youngish husbands in their starched button-down shirts, pressed jeans, or requisite khakis. Their teeth were very white—laminated or bleached. Their necks were tanner than their faces, evidence of golf and tennis prowess, proof of how little they listened to their wives about sunscreen. Worse, each of them was tainted with a dose of misogyny. Caroline knew too well and pretended it wasn't so. Overlaying all of it was Samuel's death, an unrelenting downer. Had anyone in her immediate family the courage for other joy, she wondered? And when would it, if ever, resurface?

"Is Julian around?" Maribelle asked, suddenly near to Caroline.

"God, I hope not," Raleigh appeared too. "We're supposed to be at a private party, a fun party. He doesn't belong here. Besides, what has he done for us?"

"Julian isn't coming, Lucinda didn't want him to," Caroline said. Maribelle was about to speak, then stopped herself.

"Really? Mom had an opinion about that?" Raleigh asked.

A Donna Summer's rendition of "MacArthur Park"was up, a favorite of their mother's when they were growing up in Kesgrave. A soggy spell fell over Raleigh and her sisters.

Caroline shook herself out of it. "Listen, I've got to get back to the guests. Tomorrow we'll talk."

As she walked off, she heard Maribelle say to Raleigh, "Once I get the money from Samuel's estate, I'll help you. No matter what happened with Samuel, there's life insurance, his portfolio . . ."

"No, please, I can't take your money, Maribelle," Raleigh said.

"You need it more than anyone else in the family. You're my little sister," Maribelle said. Caroline thought she sounded saccharine and unsure of herself.

She stepped back so sharply there was a searing pain at the base of her neck. "Could you two please quit this topic? Honestly! Can't you just *be* at my party without the misery?"

After that, the cocktail hour moved ahead without Caroline, as if she were not there at her own custom-designed soirée. Although she reminded herself that she was the sister who worked at Barrows, the one with two daughters she was raising in Palm Beach, she felt sideswiped. Meaning no matter what went on, her "PP" (perfect person) image was at risk. Made more so by the man she had married. How late in the game she was to own he was a dick, so she feigned he was good enough. It was easier than digging for accuracy and having to live with that.

Travis had moved across their patio to where most of Caroline's friends and their husbands stood in the dimming light. He was waving her over enthusiastically, underscoring what Lucinda encouraged about acting like a golden couple until even you believed it. A good, Oscar-worthy show was best. Caroline walked with grace to where her husband stood, waiting.

"People seem happy," Travis commented when they were almost through the dinner hour. "Our party's a hit. Larger than life."

Everything was oversized, from the croutons in the arugula salad to the vast platters of oysters to the rows of gas flares angled over their pool and waterfront. A gaggle of mothers from the Academy, Violet's class, had been pointing to the giant chandelier in the ceiling of the tent surrounded by floral arrangements. Caroline was pleased with this pseudo-Alice in Wonderland tone. It was exactly what she was after.

Travis tried out a charming smile. A scent of garlic permeated his skin—he must have overeaten the spicy prawn dish. Too late, Caroline wondered if it was an error to have put it on the menu, half her friends refused to eat onions, garlic, or gluten.

"You mother made some remark, a positive one, about the decorations. She's chipper," Travis said.

"Chipper?" Caroline repeated.

They glanced over at Lucinda, who was with her card game friends. In the polished lights, she appeared soft and caring.

"Great," Caroline said. "That's a relief." She was getting a splitting headache.

He leaned too close to kiss her near her mouth. She resisted, freezing up. Although only for show, they both knew that Caroline was far from receptive to any type of affection Travis tossed her way. Were they less visible to their guests, she would wipe her face. People were beginning their dessert medleys—butterscotch pudding, flourless chocolate cake, and starfish cookies. Whenever the band paused between songs, a high-decibel chatter rose. Caroline was proud, she had put her best Palm Beach style out there.

In the theme of *does-it-ever-end*, as she was about to be relieved, confident, Aunt Bryant came to find her. "Caroline, your sister is stirring up trouble," she whispered.

Without moving her head frantically from side to side, Caroline felt a pulsing anxiety. Within a minute, the night air became too moist, thicker, filling up the party tent. The intentionally subtle lighting changed to greenish.

"Where's Raleigh—what is she doing?" Caroline asked.

"Not Raleigh," Aunt Bryant said. She pursed her lips. She was filled with pity. "Maribelle."

Lucinda was behind Aunt Bryant, fuming. "Corral your sister, Caroline, before she spoils your night."

Travis shined the flashlight on his cell phone, holding it low. "Where is she?"

"By the house, practically stalking Collette Nayers," Lucinda said.

Maribelle. A sickly sensation—that what one had carefully honed and crafted, like an art project made of popsicle sticks, was about to crumble—overcame Caroline. She was doubly pissed because it had to do with Maribelle. Not the wayward, younger sister, she was the one who belonged in this life. Or did, before Samuel died. Caroline realized that her efforts, her purposeful plotting and planning to belong, were jeopardized by not one but both sisters.

"I'll go," Caroline said. She walked at a deliberate pace when she knew she should be racing.

Maribelle was out in the rose garden with Collette and Tina Steffen.

"We're going to the powder room, Maribelle," Tina's voice was tired.

"I'll wait," Maribelle said.

Her hair had come out of a knot at the nape of her neck, her face was flushed, she looked ready for a cat fight.

"Not necessary, Maribelle," Tina said. "We'll come to your table and find you."

"Do you expect me to believe that?" Maribelle sounded fierce, primal. How the girls had spoken on the cheerleading squad in Kesgrave.

"Could we not have a scene?" Tina was in front of Collette,

like she was her bodyguard. "There's nothing to discuss. Let's not spoil your sister's stunning party. Such an elegant night."

"It is elegant," Raleigh appeared. She inserted herself between Maribelle and Tina. "Maribelle, please, please don't do this."

"I'm sorry, I've waited for the right moment," Maribelle said. "I won't backpedal."

"What is it you have to know, Maribelle?" Collette asked.

"I only need to know if you were having an affair with my husband. Just fucking tell me. Then I can quit searching for the one who stomped on my marriage. I'm sure it was you."

Collette started laughing a birdlike, high sound. "You mean was I Samuel's mistress when he died? I was not."

Where we were standing, Caroline thought, the night air had shifted to a different climate. Drier, antiseptic, as if they were congregated in an air-conditioned lobby of a conference center.

"Why are you lying?" Maribelle raised her voice. "Why? Why not admit it? It would help us both. Tell me what happened so I don't have to guess anymore, haunted by Samuel's mistress."

Collette slinked, closer to Maribelle. "Sure, it's true. I was with Samuel, and it was great. We had a good time—a fine time together. We ended it over a year ago, and neither of us was upset. A mutually happy undoing of a tryst."

"Maribelle let's go. C'mon. You don't have to listen." Raleigh pleaded.

"Raleigh's right, let's break this up now," Caroline said. She tried to get Raleigh's attention, fairly sure she would agree and they could influence Maribelle.

Collette gave Maribelle a studied gaze. "Let me clarify for you, Maribelle. It was a fling, lots of fun. We wanted to avoid any mess, so we stopped. There were no hard feelings."

"No hard feelings?" Maribelle was beside herself. "What about me, what about your husband, your child?"

Collette shrugged. "That's what I said. We didn't want any of you involved. I'd call it fun while it lasted."

Raleigh began tugging on Maribelle's arm. "Thank you, Collette, we don't need anything else. C'mon, Maribelle. We'll cut out, the two of us, go to Jay Jay's on Clematis."

Maribelle ignored Raleigh, fixated on Collette. "I'd like the details, at least give me those."

"Collette, don't you say another word," Tina tapped her friend. "Caroline, why don't your sisters go back to their tables?"

Saige was making an announcement. She was about to sing "Rhiannon," Caroline's favorite Fleetwood Mac song. The first chords rang out, and Caroline remembered it was only this morning that she had requested it.

"Raleigh . . ." Caroline said, "that's not a bad idea. You and Maribelle might want to leave."

"How many months were you with him, where did you go, how did you lie?" Maribelle pressed.

"Maribelle, please!" Raleigh began to cry. Caroline was surprised she hadn't begun earlier.

Collette frowned. "You'll have to keep looking for her. I'm sure she exists. Like I said, I'm not the final one."

Caroline stepped in. "No hard feelings then? Can we all move on?"

Everyone got quiet, except that Raleigh kept sniffling and weeping. Tina, contained and certain, said, "Of course we can. That's the solution."

She led Collette back to the alluring chaos of the party. Caroline, left with her sisters, her mother, and Aunt Bryant, wished she could follow them.

Aunt Bryant shivered. Lucinda began patting her face with a linen, monogrammed handkerchief.

"I'm confounded," she said. Very confused, Caroline thought, for her to have been so quiet throughout.

"I'm appalled," Aunt Bryant said.

In the lamplight, both Maribelle and Raleigh's lips were bluish.

Maribelle lifted her phone out of her clutch and read the screen quickly. Julian soundlessly appeared on the terrace as if he had aced the part of the long-lost hero.

"What is he doing here?" Caroline asked. She was rude, she knew, to refer to him as "he," to speak of him as if he were not in her presence.

"I texted Julian to pick me up. I'm going with him. You've got a husband, a family, a new addition pending. I'll take this opportunity, the one in front of me," Maribelle said.

"But Julian is . . ." Raleigh began.

"Julian has come to get me," Maribelle said.

As if she had choreographed the entire evening, Maribelle seemed proud.

"You know," she said. "It's not just about offshore accounts. Julian might whisper something else in my ear."

Julian looked at Caroline, Lucinda caught it. "Go, Maribelle, enjoy the night," she said.

"Caroline, you had best get back to your guests and family," Aunt Bryant said. She took Raleigh's hand in hers.

"Ready?" Julian asked.

He came nearer. They were invisibly looped together, anyone watching knew.

CHAPTER TWENTY-TWO

Raleigh

R aleigh had never been summoned by Aunt Bryant before. When she got to Manalapan, it felt like she had crossed a time zone. Only six miles south of where Lucinda and William lived, it was a tiny town with some fairly major homes. Aunt Bryant lived alone in a modest house by Lucinda's standards. Still, there were five bedrooms and a pool in a sprawling one story with water views. "Splat, flat," is how Lucinda had described Aunt Bryant's choice when they first migrated to Palm Beach. Aunt Bryant had deliberately chosen to stay away from the estate district. "Smothering to be that close," she once whispered to Raleigh after she'd had too much tequila at a book launch at the Dish Art Gallery. Raleigh hadn't been sure what she meant.

Aunt Bryant, Raleigh's official godmother, did laps early every morning. Before Caleb was born, Raleigh used to drive over to swim with her. The mornings had an openness then. Raleigh could do whatever she wanted—yoga, Pilates, the Lake Trail—before she gave birth to a living person who depended on her.

There was a dreamy feel to being at Aunt Bryant's. Her house was peaceful because she was—tranquil because she was comfortable with her life. Raleigh respected her aunt's oblivion to gossip and rivalry, it meant nothing to her. Everything was mellow, including the music she loved. Right now, at the lowest decibel, she was playing "Uncle John's Band." The tune put Raleigh on edge; things felt that turbulent. Ever since Caroline and Travis' party two nights ago, she had been sleepless. A hollow sleeplessness, worse than after a night of Alex's soft snoring, while she remembered North. How she had run her hands along his neck where the skin was almost plaid, little vertical and horizontal lines from too much time in the sun. North. He was a vulnerable warrior, a Lancelot in King Arthur's court.

"Let's sit on the dock." Aunt Bryant said. She wore white pants and a white Lacoste sport shirt. Her sunglasses were the black, boxy vintage Ray-Bans she had worn since Raleigh was in grade school.

"Sure," Raleigh followed her.

Had Caleb come along, it would have been a catastrophe. Raleigh imagined him running up and down these planks without a railing. But he was uninvited, Aunt Bryant told her to arrive alone. A tell-tale sign it wasn't going to be the usual conversation about women artists—Georgia O'Keefe, Lee Krasner, Bertha Morisot. Or more prosaic talk of why everyone in Manalapan called the Intracoastal the Lake Worth Lagoon. This made Raleigh distrustful. Her aunt knew something before she had gotten there to confess. Raleigh was filled with guilt, then longing. A longing for North that wasn't about to subside.

"The air today," Aunt Bryant exhaled.

"I know, ideal." Raleigh pretended she was okay. For her, every day was humid with something rotted beneath the breeze. "It's always beautiful here, isn't it—no matter what," Aunt Bryant said. She poured iced peppermint tea from a thermos into paper cups.

Aunt Bryant sat on an Adirondack chair and motioned for Raleigh to sit on the other. There was cloud coverage that dulled things, then blew off. Raleigh took the tea and considered Aunt Bryant's profile. While Lucinda described "the Barrows nose," one that turned upward, as "enviable," Raleigh preferred Aunt Bryant's strong nose any day. Reed used to say everyone from Kesgrave was a third cousin once removed no matter what their features were like.

"What's going on, Raleigh?" Aunt Bryant asked.

"I'm working on a portrait for the Miller family, two girls and a boy, on schedule."

"That's not what I'm asking," Aunt Bryant gave her a look, like it was fourth grade and already she had become a smart yet wayward student.

"Caleb is in a Mommy and Me class that he loves. Alex is doing better with work. You know about the portrait of Mom and William . . ." Raleigh said.

"Raleigh, please. Be honest, that's not what I'm asking." Aunt Bryant sighed patiently, she was not pleased. Raleigh realized she was way outside her personality, asking for an audience, appraising, digging.

"I saw you with your sisters at Caroline's party," Aunt Bryant said. "You aren't yourself. I'm wondering why."

"I don't know, things have been tricky, complicated."

"Well, yes, the family *is* bewildered from Samuel's accident. I know how close you and Maribelle are, and she isn't easy to console. I have tried."

Raleigh watched the slightest wave movement on the waterway, wondering if Maribelle had a "session" with Aunt Bryant first. Due to birth order, she was last.

"I'm trying with her—trying to be there for her," Raleigh said.

"Yes, of course you are." Aunt Bryant said.

"You know I've always considered myself your advocate, Raleigh. Remember when you wanted to go to that sweet sixteen, years ago, for that Palm Beach snowbird . . . from Fairfield County, wasn't it? Lucinda said no. No traveling that far for a party weekend, a June weekend. You were crying and crying. You went on and on."

"I remember," Raleigh said. "You told me to stop, and then you talked Mom into it. I met the cutest boy on the plane ride, more cute boys at the party in Darien. We stayed up all night, and lots of kids smoked pot."

"What is it, Raleigh?"

"I was having an affair, it's been consuming." A memory click—in some ocean villa in Fort Pierce, where North and she had met one afternoon. How they swore it was the last time, they had to stop, they would hurt people if it kept going. Except once they were naked and together, they knew it couldn't be stopped. Betrayal felt far off—they were stirred and drawn in, engulfed. What was theirs belonged to them wherever they would go, whoever they would become, before or after. Raleigh was desperate for after, he less so.

There was that day toward the end of their time together, when he handed Raleigh a note, folded into a tiny square. "Read it," he said, "then tear it up." *I will always love you.*

"And I you," she said. They kissed madly before he led her to the beach, and she tossed the pieces of paper into the ocean. She knew then it would never be the same, she couldn't breathe without him after that day. Or so she believed.

Aunt Bryant adjusted her left earring with both hands. Seaman Schepps. The half hoop that Lucinda credited as day or night jewelry, including for a tennis game. Aunt Bryant looked around like they might be interrupted. "Who hasn't?"

Raleigh took a deep breath, she felt better after confessing.

"The guilt—it's close to a disease. Yet it won't stop me from missing him."

Warblers swooped in toward the dock and flapped away. Her aunt paused. There were crow's feet around her dark blue eyes and delicate lines across her forehead. Bryant was a rebel, Lucinda liked to say, she refused any measures to combat age. At this moment, Raleigh decided to do the same, no interference. While her mother was still coloring her hair, she, the youngest daughter, would go grey. Briefly, she wondered what North's reaction would be, but it was Alex's reaction she was supposed to care about.

"What I miss is how he loved me," Raleigh said.

"An affair has a life of its own," Aunt Bryant said. "You lose yourself while it's going on. Locked in a different life, a dual existence."

"For me, he's always there, Aunt Bryant."

"The *idea* of him, that's the main attraction, not always the man," Aunt Bryant sighed. "We're talking about a situation— almost a seduction."

Not true about North, Raleigh wanted to shout, there was no one more specific. Why was Aunt Bryant so jarring? She had to understand. As much as Raleigh had been discreet, she needed to spill everything, to be absolved, and Aunt Bryant was the one for that.

"I'll tell you about him, why he stands apart," Raleigh said. "Why there's this haunting question of what could have been."

"Who is he, Raleigh?" Aunt Bryant asked. "Do I know him? What about your sisters, your mother, do they know him?"

"I can't . . ."

"It would be between us," Aunt Bryant said.

How was Raleigh to be pardoned unless Aunt Bryant knew the details. Raleigh was torn, but she couldn't betray him, no matter what happened at the end.

"I can't—I won't share details."

"Ah, then he must be in Palm Beach, in the circle," Aunt Bryant said.

"I'm sorry, I won't rat him out," Raleigh said like Hester Prynne in *The Scarlet Letter*.

"I appreciate how you feel—that you've been discreet," Aunt Bryant said. "Both of you."

"As discreet as possible," Raleigh said.

"Palm Beach is a heartless place, depending on the discovery," Aunt Bryant said. "One can't be careful enough. You, Raleigh, are extremely dear to me. You have always been, since you were a little girl. I don't want you judged or unforgiven."

"No one knows, I promise," Raleigh said. "I came to you because I'm not able to let him go."

Her house, her water views, her entire life without someone, Raleigh thought. How would she understand a husband plus a lover?

"Oh, you think it's outside my wheelhouse," Aunt Bryant said. "You have figured me out, convinced I've never sneaked around with someone, I've pined away alone?"

Yah, I am convinced," Raleigh said. "You're on my side without knowing what it's like—that's how it seems."

"Well, we can't compare risk levels," Aunt Bryant said. "My affair was with a married man; I wasn't married. I was the other woman for decades. Once, years ago, we were in New York in August, deliberately, to not run into anyone—everyone was in the Hamptons, Greenwich, or abroad. Yet, there were his neighbors, standing in the lobby of the Four Seasons when we walked in. After that, he couldn't stop worrying about how it would affect his wife and children."

North and Raleigh had been petrified of being caught, Raleigh knew what she meant.

"An affair is a roller coaster ride, Raleigh. You have Alex and Caleb. The risks are profound. You could lose your life as you live it. It could be taken from you."

"I really loved him." Raleigh was trying not to cry.

"I believe you. It's beside the point," Aunt Bryant said. "Whatever went on, I'm asking you to clean things up before it's too late."

"It might be too late," Raleigh said. Because although North was gone, it never felt over.

"Well, no one gets to have everything, Raleigh. So, it's up to you, isn't it?"

Forty minutes later, at Aunt Bryant's insistence, they had swum and were drying off. Her aunt seemed pleased, as if they had accomplished something.

"Laps save your soul," she said.

Raleigh smiled. *Were it that easy.* "I've got to get back to work, Aunt Bryant. I'm on a deadline for one painting and behind on another."

Aunt Bryant pointed to the gazebo. "A few more minutes?"

Two little lizards—geckos—darted in front of Raleigh's flip-flops, close to her toes. Her skin smelled like a pool treated with salt tablets not chlorine. She needed to go. Yet she knew what was ahead, her world was in fast-forward crumble mode. Swim or no swim, water views or not.

They stood together. "It's about money, isn't it?" Aunt Bryant asked.

"Money? I'm not sure what you mean," Raleigh said. "Are you talking about the missing money at Barrows—the insanity around it with my mother and Caroline—Maribelle too? No, it's not about that."

"Money for you, Raleigh. You could use some to make you more secure, for your family. Maybe then Alex would feel better and less pressured. He's a good man, a good husband."

"You like him best of the husbands, I think," Raleigh said. For this very second on the seesaw, Alex was up, North was down.

"I do. I'd like to help get you back on track. Money to put you at ease. We can figure out an amount. It would be between us—a loan. With the distributions from Barrows diluted . . . delayed . . . who knows what? I could fix things, life would be easier," Aunt Bryant said. She sounded motivated, as if she had truly contemplated her offer.

"No, Aunt Bryant, as kind as you are, thank you, but no," Raleigh said.

"Why not? In a family where money is a ticket, *the ticket*, there is no need to resist," said Aunt Bryant. Raleigh saw that her resistance wasn't refreshing, only perplexing.

"Because it's yours," Raleigh said.

"You should take it because I have it—for you and Alex. I want you both to be secure, not pressured. Who knows when Barrows will be worked out? Short term, for a short period. If you need it for more than six months, we'll discuss how to keep going."

"You don't have money like my parents had or what Barrows makes. You don't need to save my marriage," Raleigh said, then regretted saying it.

Aunt Bryant wasn't fazed. "I have the money. I want you to have it."

She came very near to Raleigh. On one side was the house and to the left the "lagoon." Raleigh wanted to sketch a figure of a young woman who was lost in the middle. She would place her on the polished wood floor of the gazebo, barefoot. There was this sense to her, Raleigh knew already, her need to weep and be held. Instead, her subject was alone, centered in a spot where people gaily met for cocktails while admiring the skyline. Raleigh was that person whether she drew her on paper or lived in her skin.

Aunt Bryant and she were so near each other—Raleigh saw how short her eyelashes had become, that her eyebrows were completely, carefully penciled in. One smudge and she would be shown to the world for who she was.

"My idea is a good one. You don't *know* what might have been," Aunt Raleigh persisted. "No one knows the future. Whether it will work out with Alex or not, this helps."

Her remarks were pointed, Aunt Bryant suspected Alex was aware of North. That Raleigh had hurt her husband and her marriage was in jeopardy. She had to let her know it wasn't so.

"Aunt Bryant, it's okay with Alex, I swear."

"I hope so. I've been your protector a long time." Aunt Bryant was helping out of sympathy—Raleigh knew then that she had gone too far.

What she wished was that her aunt would claim Raleigh her favorite. Yet in the Barrows family, they were covert with their allegiances. It was palpable, not provable. When Lucinda bandied about who pleased her most, it was Caroline first, for being her Palm Beach follower, Maribelle was runner up for meeting many, if not every Palm Beach requirement. At least she was until Samuel's accident. Possibly Raleigh was runner up now that Alex was doing the Lucinda/William portrait and tempted to say little. As long as no one learned about North. Ever.

CHAPTER TWENTY-THREE

Maribelle

A shroud of immediacy hung over Lucinda's plan for today. She had called for a six o'clock meeting at Barrows to be followed by lobster night at Longreens. The idea of dinner together afterward unsettled Maribelle—as if they had been deep sea fishing together and, while they were still on the boat, the fish had started to spoil.

Despite the air-conditioning, which Travis ran too high—the room was set at 68 degrees—it was stuffy. If there were some horrific news, Maribelle believed, Lucinda would not have orchestrated a dinner to follow. An obscene amount of obligatory family dinners had taken place these past two months since Samuel died. No other family in Palm Beach was as insular as theirs, Maribelle was sure of that. Maybe not insular but tethered.

The sisters were resolute, coiffed and primped for dinner at a club. Caroline was ultra-chic in Proenza Schouler while Maribelle was equally so, in Victoria Beckham. Raleigh wore a tiered, sleeveless Veronica Beard; also pitch perfect. No one had consulted the other, they just knew instinctively to please their mother. Better yet, presenting as impeccable was a tool, taught by Lucinda back in the day, in the Panhandle. Seeing was believing. They were posturing as the family Lucinda envisioned.

"We're waiting for Julian," Lucinda said.

"Isn't Aunt Bryant coming?" Maribelle asked.

"She was asked, she decided not to," Caroline said. Maribelle didn't appreciate how she stared at her when she answered. Meaning they all knew when Aunt Bryant chose avoidance, it was worth it.

"I wish she had come," Raleigh said.

"Enough," Lucinda smoothed her hands over the Brunello beige shift that was a staple of hers. Maribelle took inventory of her semiprecious jewelry. After all, whatever Lucinda wore when it came to earrings, necklaces, and bracelets was a deliberate statement. Tonight, she was doubling up on Elizabeth Locke Intaglio bracelets and earrings. How she slathered her wrists was also on purpose, as if she liked the chance of disseminating migraines.

The overhead lights were strident. There was an antiseptic feel to the conference room despite Samuel's and Travis's intentions. Their goal had been to make it inviting—sophisticated, not corporate. Caroline's aesthetic was a factor too. Who could explain, thought Maribelle, why tonight it felt like they were in a skyscraper in New York or Chicago, not on a low floor on a shopping street in Palm Beach. Mood over matter, plus being here at this hour made it very corporate too. Everyone was thin lipped and cryptic in their assigned seats. They were lined up in the same order as last time, Raleigh, Caroline, and Maribelle faced Alex and Travis. Samuel's seat was emptier and more flagrant than right after the accident. Maribelle detested how he wasn't there, how he was more dead as the months went on. What seemed to be the same per meeting, however, was Lucinda. She situated herself in the Reed Chair, she was getting accustomed to it.

Then she began to pace, tapping her fingers on the Nakashima dining table. Travis was back to his nervous habit of swiping at his upper lip. Maribelle stared at the portrait Raleigh had painted of the three sisters ten years ago. When entitlement wasn't so loaded, and a Palm Beach season was something to dive into. Perhaps Raleigh's fantasy was right. The Barrows belonged in Kesgrave, living as they had circa the early nineties. A place where aberrant families weren't in hiding, and seven and a half million dollars was a sum beyond comprehension, not what Maribelle's dead husband had siphoned off.

In Palm Beach, plenty of people had merely written off what Samuel "borrowed" and absorbed the loss—what Maribelle had begged her mother to do from the start. As she looked at her sisters and mother tonight, she suddenly perceived that this wasn't the only about her husband. It was that their father had been gone too long to carry the family, his influence had waned. While their mother had created the fable and steered them to Palm Beach, their father had kept everything in line. He wasn't punishing or cruel, that Maribelle knew. She needed to get the fuck out.

"Travis, isn't that the door?" Lucinda asked.

Estelle, who won the prize for blind devotion, including working overtime, led Julian in. His style was friendly, bordering on appropriate. All three sisters, Maribelle noticed, were such scowlers lately, they each pretended not to notice. He was in narrow khaki trousers and a blue striped button-down shirt. Maribelle assumed he was dressed for the rest of his night. Afterward, his plans, as she wrote them, were to stay on the island, make the rounds. HMF at the Breakers or the Colony, if he crossed the bridge, Pastis, on Clematis Street.

Only yesterday Maribelle had told Kendall that *PB Confidential* ought to cover the music spots in West Palm. Nadia overheard and said, "Oh, sure, right after we showcase The Third Wave of Feminism lecture at the Literary Society."

Maribelle might have pushed back, except why bother? She had become wary. When she thought of the magazine, all that counted was that no one learned about Samuel's scheme. An effort that had settled into a lethal dust.

"Well, good evening," Julian said.

The part of Maribelle trained by Lucinda knew his teeth should be laminated. That his shirt was not pure cotton but a synthetic blend. He was too muscular. It must be natural, not something produced by bench pressing. Lucinda liked that, as far as body building went. She wasn't impressed by crowded gyms and all that huffing or the clank of heavy weights against the ground. The obvious part for Maribelle, her sisters, mother, and Aunt Bryant was Julian's effect. Travis, Alex, Samuel, appealing by daily standards, looked sooty and drab in contrast. Julian was handsomest.

"Will anyone want anything to drink, Travis?" Estelle asked. "I've put out some macadamia nuts and water bottles." She pointed to a few dishes placed at either end of the conference table and accompanying paper napkins. The napkins had Barrows in block letters at the bottom right.

"We're in good shape, thank you, Estelle," Caroline said

Estelle nodded. Her blouse, a half clingy, taupe number, fit poorly. Her hair was odd for her. She was not wearing her wedding band. Maribelle briefly wondered if Estelle was no longer married, then remembered she was in her own trench. It was her war, and any other soldier's story had to be meaningless. Samuel, of all people, had taught her about that.

"Thank you," Estelle swirled around and out.

"Hello, Julian," Lucinda's voice was overly even. Maribelle knew she was sharpening her claws, she liked running the meetings on Samuel's "malfeasance." She had chosen the word *ad nauseam* to describe the situation.

Julian opened a file. "I will report on my findings."

Raleigh had that deer in headlights look. Alex, it seemed, was trying to get her attention by clearing his throat, fanning himself with his hand, scraping his chair against the floor. When nothing worked, Maribelle was tense, sure he might jump over the table to calm her. If he had the instinct, it passed. Maybe at last he was having an epiphany. He froze up, as if he finally understood what a great break it was to *not* be a Barrows.

"Riptide Corporation," Julian said. "It is now dispositive, this is where the money went. Tracing money that's gone offshore isn't easy to do, and when I say it is Samuel's corporation, it is after much research and with certainty."

"Is it recoverable?" Lucinda asked.

"Five and a half million dollars will be recoverable. Two million will not. It is gone."

"Gone? Gone where?" Caroline's sounded panicked.

"It would be useful to know," Lucinda said. "Doesn't everyone agree?"

Raleigh stared at the windows, not daring to get up from the table. Maribelle knew the feeling. Just outside this room, it was dusk; the street below was quiet, safer.

Travis's eyes were murky, downward. Alex pushed his head back like husbands and fathers did when they were bored or trapped at a Palm Beach event. Lucinda's enormous push for her cause felt grimy. Maribelle had small welts on her neck, more a Raleigh thing, but hers tonight.

"You know, Lucinda," Travis said. "I'd like to focus on the money that *can be* recovered and put back into the companies without the authorities being notified. We want it to remain private, to sidestep criminal charges."

"Criminal charges?" Caroline asked. "What happens to Maribelle if there are?"

Maribelle resisted saying *how kind of you to care, Caroline, how kind of you to put my risks up front.* Another option was to be pathetic and reveal what a process grief was. No husband in her bed, at any dinner table or party. Any popularity that belonged to her was curiously gone without Samuel. She decided to offer up what she knew.

"Well," Maribelle said. "I've spoken with Daryl Dexter, and the estate is responsible for anything that's owed. He'll be pleased the money has been found."

Travis stood up to adjust the air conditioning, fiddling with the panel.

"To be clear, does Maribelle have to return the money?" Raleigh asked.

"Of course she does, Raleigh," Caroline said. "Samuel took it. So, yes, as soon as probate is wrapped up and the estate is closed."

"Exactly," Lucinda's said. Her voice tinged in meanness. "Maribelle will pay what is owed to Barrows. Fortunately, she's only responsible for a portion of what Samuel stole according to Julian's findings."

"Can't Barrows as a private company simply write it off for some reason?" Alex asked.

Another version of the same question. Maribelle was surprised it was her little sister's husband who cared enough to know. Alex, with his shadow beard and unruly hair by local standards. He had a poetic appeal, except somewhere along the path, Maribelle wasn't sure when, he had been depleted of his independent spar-kle—the one he had when he arrived in Palm Beach as Raleigh's husband. Since Raleigh was known to spill her true feelings, Maribelle wondered if she had warned him back then, if she had conveyed that while the Barrows family draws people in, one mustn't be fooled. Beneath, they were like the barnacles in the Apalachicola River, the ones that overwhelmed the oysters, robbed them of their survival.

"That's been my question for a while," Maribelle said.

"It's up to Lucinda. Your mother decides," Travis said.

Wuss, kowtowing to his mother-in-law. "Give it up, Travis," Maribelle said under her breath, *own your life.*

"I'm leaning toward Samuel's estate paying Barrows what was taken." Lucinda said.

"Mom!" Raleigh started a low-key version of her weeping. The kind where the weeper was immutable. No one paid any attention.

"That makes sense for the greater good," Caroline said. "Barrows will benefit."

Travis nodded. "Understood."

Maribelle was at the brink. She had nothing to lose, had she? Two million dollars owed by her while Caroline, Lucinda, and Travis were triumphant. She wasn't the one in Palm Beach with a child or children. She had skipped that beholden, desperate attachment spun by Lucinda. At this moment, Maribelle was propelled forward. She had to let go of whatever had been. She couldn't remember why she had loved Samuel. She stood up to speak. Everyone became hushed.

"There won't be a criminal investigation, that wouldn't work for anyone, would it?" Maribelle asked. "Nor would a feature story running locally, something like *The Truth about the Barrows.* Especially since we are pretty sure Travis knows more than he lets on."

"Hey, Maribelle," Travis stood up too. Was it a bad ping-pong game of who announced what? Did he think he had a bit part in a play? Everything about him looked skewed. He was no longer elegant and dapper. "How dare you accuse me . . ."

"Travis, stop, please," Caroline stood up next. "We won't accomplish anything if . . ."

"If what?" Raleigh jumped up and did her dancer pose.

"I've got to go," Maribelle said. She looked at Julian.

He was collecting his papers while acting as if the Barrows weren't a train wreck. As if the evening hadn't been a revelation.

"There isn't much else to go over," he said. "You have my findings."

Raleigh moved away from the conference room first. Lucinda began calling after her, then Raleigh and Caroline. Not the men. It didn't matter. Maribelle passed Estelle, who seemed stupefied, out into the Florida night air.

After Maribelle had pulled around on Royal Poinciana Way and was heading west, she texted Julian. *Can we speak tonight? Now at 212 Flamingo.*

He was waiting outside his Mediterranean style house. She followed the footlights along his walkway. "Welcome back to El Cid."

"I'm happy to return," she said.

Inside, she tread carefully, as if they hadn't been together in these rooms the night of Caroline's party. The house was an original bungalow and had belonged to his grandparents. It had a slim entry with high ceilings. Maribelle imagined halcyon days—Ella Fitzgerald singing "I'm Making Believe," Frank Sinatra singing "My Way."

"Yeah, a vacation from your life."

They walked into the kitchen with a white linoleum floor and apple green walls. He had it right, she thought, she was ready to move in.

Maribelle kept wondering was if Julian had edited his story as so many people do. She was still waiting for a dog, a child, a woman to come in and say hello, curious about her. Maybe resentful. She knew nothing about Julian. Then the practical parts started. Did she have a travel toothbrush in her makeup bag? She needed to freshen up, her hair was limp at best, frizzy at worst.

"We ought to talk," Julian said. "We have privacy, it's only the two of us."

While it was very good news about privacy, Maribelle still didn't want to. Not only did his questions worry her, but also her own. What mattered most to ask—were you ever drawn to Caroline? Is the case finally closed? She yearned only to go into his bedroom and recapture the magic of their first time together.

In the dim kitchen light, Julian was Herculean. He took off his blazer and laid it on a kitchen stool. "I know what happened with the missing two million that Samuel siphoned from Barrows."

"I do too," she said.

"Why didn't you tell me?" Julian asked.

"I didn't want anyone to know," Maribelle said. "Wouldn't it have made me look complicit if my husband poured a fifth of it into *PB Confidential?*"

"Not necessarily. Did you know he was doing it, Maribelle?"

She wanted him to believe her, not to lump her in with her family—especially with her mother. She hoped he would kiss her now and shelve the rest.

"I swear I didn't know, not until after he died," Maribelle said. "When Holly told me, I was upset and very surprised."

She didn't mention how ashamed she was that Samuel was propping her up in a job, something she was capable of handling on her own. Paying Holly off. She dreaded seeming like a loser to Julian.

"Well, no one needs to know about where the money went. Tell Holly Lamm to keep it quiet," he said.

"I have, and I'll ask her again. She knows it's expedient to not talk," Maribelle paused. "Julian, why didn't you say anything tonight at the meeting? My mom *hired* you."

"To protect you. Somebody has to look out for you," he said. "Do me a favor, Maribelle? Anything you learn about the rest of the money—the other five and a half million—be careful who you confide in."

"How will I find out if you haven't?"

He shrugged. "People confess, letters are found, emails . . . something."

"There's been enough to untangle," she said.

"Agreed. Still, someone knows. Luckily there wasn't enough proof of foul play beyond the fact that Samuel took it."

Samuel proved to be a brilliant chameleon, Maribelle thought. The ultimate duper.

"Do we have to talk about this—try to yet again imagine what Samuel did and why?" she asked.

Julian put his forefinger against her mouth. "No, no more."

Again, there was the idea of Julian without his investigation. What else made this tension between them acceptable, Maribelle thought. What sort of person was she? Julian came into her life because of her husband's dubious death and deceit. Especially when Lucinda's theory that handsome men were rarely kind could easily apply.

He was leading her toward the bedroom. They were as far as they'd gotten the night of Caroline's party. She looked at the plain room with sturdy, wood furniture, the kind Maribelle had not seen since Aunt Bryant's house in Kesgrave. Only a lamp was lit on a desk. Piled high were books, a few were library books, bound in plastic. It felt remarkably safe.

"You okay?" he asked.

"I am," she said.

Julian unzipped her dress while she unbuttoned his shirt. They were kissing, laughing until he carried her to his bed, where Maribelle prayed she would stay—in this place, this room, his arms—for unending days.

Afterward, Julian held her. They spoke in tapered voices as if they were guests in someone's house, or they shared a three-year-old who had nightmares and roamed around.

His chest was tighter than what she knew, he was unlike anyone else—from another planet.

"It's something, how we met," Maribelle said. "Because of what my husband did to my family, it's surreal . . . "

Julian leaned on his elbow and did that gaze into her eyes move.

"What is it?" she asked.

"You know, I saw you before we were introduced by Bryant. I remembered you—the shape of your face, how you walked with Samuel into the Trents' party—about a year ago," Julian said.

"I don't remember seeing you there."

"It was crowded, I was with a date," he said. "I venture to say we were talking with different groups of friends not about to overlap with my crowd. Anyway, when your godmother—right, your aunt—called and wanted to know if I could take the case, I said sure. I wasn't really into working with another Palm Beach family, except for you. I remembered you, that's mostly why I took it on."

"And now you know *too much* about me and my family," she said.

"I do know something," Julian agreed. "But it's complicated."

"I was the one who wanted to leave Palm Beach," Maribelle said. "I was begging Samuel to try somewhere else for one year. Away from Barrows, the family, his mistress. Meanwhile, he was stealing money and with other women. That's the truth."

"What did he say?" Julian asked.

"I don't know, it seemed that he might have been okay with it, or I was dreaming," Maribelle said. "And then, there was the accident."

She wasn't able to read Julian, was it in sympathy, disbelief? She touched his hands like she used to touch Harper's when she was very young. A delicate, hopeful touch. "Please don't judge me by Samuel, or my mother, or my sisters."

"I don't mix it together. Not any of it."

She believed him, meaning he was just placed on a very short list of people in her life. She believed Raleigh. She believed Caroline two-thirds of the time. Aunt Bryant always, Lucinda, very sporadically.

"Hey, please, listen, don't worry, Maribelle," Julian said.

What kind of wife was she that he wanted someone else—had she failed him?

She had some choices. She could express her thanks; she could confess how miserable it's been. She leaned into him, and they started kissing—insane kisses like lost lovers who were torn apart by a continent. Reunited after years, starved for one another.

Julian swooped her into his arms, and they were at it again. She was his unbride, Maribelle thought, and he was a total stranger. How fitting it was for the pile of lies she came from.

CHAPTER TWENTY-FOUR

Caroline

O ut on the deck, Lucinda was pacing around her new pizza oven when Caroline arrived. Denise was rolling dough, a six pack of Boozy Tea sat on the bar. Clearly Lucinda oversaw every detail. Caroline might have missed something on the calendar unless this was simply a trial run for a luncheon or party. Not that she cared. All that counted was a private conversation with her mother—she needed her full attention. To the left, the pool maintenance crew was packing up. Caroline vaguely wondered if her mother had already swum today. To her right, the Intracoastal beckoned as always. A body of water that existed no matter what it yielded. A tributary. Samuel was wracked by it and on it flowed.

Caroline, in her linen beach cover up and peach-colored straw hat, a sixties look that she favored, approached.

"Caroline!" Lucinda said." This is a surprise." She did a quick intake, offering her company smile. She despised it when anyone, including her daughters, was impromptu. She hadn't rehearsed her script. The worst part for Lucinda was not being in charge of the agenda.

"You are in resort mode—excellent. As you see, I'm practicing my pizza skills. A thin crust, fresh mozzarella and ricotta, broccoli that Denise has charred. Last summer, the Norrics and Damons both raved about doing this in the Hamptons, made from scratch. I decided William and I should finesse it for entertaining."

"Nice," Caroline said. She resisted any reminder of the frozen foods of her childhood. The Lucinda of long ago, in Kesgrave, had taught her daughters that frozen was a step above canned goods, a way to go. Her selection extended to frozen pizza on a weekly basis.

"Look at the size of the oven!" She beamed.

This was their third conversation about pizza making, Caroline noted. Her mother's crushes and whims were varied. In the late nineties, she had been obsessed with reading Stephen King and Danielle Steele while eating cheddar-filled pretzels. Years before that, she was faithful to the Jane Fonda exercise frenzy. Now, in Palm Beach, the obsessions were fancier, more elegant and, of course, appropriate.

Caroline was apprehensive, her petition, however it went down, had to begin. Lucinda peered out of her binoculars, palm warblers and green herons swooped low. These birds practically belonged to Lucinda, Caroline thought. There had been offspring for years, literally nesting beneath the roof of her pool house.

"I was hoping to find you alone," Caroline said.

"Ah, you calculated that William would be on the golf course," Lucinda said.

She was in tennis clothes. Caroline had planned to get over in time to talk before her mother headed off to her weekly game. She had counted on no one being around, including Aunt Bryant, who was invited reluctantly and showed up regretfully. This moment couldn't hold forever, she and Lucinda needed to speak.

Lucinda glanced at her phone, placing it down on the outdoor bar. Overhead a helicopter whirred.

"Why are they flying this path?" She pointed. It was a freefall to the chair. They waited for the noise to finish.

"What I want, what I came here to ask for is Samuel's job—to be the CFO of Barrows." Caroline's words tumbled together.

The steely stare, the one Lucinda saved for housekeepers or hairdressers who ran late and others who irritated her, was directed at Caroline. She turned to Denise, who was slicing tomatoes. "Denise, we'll finish later."

"Yes, Mrs. Barrows." Caroline felt Denise's compassionate glance as she headed toward the house. Once she was too far off to hear, Lucinda adjusted her visor.

"Samuel's position as CFO? Why, Caroline? Travis is working with Heidrick and Struggles out of Chicago on a search to fill the position. They're very good with a large network."

Headhunters. How could he? In the moment, Caroline loathed him, it was close to inspiring.

She paused, inhaled. "Why do that? We need someone who knows Barrows inside and out. I've been there since I was five, and Dad brought me to work on Saturdays. I sat at the little desk he had made for me and stamped envelopes for payroll."

"Of course, you did, how charming it was. Those father-daughter Barrows weekends."

"*I* was groomed by Dad," Caroline insisted. "My sisters weren't enticed, you know that. They didn't show up. They didn't care in the least."

Lucinda was gliding, as if nothing said was significant, toward the wrought iron garden chairs. She signaled for Caroline to follow. They sat as equals, yet Caroline sensed they were inches from being foes. Foes over Barrows. No one loved it better than the two of them, that was the thing.

"More to the point, you have the girls and Travis," Lucinda said. "The new addition you'll build is very exciting. There's a certain life in Palm Beach for you to live. You're going with your family to Nantucket this coming summer. You'll be at the Barrows house there. You'll want less work not more. There is enough responsibility. There's enough on your plate. Who among your friends works as a CFO? I've taught you the ropes, and you have the position you have."

"I should be CFO, I've earned it." Caroline spoke as though she were brave.

"You have a good position—prestigious without being *too* demanding with room to be a Palm Beach mother. Why should work obliterate other parts of your life? Go shopping, redecorate, play golf."

Lucinda viewed her surroundings as if her privileged life stated the case. "About fifteen or twenty years ago, Caroline," she sighed, "women took cooking classes, went to wine tastings. What designer bag you carried mattered. Travel, restaurants, wardrobe, whatever measure kept things intact. Trust me, it's worth it, it's easier. Where does your overwhelming ambition come from?"

Was she joking? A rhetorical question, a tone-deaf question.

"Where does it come from? Mom, you know it's from you," Caroline said. "And things have changed, I can do both. *You* did both. You didn't have a title, yet we know Dad created Barrows with you. Maybe, actually, *you* created Barrows with Dad fronting it."

"Well, not exactly, Caroline. Let's let Dad be remembered as the founder. But yes, Barrows matters to me so much."

"I get that because it matters to me—to the same degree."

Lucinda smoothed the hem of her pale blue tennis skirt. Who but their mother paraded around in tennis clothes at her age, Caroline thought. In the hushed, wood-paneled women's dressing rooms at Harbor Club and Longreens, members whispered how Lucinda Barrows hadn't any cellulite. She prided herself on it—she worked at it. When her daughters turned fifteen, she instructed them to thump on their thighs and butts to stay in shape. Once they were in college, she taught them to do Kegels too, stressing inner and outer effects.

"There is nothing more to discuss, not now," Lucinda said. "We'll change the subject. We'll talk about your house."

"The house, I'm grateful to you, but I never asked for an addition," Caroline said. "The time isn't right. I can't take this money when Maribelle has Samuel's debt and Raleigh—we all know she and Alex are struggling. I think they both suspect *I* came to *you* about the renovation."

"Does it matter what the genesis is?" Lucinda asked. "I want this for you. Laurit is the contractor, Margot Damon used him, she said he's stellar. When you meet with him, I can join you."

She pressed her lips together. Her hair blew off her forehead, which seldom happened. How she had infiltrated this place, Caroline thought. What motivated her mother? Was it some Mahjong game where her friends' daughters were getting bigger houses?

The wind was whipping up from the west. The Intracoastal was getting choppy. Caroline remembered Maribelle and Samuel steering the *Vertigo*, blissfully. How lonely it was convincing her mother of anything.

"Caroline, if I speak to Travis about the position, you'll need to follow through on your house expansion," she said. "You'll need to be emblematic, a representative for our family—success, respect, a moneyed young mother with her family."

"Listen, we're each doing what we can. I happen to be the daughter in the trenches in Palm Beach."

"Clearly, but at the moment, you are the daughter who exceeds my dreams." Lucinda stood up, squinted. "I'm off for doubles. You'll let me know how the house plans are coming along."

Since she was a trained acrobat in the best side-show at the circus, Caroline knew she would contort herself. If the Barrows act intrigued outsiders, so be it. Most of all, she wanted to remain in the game.

CHAPTER TWENTY-FIVE

Maribelle

The shops at Royal Poinciana Plaza weren't open yet when Maribelle crossed the terrazzo patios, the morning light slanting toward her. Despite what she knew about *PB Confidential*, Samuel's underwriting of the magazine had to work in her favor. She decided to fight one more go-round for the content she wanted. All this after speaking with Julian, who assured her with his radiance that all inquiries are over—including Officer Breeley's.

"A hundred percent finished?" Maribelle asked.

This was an hour ago, when they were on his porch drinking espresso.

"*I promise*," he said.

The air seemed cleansed in the office, the filters were changed two days ago. Tanya booked a company to come after hours and scour. And while Maribelle had been on an invisible break, not as focused as usual on the magazine, she was relieved to be back.

Carrying her iPad through the reception area, Tanya was the first to notice Maribelle. "Ah, you've arrived!"

Nadia was next, coming through the conference room in a long, lime-colored skirt, fitted by Marina Moscone, Maribelle suspected. She did not eye level with Maribelle.

"Sure, she's here," she said. Her hair was glistening as usual, her torso, pitched like a dancer's. "You called the meeting. True, Maribelle?"

Kendall was already in the conference room at the wall of framed *PB Confidential* covers, three chosen editions per year for the past four years. Palm Beach women graced the covers— mother and daughter duos, dowagers who stood alone, including Mrs. A in a feature article on philanthropy. There was a cluster of issues focused on restaurateurs and shopkeepers, a story Nadia did on Vintage Tales when she had first started.

"Sometimes, I come in to visit this array, to get ideas. You must be so proud, Maribelle," Kendall said.

"I am," Maribelle said.

"We are brainstorming, I assume—the three of us?" Nadia asked.

As Maribelle chose to sit at the head of the table, she flashed to Lucinda filling the Reed Chair at Barrows, her tone at those meetings, how imperious she could be.

"Right, Holly won't be joining us," Maribelle said. "I'll let her know."

"We're just meeting for the best topics, ones that knock everyone out," Nadia said.

While Maribelle had been avoiding her, she'd not forgotten her ambition for a Barrows story. Damn Samuel, who stealthily buoyed *PB Confidential*, enabling Maribelle for his own good. Arranging for his wife to believe her work was elemental while he busied himself with his secrets!

"We know how juicy things are in Palm Beach, especially when everyone knows the players," Nadia looked at Kendall.

Although the lighting in the offices was not fluorescent, it was sour today, Maribelle thought. Each woman seemed too squished in her chair. Both Kendall and Nadia had circles under their eyes and a ghastly pall, meaning Maribelle did too.

"That's the goal, isn't it?" Kendall asked. She was tapping her pencil, something she did too often.

"Yeah, except this has to be *our* feature—*our* cover story for the last hard issue," Nadia said. "Big, sensational. That's what will entice everyone to follow us online."

"What are you considering?" Kendall asked.

"Well, it's about an investigation, a family company, a mysterious death—in Palm Beach," Nadia said. Her feigned sincerity was challenging, Maribelle gave her that much.

"I don't know . . . Maribelle?" Kendall was speaking too quietly.

"Oh sure, people will be shocked, town will be buzzing." Nadia kept on. "We know how the players like to protect their confidences."

"Except, Nadia, there's Maribelle to consider . . ." Kendall said.

"It's fine—it's worth it. You'll see when this feature makes it our biggest seller ever," Nadia said.

Had Kendall missed how supercilious Nadia was? As if one day, if Kendall played her cards right, she too might have a shot at what Nadia was about to achieve.

Maribelle's anxiety was ramping up. She needed to stop this. "That's not the focus right now, Nadia."

Nadia tossed her head. "Why not? The boating accident, who knows what really happened? Your ambitious mother could kill anything in her path—unless someone else were to stop her."

"My mother?" Maribelle said. "Are you insinuating . . ."

"I'm not insinuating anything," Nadia said. "I'm questioning what other Palm Beachers are questioning, reflecting what's going around."

Nadia stared past Maribelle, who was obstructing her path. Maribelle realized Nadia might never have had scruples. What about Holly, who had turned Nadia down for this story up to this point?

A slow sensation, like melting away, began for Maribelle. Lucinda's biggest fear, invisibility, was suddenly understandable. The control she had at the magazine had shifted. She now questioned herself. Wasn't she, Maribelle, the architect of the magazine's rise from a giveaway at supermarkets and chain pharmacies to what it was today? Or had Samuel and Holly simply convinced her that she was in charge? Another ploy. Had her editorial decisions made *PB Confidential* the most popular publication, or was it not the case? Maribelle decided Nadia would not undermine her. She stood up.

"Nadia, we've been over this. It won't be happening. Here at *Confidential*, we're focused on the season—events, charities, parties, fundraisers, places to be seen. What you do so well, Nadia."

"We aren't covering the Literary Society?" Kendall sounded crushed.

'We can do that, we are planning soft stories, local interest," Maribelle said. "Nothing outrageous or unkind."

"I can take my idea elsewhere," Nadia said. "A lead piece about a morally bankrupt do-gooder with a hidden agenda, a key member of the female-laden Barrows clan. Who can control the presses anyway?"

What did Nadia know precisely? And with whom had she spoken at Samuel's memorial? What had she been told? That feeling again, the same as the morning Travis came over to announce there had been an accident. As if there was no foundation beneath the structure. The structure of her marriage, now the structure of her work. She tried to remember what it was like with Samuel, a man who never appeared the same way twice. Each morning, she woke up unsure of which Samuel would appear—aloof and uncommunicative, joking and wide-smiling, short-tempered and enraged, or charming and sexy.

Nadia rotated her head. "Oh, come on, Maribelle. I'm about to call a guy named Julian, a forensic accountant, and see if he'll talk. If he won't, either way, I can get to the police reports, the Coast Guard. A few friends at the *Daily Sheet* are sniffing around, I want to beat them to it. What if they've heard that this family . . ."

"I don't care what they've heard at the *Daily Sheet*. We won't be doing the story. You can stop threatening me. There is nothing to uncover. My husband died in a boating accident. There is no mystery, Nadia. It's a tragedy," Maribelle said. "Kendall covers the jewelry show and the poetry festival. You can do a front page on thriller writers in South Florida and the three novels that take place between here and Miami. Plus, your charity party beat."

Nadia clears her throat. "Maribelle, I remember when I first came to *PB Confidential*. Our first conversation was about getting the best story before anyone else does. Not that we're a newspaper, but a dishy story about a prominent Palm Beach family? This is the kind of thing you've sought out."

Her floral wrap dress was sticking to the back of her knees when Maribelle stood up. "You know, Nadia, we'll need a few minutes," she said. "Kendall, there's no reason for you to stay. You're good, right?"

As Kendall gathered her things, Maribelle remembered the week she hired her. She and Samuel had argued over something ridiculous—Maribelle's decision to beg off a Barrows family business trip to Bermuda. He kept insisting it mattered to her sisters that the whole family be together. He called Lucinda a battle-ax yet claimed they had to go. While they were there, Samuel was riding around with Raleigh and Alex on mopeds. Maribelle stayed behind to FaceTime Kendall, who was working on her first piece about local beach hopping. Since she wasn't out and about on the island, Maribelle was charged with watching Caleb, which meant giving him too many unallowed sugar cookies. He watched Maribelle's iPad for hours.

When she got to the door, Kendall asked, "Is everything okay?"

"Sure," Maribelle lied.

"Absolutely," Nadia chimed in.

"Why don't I just interview you, Maribelle?" Nadia asks. "That way you can contain the story. I had no idea your family was experiencing such strife after Samuel's death. It must be hardest for you. Still, it will sell copies, right? I've wanted to do an exposé on the Barrowses from the Panhandle for a while."

"Holly has already killed it, Nadia," Maribelle said.

"Definitely that was true before, except she wants to sell copies. As I said, the fascination, the questions, they float around. An *it girl* loses her husband when he's in his late thirties, a guy who created a stir. Add to that how no one has ever quite understood the family's arrival in Palm Beach. There's talk that someone has been hired to dig around," Nadia said.

They were practically embryos on the social ladder by Palm beach standards when her family arrived, Maribelle realized. There were rope burns to climb the ladder, sure, but Maribelle knew she couldn't be stuck in this Samuel plight much longer, putting out the fires. She had to get beyond it—onto something jubilant. What was it Aunt Bryant believed about joy?

"You know what, Nadia? You should run *PB Confidential*," Maribelle said. "You have a vision, you love Palm Beach."

"I do." She took a swig from her Voss bottle. "Not exactly as you see it."

"I know that."

An odd shadow fell across the table, dividing them. Maribelle was very tired. "I've no more tricks for defending my family."

Nadia looked at her sympathetically for a brief second. "Maybe you don't have to defend anyone. Wait to see what I write."

"Maybe," Maribelle sighed. "Except, I don't believe you. Here's the deal. If you would like to be editorial director, I can make that happen, soon. All you need do is *not* write about my family. As long as there is nothing about our family in the future. Ever. Those are the terms."

"What?" Nadia asked. She pulled herself up in the Hans Wegner chair, astonished. "Why would you do that, Maribelle, after what you've achieved? Where would you go?

A wretchedness came over Maribelle, not quite like the morning that Samuel drowned, but another kind of loss. Another version of what wasn't hers and was only borrowed.

"I'm not sure it matters where I'm going, just that I know to go," Maribelle said.

"Maribelle, listen . . . you and I, we . . ." Nadia said. She jumped up. "I mean . . ."

"I'm meeting Holly for breakfast tomorrow," Maribelle said. "That's the first step."

As Maribelle left, Holly's dog, Toto, leaped down the hall. Tanya was behind her, holding out delicate biscuits, the type Supy would gobble up in one mouthful. Suddenly, the air conditioning was feeble, there wasn't enough ventilation. The lime green script on the *PB Confidential* banner reminded Maribelle that nothing was what it seemed.

Outside, the stores had opened, women were strolling about, beginning their purchases. Yet, none of the show-stopping dresses had to belong to her. Not even the sumptuous windows of Kirna Zabête or trendy Alice + Olivia seduced her.

About this moment, it was laden with choices. Maribelle could be elsewhere—a ceramics class, a lecture at the Four Arts, a walk through the Shelteere sculpture galleries. Another part of the country, another continent. Any cliché about moving on. Leaving what was for what might be.

CHAPTER TWENTY-SIX

Caroline

"**R**ight this way," the host smiled, holding breakfast menus in the air as if they were fans.

Passing the orchids that graced the tables, she led Caroline into Café Boulud at the Brazilian Court. Since this was Caroline's favorite spot for breakfast in Palm Beach, she ought to be pleased. Instead, she was filled with dread, knowing the essence of her meeting with Maribelle.

"Do you prefer inside or out?" the host asked. That's when Caroline noticed how tall she was, that her wedge sandals with crossed straps, like band-aids, make her more so. Her dress was simple, off-white and gathered at the waist. She was probably no older than Caroline, yet a part of her wanted to fall into her arms for asking the question, for caring. Before Caroline was able to voice her preference, Maribelle came rushing toward them. It was ironic, thought Caroline, how people without children either appeared early, completely composed, or they were more frazzled than young mothers and rolled in late.

Caroline and Maribelle air-kissed. "This is your haunt, where do you want to be?" she asked her.

"Where it's quiet, facing the courtyard, and where the air conditioning doesn't drone on," Maribelle said.

When was the last time she and Maribelle had been alone— without Lucinda, Raleigh, or Aunt Bryant, Caroline wondered. Lately, Travis and Alex were constantly around too. She stared at her older sister, who was drained rather than melancholy, as if her heartache had morphed into the next phase. Only yesterday at Barrows, Estelle was talking about the stages of grief, according to Kubler Ross. Maribelle wasn't presenting in exactly that trajectory. She seemed remarkably preoccupied. That wasn't one of the stages, as Caroline recalled.

"How are things?" Caroline asked.

"Okay," Maribelle chose to face her. They were across from each other. "I mean for a tough period."

"Better lately, though, right?" Caroline asked. She almost mentioned Julian then stopped herself. It wasn't a good idea.

"Hardly," Maribelle said. "What's tense is *Confidential.* I have a meeting with Holly at nine-fifteen, here, right after this."

"Ah, about your new layout and book reviews, moving away from the charity bashes? Fewer pictures of Lucinda and William and their pals?" Caroline asked.

"You remembered!" Maribelle said.

The sisters share a staccato, trained laugh.

"Sure. If only it were about that," Caroline said.

She knew she should push on, show interest, but she was too hellbent on her own mission with little room for much else.

She began. "Listen, I've come to ask you something important."

Maribelle frowned. "Oh, God, Caroline. Your girls. Am I remiss? I'll take them to Longreens on Saturday for the scavenger hunt. I owe Harper a text."

"No, no," Caroline said. "They've been so busy. I should have called you. We should have gotten together—you and I and the girls. A Cucina lunch or something."

The way Maribelle sat there, absorbing the information, made Caroline think of Raleigh's works-in-progress. Like she was painted a crisp person before Samuel's accident, and since then, she's sodden. Absent. The old Maribelle gone, the replacement an interloper.

"What then, I'm exonerated, aren't I? Once Samuel's estate is closed, I'll settle up,"

"I know that," Caroline said. She hated the weight of her news, pulling her down. None of this was Maribelle's doing.

Maribelle sighed. "Do you ever feel like you don't know anyone for real? Like this is all some phantasmagoria?"

"Do you mean Samuel? Because I find it's true with Travis too." Caroline was tempted to elaborate. How between Travis crunching on pretzel sticks and stalking the grounds of their house for the new addition, intimacy seemed a losing proposition.

"It's not husband specific. Lucinda is included," Maribelle added.

"She's always part of it," Caroline said. "But for me, lately, it's Travis. We work together, we're married. I should know him, still I don't."

"Well, if you ever figure him out, let me know what Samuel told him. I'm sure they were confidantes," Maribelle said.

A segue, Caroline thought, to explain why she had come to Café Boulud. But she was chicken, anxious. She needed another minute or two.

"I've asked Travis about it, over and over again."

In real time, Caroline and Maribelle were united—they both suspected Travis, there was nothing to be done.

Nearby, a blonde mother and her two teenaged daughters, on their phones, sullen, were being served pancakes, omelets, side orders of bacon. There was no avoiding how pungent bacon was, even at Café Boulud. Caroline assumed they were hotel guests. She had this urge to warn the mother that expectations keep shifting for mothers and daughters, it was a never-ending story for both sides.

The restaurant was busier, Caroline took a swift inventory to make sure they didn't know a soul. Maribelle said, "Don't worry, Caroline, only tourists come here. We won't run into anyone."

"That's fine," Caroline said. She breathed in, out. "Maribelle, were you on the boat with Samuel that morning?"

Maribelle was suddenly sharper, offended by the question. "Excuse me?"

"I wanted to ask, to make sure," Caroline said. "Let me say it once more. Were you on Samuel's boat the morning of the accident—were you at the pier with him?"

"I wasn't. I told you what I've told the Coast Guard, the one who came around, Officer Breeley. And the local sheriff. What I've told Julian. I dropped Samuel off and rushed to Sunrise Yoga," Maribelle said.

Her sister wasn't offended. She wasn't bothering to pay complete attention, Caroline realized. Why was she fidgeting with that slim pad she carried around, glancing at her work notes?

"Maribelle, what I'm asking matters," Caroline said.

"I understand, except my entire career is on the line. My breakfast meeting with Holly is in a few minutes. It's critical . . ."

Maribelle checked her phone, held it up like a mirror. "Oh, shit, I'm decrepit, aren't I?"

Caroline had to ignore Maribelle's drama, she had to stay her course. While Maribelle rooted through her work bag, a beige canvas number, Caroline lifted her bucket bag from the floor, ready for her own presentation. But Maribelle was hurrying. She pulled out a flannel jewelry pouch that read *David Yurman*, shook out a pair of gold hoop earrings, and started putting them through her ears.

"Trying to be half human," Maribelle said. "Lucinda would tell me it's rude to do in a restaurant."

Next, she lifted two white enamel bangles out and slid them over her left wrist. She shook the pouch once more. The aquamarine pear-shaped pendant glided onto the table. The same one Roger had given Caroline at the dock. The same one Lucinda had bought for each of her daughters. The same one Caroline was about to produce as proof that Maribelle was on the pier.

Maribelle held it to her neck, reaching around for the clasp.

"You know what Samuel did tell me that morning, Caroline? He said he loved me, and we'd work things out, set our plans straight," Maribelle said. She was almost crying. "I'd been waiting, hoping he'd come back to me. He said we'd head to LA for a year, he wouldn't put it off anymore. He knew how I wanted to leave Palm Beach. That's why I can't believe he died. I can't believe he was taking money. Why would he? Then the fucking wind squalls, his fucking deluxe *Vertigo*, and he was gone, poof, drowned. I don't know what to think anymore. I don't know what to believe. Everyone is adamant that he loved me. They keep telling me in these oozy voices. How the hell would they know? How would you know? How would Raleigh know?"

Raleigh. Maribelle's bangles clashed together like cymbals when Caroline reached for Maribelle's hand. "I'm sorry. So sorry."

"I know," Maribelle said. "It's like I'm wading around my backyard filled with mounds of invisible debris. And I've got to get through."

She broke Caroline's grasp and started putting on Le Rouge Duo Ultra Tenue lip gloss—the color the three sisters wear every day. Caroline followed Maribelle's gaze. Holly, in haute couture, was fluttering toward them.

❧

Never before had Caroline sped on the A1A. There were too many police cruising about in hopes of scoring a speeder. This morning, she took the risk, making it to Raleigh's on List Road in record time. The sun was more potent this time of year. April in Palm Beach, the sky was cloudless. In her bewitching, careless style, Raleigh was in the kitchen with Caleb when Caroline walked in, unannounced. Caleb was smearing bananas on the kitchen counter from his toddler seat.

"Caroline, what's wrong?" Raleigh kept slicing strawberries, adding them to a bowl. A yogurt pop was melting on a plate. Caroline imagined the breakfast she had left behind at Café Boulud.

"Where's Alex?" she asked.

"On a run around the Lake Trail." She put down the knife, tilted her head. "Why, what is it?"

"We have to talk," Caroline said. "The two of us."

"Ma! Mama!" Caleb was listening. "Gold fishies?"

Raleigh wiped her hands, opened a bag of Pepperidge Farm Goldfish, and sprinkled them on the counter in front of him. "I know you don't approve of his snack."

"Let's talk before Alex gets back," Caroline said.

Did Raleigh flinch slightly? Was she panicked, ready to grab her child and make a run for it? Caroline wasn't able to judge.

"Okay," Raleigh said. She half-wiped Caleb's face and hands, then lifted him out of his chair.

"C'mon, Potato, you'll sit outside with us."

He started flailing, reaching for the goldfish until she handed over the iPad. "Extra time today, you've been such a good boy."

Raleigh guided Caleb to a corner of their screened-in porch, the one that Lucinda complained about, saying homeowners on the island of Palm Beach do not *do* such porches. Islanders preferred spacious terraces, patios, spaces that showcased their grounds. Caleb became distracted and quiet. Paints and easels were everywhere, two stretched canvases were landscapes. One was of the banks of the

Apalachicola River. Caroline felt this pang. Had she, along with the family, missed how much Kesgrave meant to Raleigh?

"Sit, please," Raleigh gestured.

Raleigh let her hair down, it was mangled and beautiful. Her yoga pants were a charcoal grey. Her rose-colored tank top was too large. She knotted it at her waist and sat on the edge of a wicker chair.

"I can see Caleb from this angle," she explained.

When they sat down, Caroline felt half-corporate by comparison. She wore an ivory blazer and a Love Shack flowy pale blue maxi dress beneath. She was about to start a conversation she hadn't envisioned until twenty minutes ago.

"When we lived in the Panhandle, and you were a little older than Caleb, do you remember I loved intricate puzzles and, later on, crossword puzzles?" Caroline asked. "When I was in seventh grade, I was the one who played chess with Dad?"

"I do. You were beyond amazing," Raleigh said. "Maribelle and I couldn't play chess with Dad, ever."

"So yes, well, I suppose it makes sense that I'm the one who figured out who Lara is," Caroline said.

Raleigh trembled, as if hearing the name was too painful for her. Caroline got it. Without Samuel, the name was misused, grating. But what Caroline couldn't get past was Maribelle and Samuel. They had been a couple for too long. They were imbedded in her brain. Raleigh and Samuel together made no sense, it was insane.

"You and I, we have our husbands. I'm with Travis, you're with Alex. Maribelle was with Samuel. Kind of like being served a dish at Café Europe. Remember Dad said no sharing there, no second guessing. It was too serious a restaurant. You choose, you make a commitment."

Caroline took the necklace from her blazer pocket and placed it on the wicker coffee table.

"Have you been looking for this? Since we each have one? I'm fairly certain Lucinda's is with her many other necklaces in her jewelry drawer. Maybe stashed in her vault. Mine is in my jewelry box. Maribelle's is around her neck at the moment. I've come to return yours. After they brought in Samuel's Riva Rivamare that day, your necklace was found on the planks of the dock."

She lifted it up. Raleigh stared, lurched toward it, and fastened it around her neck. She was crying without gulping or making a sound.

"I figured it out," Caroline said. "I know about Samuel, but Maribelle doesn't. You said you were having an affair; that part I understand. Who wouldn't want a lover at some point, even with a nice husband? Which you have—a really good husband. But *Samuel*, Raleigh? *Samuel?*"

"You don't have the facts." Raleigh started shaking her head vehemently.

"I might not," Caroline said "The fact I have is that Maribelle adores you. *She's never going to know.* Never will she know that you were at the marina that morning. You must have gotten there right after she dropped him off on her way to yoga. You barely missed one another. Why Lara? Want to explain that?"

Raleigh was still crying.

"I deserve to hear this," Caroline said.

"Lara is from *Doctor Zhivago,*" Raleigh said. "He called me that, and I called him North. I wanted to tell someone. I tried with Aunt Bryant, but I chickened out on naming him. She didn't want to know anyway."

"And that morning?"

"I was going on the boat with Samuel. When I got there, he started talking. I was still on the dock. He said he couldn't leave Maribelle, she was onto it. That morning, she'd said something, he acted like he didn't hear her. But he did hear her—it made him change our plans."

"What did she say?"

Raleigh sighed. "That she and Samuel were planning an exit until this woman came along. *You and your fantasy girl.*"

"Maribelle knew something," Caroline said. "How much though?"

"Well, she knew he had a lover—not who it was. Samuel decided it was getting too complicated. He'd thought it through and decided no one would be making any moves." Raleigh sucked in air. "I asked him about his promise to me to leave for Kesgrave together. He'd buy property there for us. He'd been telling me all along he would. But that morning, Samuel laughed. 'Kesgrave, that shithole?' he said, 'You've got to be kidding, why would I?'"

Whatever Raleigh told her, Caroline knew, only made it worse. The details she was offering were blighted.

"I'd never heard him mean like that, especially about the Gulf Coast," Raleigh said. "We'd gone there together. We'd visited the old spots. With me he was always seductive, caring. That's why I was shocked. Right as he was blowing me off, he held out his hand for me to get on the *Vertigo*. Supy was barking so loud, it wasn't friendly. I was weeping. I said, 'Go, it's okay. I don't want to get on. It's okay.'"

"Samuel was yelling, 'Get on the boat, Raleigh.' The wind had picked up. He sped out of the marina. I saw him steering toward the channel markers, a big wake. He was speeding. He seemed fine. He knew how to be in the waterway. When I got into my jeep, the wind was really strong from the west. I thought that North—Samuel—would like the challenge. He was free. We were going to quit and not harm anyone, especially Maribelle."

"You didn't know about the millions that he was stealing? *From our family company?*" Caroline asked. "There were emails, a scheme about money, Julian found out. It didn't lead to anything except the initials MBW, for Maribelle Barrows Walker, and Lara, meaning you."

"No, I swear I didn't know. Later, after the accident, I learned through Lucinda and Travis at the Barrows family meetings. I didn't know why Samuel risked taking money or what he was doing with it," Raleigh said.

"You know that morning, I drove there to tell Samuel what he ended up telling me, to stop what we were doing. I knew it was ... odious ... wrong. He said it first. I didn't believe he'd leave Maribelle anyway. Afterward, what would have happened?"

"Our entire family would have been splintered, destroyed," Caroline said.

"It didn't come to that. North—Samuel—wouldn't have it. We know who he was, don't we?" Raleigh asked.

"Not really," Caroline said. "Remember at his memorial service when those people spoke about him, and our family was stunned?"

Caroline was taking in shallow breaths. She watched Raleigh carefully, checking on Caleb, who continued on the iPad like he had joined a cult. Then she returned to the question of Raleigh. *Raleigh with Samuel.* How could she? How could he?

Alex appeared, standing on the grounds beyond the screened in porch, sweating and wiping his brow with a white hand towel that read *Raleigh and Alex* in blue script.

"Hello, sisters." He smiled.

He was so young, so unencumbered, Caroline thought. She and Raleigh did their best at a fake hello.

"How was your run?" Caroline asked.

Raleigh was weeping again. Alex noticed yet said nothing.

"Five miles, just a sprint," he said, "Being a runner is efficient."

"Hey, Caleb," he said. His teeth were very white.

"Daddy, Daddy!" Caleb abandoned the iPad for his father, pivoting in his direction.

Alex came onto the porch, gathered Caleb, and gave Raleigh a kiss.

"I'm off to shower. C'mon Caleb, let's go, buddy. You can sing along with me."

After they left, Caroline turned to Raleigh.

"Alex might know about an affair. He must not find out it was Samuel. No one can ever know, Raleigh. Agreed?"

Raleigh was shivering. Her lips were blue, just like when she'd been in the river for too long as a little girl. Caroline knew she ought to hold her, ought to be calming. She was unable to forgive her.

"I wonder if you wanted Samuel to prove you could have him," Caroline said. "Isn't that the question?"

Her sister took a wet wipe from a canister on the wicker table. She cleaned the aquamarine pendant and tugged slightly on the chain. It was secure. Her eyes moved past Caroline.

"I had been in love with him since I was a little girl, since I was seven. You all knew, didn't you?"

CHAPTER TWENTY-SEVEN

Raleigh

An unspeakable day. Once Alex came back from painting Lucinda and William, a project he had come to loathe, Raleigh announced she was going over to Maribelle's. There was something about her intensity, so he simply nodded. It wasn't as if she frequently drove to her older sister's for a visit at dinnertime. Rather, they were out together at night functions for charity or parties or family gatherings.

Raleigh had never known misery like this morning when Caroline came over. Not when her father died or when Samuel drowned. There was a dread that washed over her, a gnawing, grinding feeling that beat her down. Her regret was infinite and too late.

Raleigh asked Alex if she could drive his SUV because hers was low on gas.

"How could that be?" he asked as she was rushing out.

"I don't know," she shrugged, "I have a lot on my mind."

Alex was staring at Raleigh. She must have looked deranged for an evening in Palm Beach, let alone anywhere. She was in a long, swingy grey skirt that she usually wore to paint, paired with one of Alex's white V-neck T-shirts that she knotted at the waist. Her hair, pinned on top of her head, was very dirty. Again, Alex said nothing.

Caleb was clinging to Raleigh's knees. Why would anyone cling to her or want to be near? She was radioactive, she knew it.

"Caleb, sweetie, I'll be back before bedtime." She used her most patient Mommy voice.

He clung tighter.

"I promise," Raleigh said.

"Are you sure, Raleigh?" Alex gave her a piercing look meaning it was not a good idea to make empty promises.

She said it anyway, knowing her promises needed to be real. "I'm sure."

Alex came to where Caleb held onto her legs and tickled, then lifted him. "Caleb, come on, we'll go read *Corduroy*."

When Raleigh started the engine, Alex's radio was set to Sirius. The lead singer for Abba was singing "The Winner Takes It All." Raleigh wished the singer and she knew one another. They could be friends, every lyric proved it was the case. Driving along the A1A, Raleigh sobbed. The sky darkened over the ocean, the mansions to her right receded in the dusk. The road wound along the ocean side. No stars were out, nor was the moon. Raleigh remembered the river in Kesgrave whenever she drove along the ocean road, yet she loved this too. The constant push of the waves, it was like being in a line surge. She began to pray.

When she reached Maribelle's, she texted she was outside. It occurred to her that she had not been here since the day they had sorted through Samuel's things. *Samuel, North. North, Samuel. Her sister's husband, her lover. Lover, husband, traitor, sister.* All of it shattered in her head, swirled around her being.

?? Come in. Maribelle texted.

"Why are you here?" Maribelle asked when she opened her door. Supy was beside her, ears upward, her dog eyes quizzical. "Did something happen, is Lucinda okay, the girls?"

"I want to tell you something. We have to talk." Supy started sniffling around Raleigh's feet as if she had not seen her before. Or had no dog memory of her.

"Super Dog, please, stop this," Maribelle sounded severe, but Raleigh knew she didn't mean it. Supy underscored why people treasure their pets, although Raleigh had ignored Alex and Caleb's plea for a family dog.

Supy wasn't letting up. "Supy, please," Maribelle said.

Raleigh fiddled around in her bag to find a travel pack of peanut butter filled Ritz Bits. She held out her hand out for Supy to take one. Supy whined questioningly at Maribelle to make sure it was allowed.

"Okay, sure, this one time," Maribelle patted the top of her head. Supy came to Raleigh and ate the handful of mini crackers. A second later when they stepped through the front entrance into the living room, she was half wagging her tail.

"Raleigh, I'm going out, soon," Maribelle said.

When she backed up, Raleigh realized how good her sister looked in a wavy print dress and chunky tan boots. Her face was different than it had been lately. She was something else, could it be *happy?*

"With Nadia?" Raleigh asked.

"Nadia?" Maribelle laughed fast, then stopped. "No, not on the calendar."

There was a sense that Samuel was about to saunter in, back from somewhere—a drink with the players after a late day doubles match. He liked to twist his racquet and hum off key, he bordered on jolly. Other times, he was back from being on the *Vertigo* or a day at Barrows. The three of them had stood here together over the years at different hours of the day—she and Maribelle; she and Samuel; Maribelle, Samuel, and Raleigh.

After the months and months of maneuvers and lies, Raleigh wasn't able to stand it any longer. That's what Caroline's confrontation with the pendant had done. She had to confess this second, absolve herself. Instead, her memory jolted her to a hotel room last spring. The sheets were 700 thread count, she and North had slid against the cool white cotton into one another. His breathing was deeper than hers. They were over the moon to be together, there was magic around them. He whispered *Lara,* and she whispered *North.* His body over hers, the one man whom she had always wanted. No one else mattered, obviously. They were trespasser-lovers. They were not only illicit, they were wrong, terribly wrong. How had they dared? How could they not?

"I've got to finish getting ready," Maribelle said. She was holding a Maybelline lash thickening mascara—the popular one that everyone from Kesgrave to Palm Beach knew to use—in her hand. She motioned for Raleigh to follow to her bedroom. Supy pranced ahead through the hallway as if Maribelle was talking to her, too.

Raleigh stood in the doorframe while Maribelle twirled around her walk-in closet, checking out her clothes, her hair. She didn't ordinarily primp like this, it was something Lucinda was against. *Mind the fuss,* she coached, *be effortless.*

Since the last time, Maribelle's bedroom, their bedroom, hadn't changed. The layout still seemed wide and empty; the shades of pale remained. No one had been hired to haul out the king bed, so broad one might not find the other sleeper until morning. Tonight, it made Raleigh queasy, separating it out was impossible—Samuel and Maribelle, North and Raleigh.

"Maribelle, listen, there's something awful and hard, really hard, that I need to tell you. I came tonight to . . ." Raleigh tried not to cry.

Maribelle's phone was receiving a string of texts at the same time as Raleigh's phone. But Raleigh didn't want to check. The conversation that was about to begin couldn't be interrupted by a text or a call. Raleigh had to tell Maribelle this very second, it was like acid eating at her skin. Holding up her phone, Maribelle motioned she had to see who was frantic to reach her.

The French doors opened, and Caroline, who looked furious and sloppier than ever, stormed in. She was in leggings and a T-shirt from the Academy.

"Raleigh, goddamnit. You never listen. I warned you not to come. What are you doing?" Caroline was screaming, her voice rose to the ceiling and crashed over them.

Maribelle was astonished. "Caroline, what is going on? Am I being ambushed, is there something remarkable to tell me? Because I have plans, soon, for tonight."

"I kept trying to reach Raleigh to reel her in. Finally, I texted Alex, who said she'd come over." Caroline was still shouting. "I gave up *my plans* to come to you."

"I have none," Raleigh said. "No plans."

Caroline collapsed on the edge of the bed. Raleigh stood like a soldier. A defector.

"Where are you going?" Caroline asked. "I mean, did I miss a dinner, or miss locking something in, somewhere tonight?"

"That's unlikely. Anyway, you didn't miss anything that I know about," Maribelle started applying mascara. "I'm going out with Julian."

Maribelle and Caroline looked at one another through the mirror, like undeclared female rivals in a limited series on Netflix.

Caroline flexed her knuckles without cracking them. "Has Raleigh told you?"

"Told me what?" Maribelle wasn't paying total attention.

"I was beginning to tell her," Raleigh said. Her head was pounding in a dangerous way.

"Okay," Caroline said. "Go on."

Maribelle adjusted her dress like she might take it off, over her head. "Should I change, what do you think?"

She pointed toward her closet. "After your news announcement, Raleigh, want to take these two Vince dresses? They're no good on me and quite good on you."

Caroline was mouthing at Raleigh, or so it seemed. *Fuck you.* Raleigh's head was about to split open.

"Maribelle! Don't change, you're fine, great. Let Raleigh talk," Caroline said.

"Okay, got it." Maribelle came to the other edge of the bed and sat down.

Raleigh began pacing, every part of her ached like she had been poisoned. "You know how you've been saying Samuel was unfaithful?"

"Yes, we know it was Collette, who knows beyond her." Maribelle said. "I've about given up." Maribelle examined her hem, checking it out for some reason. Raleigh wanted her to quit fussing.

"Maribelle, listen . . . listen. I'm the one," Raleigh said.

"Excuse me, the one what?" Maribelle asked. She was focused on her reflection in the mirror. "Kind of questioning the mood of my dress, the shoes are . . ."

"*The one.* The one Samuel was with," Raleigh raised her voice.

Maribelle's entire body became ice, or wax, as if she were no longer real. She didn't know this language, this truth. "What did you say?"

"Yeah, I was the one. For the last year. The one you said you couldn't find," Raleigh said.

Maribelle swatted at the air as if she could disperse the words—like a swarm of gnats.

"*What are you talking about, Raleigh?* He was my husband. Your brother-in-law. You're *my* little sister. I can't believe what you're saying? *Why* would you do that?"

Her voice was too quiet, Raleigh wasn't a hundred percent sure she had heard her. Caroline seemed to be trying to hear her too.

"I'm very sorry," she said. Her lips were thinning into one narrow line.

"*Sorry?*" Maribelle whispered. "*You*—with *Samuel*—and that's it? *Sorry?*"

Caroline gave them a sweeping stare. "There's more, isn't there, Raleigh?"

Her sisters stood near the window overlooking the terrace. Although it was nighttime, the shades weren't drawn. Raleigh disliked the dim sky against the panes, at her house, she pulled the shades every night in every room. At Maribelle's, a ring of darkness was settling around them.

"Raleigh?" Caroline asked. "The rest?"

She opened her mouth, nothing came out.

"Raleigh, for Chrissake." Caroline said.

"My confession, yes." Raleigh said. "I saw Samuel at the boat that morning. We were going to go out together. When I got to the dock . . ."

"Wait, stop it," Maribelle said.

Her hand was up, she came too close, about to slap Raleigh across the face. Raleigh cringed while Maribelle stopped herself in time.

"You have ruined everything. Whatever trust I had in you, in our family, is gone," Maribelle was shouting. "My whole life, I've tried to protect you, to love you."

The night was engulfing Raleigh. "I know," she said. "But he wasn't going to leave you, Maribelle. Samuel and I were going to end it. That morning at the dock. We decided to end it. It was for the best."

Maribelle screamed louder. "Go to hell, Raleigh. Get out! Get the fuck out!"

She charged at Raleigh, her hands on her hair, dragging her by her head. Raleigh tried to unpeel her fingers, her nails were like claws. Caroline stepped in, yanking her sisters apart. She was panting.

"Maribelle, please," she said. "Raleigh can't leave, she has *more* to explain."

Walking to the corner of Maribelle and Samuel's bedroom, Raleigh saw how the angle of their bed and desk seemed distorted, the walls were curvy. She imagined Van Gogh, who had painted in this wavy perception, all in his mind's eye. Tonight, she understood, to Raleigh, her sisters were young and old, vivid and murky.

"More, Raleigh, there's more to tell," Caroline snapped.

"He loved you. Maribelle, he loved you. I always knew, always believe it," Raleigh said.

"I'm not soothed or comforted, Raleigh. I pity your very pleasant husband and sweetest son." The tone in Maribelle's voice made Raleigh wonder whether after this, they would ever speak again.

"Is there anything else? Because if not, I want you gone. Caroline, you too," Maribelle said.

"No, not yet," Caroline said. "We need to keep talking."

"Really? After you've ruined my evening, my entire life?" Maribelle started pacing. "I don't know what I'll do with this kind of betrayal. What would you suggest, Caroline, since you always try to fix things? Should I call a shrink? Spill it to Lucinda or Aunt Bryant? Both? Neither? Separate from the family? Everywhere I look, there's pain."

Raleigh was crying in a soft way, so were her sisters. Supy came to her for more Ritz Bits. She got up to find her bag in the hallway. When she fed her another handful, Supy ran ahead to Maribelle and whined.

"We used to talk about clothes, books, body fat, Pilates. Now we talk about Samuel. *Samuel drowned, Samuel and Barrows. Now, Samuel and Raleigh.* Who was he really?" Caroline asked.

"I have no idea," Maribelle says. "Nor who you are, Raleigh."

Raleigh put her head in her hands without an answer.

Someone was getting texts. No one moved. Outside, it had begun to rain, the wind was kicking up from the ocean side. In a better world, not long before, Raleigh thought, the three of them would be trading secrets, huddled together. Some kind of team. A love fest.

"I've spoiled everything, haven't I?" Raleigh asked.

"I think so," Maribelle was crying harder. It made Raleigh sorrier than any other part of what she had done.

"Suppose that Samuel was simply another controlling, good-looking guy," Caroline said. "And Raleigh was too vulnerable to resist. Samuel was seductive. Lucinda never got over how handsome he was. Aunt Bryant said to beware the man who is noticed before you. Her example was *Saturday Night Fever.* Remember when we were kids? John Travolta's character, storming the room with his dance moves."

"Meaning no one ever got over that he married me, not either of you," Maribelle said.

She focused on Raleigh. "You didn't have to have an affair with him, Raleigh. You've ruined everything."

"Everything," Raleigh sobbed.

There was that seesaw again, except the players were changing. Caroline and Maribelle were up, and North was down. North, Raleigh realized, was *too* Samuel in this room—it obliterated what essence they had shared.

"Why, Raleigh? Why did you do it?" Caroline asked.

"When I was small, like seven years old, and I'd see Maribelle with Samuel, I thought he built the world," Raleigh said. "I wanted to be with both of them, I wanted to love him, too."

When Raleigh said *Samuel,* Supy started howling.

"Who knows what Samuel felt, what he believed in," Maribelle said. "He used to quote these lines from a poem, one that was packed with meaning."

A sick, sticky sense overcame Raleigh. "What poem?"

"Are we reciting poetry?" Caroline asked. She had stopped crying, she straightened up. Raleigh saw her as a possible referee. This could be a diversion or a waste of time.

Maribelle was calmer. "Oh, the one stanza of a short poem. Something like 'The sea is a room . . . back in time,' then this line about headlights. The last lines—how Samuel would say them slowly, looking at me."

Raleigh clapped her hands together. "You mean this?" she began.

The sea is a room far back in time
Lit by the headlights of a passing car.
A glass of milk glows on the table.
Only you can reach it for me now.

Maribelle and Raleigh were petrified, lifeless.

"You know it, too," Caroline said flatly.

"I do. Charles Simic," Raleigh said. "Samuel gave me a signed first edition."

"Oh, how romantic," Maribelle's voice was a scalpel. "Was there an inscription too?"

She stared at Raleigh as if they had just been introduced. As if a wand had been waved and having been the big sister, Raleigh's ally for her entire life, had never happened. *We did not mean to hurt you*, Raleigh wanted to tell Maribelle, yet it would only make things worse.

Maribelle marched out with Supy following in a sad, sorry dog style.

Caroline glared at Raleigh. "Was that necessary? You said you wouldn't . . ."

Raleigh started to cry again. "I had to tell her. My brain was exploding."

"It's always about you, isn't it, Raleigh?" Caroline stopped herself when Maribelle re-entered. She held up a copy of *Return to a Place Lit by A Glass of Milk*. Raleigh knew it in two seconds—the same red and purple cover, except Maribelle's was worn, older.

She opened it to the title page and read, "To Maribelle, the one who counts for everything, always. With love, Samuel."

"How creative," Caroline rolled her eyes.

"And *exactly* what he wrote in my copy," Raleigh said.

"What a turd," Caroline said.

Maribelle dropped the book on the floor. Supy sniffed and brought it back to her, like fetching a tennis ball.

"I'd prefer if Supy had peed on it." Maribelle started laughing. She laughed louder, the way they did when they shared a joke. Caroline joined her in that *sisters only* way. It was contagious, no one could help it. Raleigh wanted so much to be a part of them, to be entwined with her sisters. To forget the recent past, cleave to what was further back in time. When they were young and safe, and anything was within reach.

In the middle of Maribelle's antiseptic, meticulous bedroom, they were rolling in laughs. When Maribelle stopped, they stopped. Caroline frowned, meaning it was about to be serious, the reprieve was over.

"Aunt Bryant believes what's not known has to be forgiven," Caroline said. "Whoever Samuel was, however we saw him, he's dead. We're not."

"I want it to be over," Maribelle said. "Every part of it, over, finished."

"Me too," Raleigh said.

"I bet it will be," Caroline said.

Maribelle reached for Raleigh's hand and tucked it inside her cool, smooth palm.

CHAPTER TWENTY-EIGHT

Caroline

After the Wildlife Conservation fundraiser at the Four Seasons, Travis and Caroline walked the length of their property. With his phone, Travis switched on the outside lights, the pool sparkled. Across the Intracoastal, West Palm seemed so alive, thought Caroline. The water lapped at the bulkhead. Their house, one of those Mediterranean classics with a peachy pink stucco, made her wistful. For the past five years that they had lived here, it has been the same. Now they were bettering their home in hopes it would elevate them, improve their status. Caroline doubted it mattered, while Travis was already a Lucinda ally, keen on next steps.

"There's where they're starting tomorrow morning," Travis pointed to the family room. He hit his phone once more, the outdoor speakers came on. Van Morrison was singing "Days Like This." "They'll scaffold to the south, according to plan," he said.

"It's not so easy to see at nighttime," Caroline said. "Let's go inside."

She wanted to check on the girls and kick off her heels. She hadn't yet recovered from the scene at Maribelle's yesterday, if ever she would. For most people, it was enough drama, yet Caroline remained in in search of Travis's version. For weeks she had been asking him, *what did Samuel tell you, what did you know?* He kept shirking away.

"Sure, in a minute. Let's take a quick inventory—a once over—before we go in," Travis said.

Her husband flashed his phone, accentuating specific spots—where the bougainvillea needed to be removed, maybe destroyed, to extend the walls. In the half dark, his face was at an angle, his chin wasn't his. He was distorted. He came over and wrapped his arms around her. Caroline pulled back.

The air was decomposing. She had to know. "I've asked before, Travis. What happened with Samuel? What did he tell you?"

"Samuel." His intonation was peculiar, as if Samuel's name was recent news to him.

"Did you rig the boat?" Caroline asked.

"Rig the boat? Christ, Caroline, what a question," Samuel said.

Her mouth was too dry. *Who was her husband?* she asked herself. She said nothing. Travis tapped her elbow. "Ready to go inside?"

He led, not something that often happened. Caroline was always ahead, in a rush. Travis unlocked the door to the kitchen. Nicole was sitting at the island, halfway through a bowl of popcorn.

"Nicole?"

"Caroline! You're back early." She crunched on a mouthful.

For a mother who scarcely checked on her children once they were asleep because she couldn't handle waking them, Caroline yearned to run to their rooms and look at them.

"How was their night?" she asked.

"Harper fell asleep a few minutes ago, say, nine thirty. Violet was asleep by eight," Nicole kept at the popcorn.

Travis, who rarely spoke to Nicole on a good day, was busy jiggering the kitchen drawer. He took out a tape measure, walked to the windows. "Hey, Caro—what will happen is, we'll pop these out . . ."

Caroline started unfastening her twin diamond tennis bracelets. Her parents had given her the first when she was twenty-five, and Travis bought the second for her thirtieth. Tonight, they felt opulent and garish.

"I'm going upstairs," she said. Neither seemed to hear her.

Caroline changed into a lavender night slip that Aunt Bryant had bought for her when she turned thirty-five. She had felt so old that day, realizing lavender was last popular when she had been in high school at Pinestream. Since Samuel died, she hadn't cared about looking good to fall asleep beside Travis. Tonight, she decided to wear it because she was in the mood for the cool, silky fabric.

Travis came out of his dressing room in a pair of boxers and noticed, even in the low lighting. "Am I getting lucky?"

A poor joke, they both briefly smiled. He climbed into bed, moving toward Caroline. He tried to kiss her, what Caroline would call a preliminary kiss before married sex. She shut her mouth, he was contaminated. Fear took over, not excitement. Caroline moved to the edge and sat up against the pillows.

"I can't do anything until we talk, I'm sorry," she said.

He was disappointed, she saw it—and beyond that, annoyed.

"Talk? We're in the office together. You come to every meeting these days," Travis said. "We're married. We're in the same bedroom every single night. What sort of conversation?"

"Travis, I've asked already," Caroline sighed. "I'm still asking *after* Julian delivered his clean report about Samuel. The Coast Guard has signed off. A little like going to a doctor and getting remarkably good news about your health, despite what you feel. Between us, please, what did Samuel tell you?"

"The information comes from Julian," Travis said.

"Right, and now you are fond of Julian, although at first you weren't," Caroline said. "You must be grateful—he closed it up, case finished."

"That's a good thing, Caro," Travis said. "We don't want any visibility."

Her hair was pulled back and too tight. Caroline took it down. Of course, it would be simpler if she left the situation alone. She was the only one who knew the mess with her sisters and Samuel. Her father used to say the truth was overrated. She needed to apply it to this night, this moment with Travis. Why would she want this conversation instead of an easy path forward?

Caroline jumped out of bed, snaking their bedroom from corner to corner like some crazed modern dancer during rehearsal. Travis stared at her.

While in motion, she said, "Yeah, sure. You must totally appreciate what Julian did."

"I do," Travis said. "The family—everyone—is majorly relieved."

Caroline paused to picture Julian and Maribelle together, then let it go. There was her husband, the one she had to have, the one who used to say they were a team. Frenzied memories of Travis and Samuel flooded her mind. Back in Kesgrave when they were playing football, wrestling, after games, guzzling Pabst Blue Ribbon in Travis's father's souped-up truck. She and Maribelle beside their guys. Maybe Raleigh was instinctive about who the Barrowses truly were. Living the Palm Beach life, *pretending*, because money did a mind trick on people, wasn't that what lured Samuel?

"This is a test, Travis." Caroline sat on the edge of the bed and lowered her voice. "Tell me why Samuel did what he did. Why would he hurt us?"

Travis ran his hand over his upper lip, that habit he had.

"Over a year ago, I was looking at the books, analyzing spread sheets," he said. "I discovered Riptide Corporation and figured it out. I confronted Samuel. I told him not to do what he was doing—funneling money into a shell company, taking from Barrows. He wouldn't explain his motivation. I had a sense he was doing it because he could get away with it. You know how he resented your parents. How they thought his family was less when we were growing up. Beneath the surface, he was angry. It didn't matter that Lucinda liked Samuel because he was good for the company. Maybe it kind of made it worse. Samuel never forgave her for not letting his parents sit at their table at his wedding. And he couldn't stand how Reed let us in but never gave us any credit, anything extra. After he died, your mom wasn't any better."

"My mother's style, she picks and chooses," Caroline said. "Look at where the company is because of me and the marketing team. Have I been praised for my work—by her? By you?"

Travis took her hand, she took it back.

"Caro, we couldn't have done it without you. You deserve credit."

He was right. She resisted saying, *too little, too late.* Instead, she folded her arms over her chest. "Go on," she said.

"Well, Samuel sort of loved Barrows, the business, and Barrows as in having a Barrows wife in Palm Beach. He resented it all too. When I told Samuel I was worried and against what he was doing, he said it was between us, to look the other way. He said I had to trust him."

"Trust him," Caroline repeated. Tonight, Travis seemed old, he had prematurely aged and she had missed it.

"I thought Samuel wanted one or two of his women to have money," Travis said. "When I asked, he was amused. He said it was the opposite. He wanted to escape every one of them. They weren't at the heart of it. I almost wish it were the case, you know, some guy stealing for his wife and his lover. Samuel wanted for himself."

"What did he want?"

"A yacht—a Turquoise Go—a Lear jet, a place in the Hamptons, Aspen, somewhere abroad. To be equal with the wealthiest Palm Beachers. To have more than Lucinda and Reed. He told me, "As soon as Lucinda kicks the bucket, we'll change the name to Walkers. It will be our empire." Travis said.

"Walkers?" Caroline asked. "What about you?"

"He didn't bother to make me a partner in his fantasy, to call it Walker Sears. He tried to talk me into it. He told me we were unbeatable—the Dynamic Duo. We could go anywhere with it. I told him I wasn't leaving you, my kids. I wasn't leaving Barrows."

"Except Samuel got along with my parents. He learned from them. He was Lucinda's favorite."

"Favorite sure is a big deal in your family. Samuel had power—he was everyone's favorite. That was the con. Lucinda was duped, too."

"Lucinda, duped," Caroline said.

Little circles of sweat covered Travis's forehead. His posture, the pupils of his eyes—Caroline found him so unappealing.

"Aren't you complicit?" she asked.

"He swore, Caroline—and I swear to you—he'd pay it back. My job was to make sure no one else found out. Samuel was my best friend, but he made a mistake. He should never have done it." Travis's voice trailed off in a long apology.

Caroline listened as if he had returned after an extended business trip, ready to confess. In fact, they had been in each other's path since Samuel's accident. Whether they were standing in the library in their own house, at a meeting at Barrows, or partnered for mixed doubles at Harbor Club, it had been unnatural. Travis could have told Caroline about Samuel at any point. Instead, a coated, heavy distance had come between them. Travis's ties to Samuel ran that deep.

"I'm sorry, why did you protect him?" Caroline asked. "To the point where you never told anyone, including me? Your *goddamn wife*, Travis."

"I thought it was for the best. I didn't *want* the company to have missing funds with new locations in Texas and the Carolinas. I didn't tell you—or anyone—because I wanted to protect Barrows. Samuel wasn't careless, he was careful. I believed he would repay what he had borrowed. He was too afraid of being caught to not pay it back—he promised."

"Borrowed? Promised? You give him so much credit. He *stole* the money!" Caroline was flushed, angry, her heart ached.

"I threatened to expose him, Caro," Travis said. "All those years we were friends, I covered for him whenever we got in trouble. I always took the blame. I never ratted him out. He came across as the Good Kid when he was always the ringleader. I was the one who got suspended from school. I was the one who got kicked out of Boy Scouts.

"I told him 'not this time.' I didn't blame him for resenting Lucinda and Reed—they did treat him and all their sons-in-law shabbily. Still, Samuel acted out. He used to take their stuff— Reed's watch, his camera, whatever he could get that was Lucinda's. Sometimes he'd return them, sometimes not. I'd tell him it was foolish, pathological. He really detested parts of what your parents did. Except the money, he wanted that. Money was another story altogether, a strange head trip for him. I wasn't going to let him steal from you, from Harper and Violet. Whatever he did, why ever he did it, he was planning to pay it back, Caroline." Travis sounded more himself. He was convinced.

"How would you know?" Caroline asked.

Her husband lifted his phone from the dresser and put on his reading glasses. "Samuel texted me that morning, probably the last text he ever sent."

Travis began scrolling through his phone, holding it up for Caroline to read.

On Vertigo: Returning money this a.m. I'll explain.

"Except he never got there." Travis studied the screen. "You have your sisters. He was a brother to me. Do you know what that office is, day in and day out, without him? Your mother's fury, your sisters unrecognizable? Who are you in the mix, Caroline? Where'd you go?"

"Where did I go? Not to some recruiting firm to find someone from the outside. How do I forgive you for that? An endeavor to protect Barrows, fair enough, I suppose, but to not consider me for the job? And it's my mother who tells me?"

"Wait, wait a second, Caro. It wasn't ever my idea to use Heidrick and Struggles. Lucinda chose them. I suggested you for Samuel's position after you and I had the tiff. I started lobbying for you. I thought if I surprised you, it would be great. It would help. I'd win you back somehow. Your mother listened, then said you had too much to do as a working mother already."

Caroline watched her husband with his body language and his bruised morale. She thought of Lucinda's plan that she and her family be the showpiece of the Barrowses in Palm Beach, what it entailed.

"I believe you," she said.

It was tempting to tell Travis about her sisters, the aquamarine pendant, Raleigh at the pier that morning. Aside from how sacred it was to keep it among themselves.

"What do *you* want, Travis?"

He hung his head. He was pathetic, wasn't he?

"Okay, well, it's clear to me what *I want*," she said.

"Is it?" Travis started crying—a primordial sound—not sobbing, rather, some pent-up misery let loose.

"A simpler life?" he asked.

Caroline began pacing. "Not simpler. Better. I want Samuel's job. I want to grow Barrows with you, to be someone who runs the company, one of those people."

"One of those people. It's hyped-up, you know," Travis said. "There's stress, constant expectations. Vendors are a pain in the ass, tending to each Barrows location is grating. Answering to Lucinda these days is torture, she doesn't make sense."

"I'm aware."

He looked up, straightened somewhat.

"If you were to fill Samuel's chair, the marketing team would have to be as good as you are. You'd have to train someone first, like you suggested. Your schedule wouldn't be flexible, you'd miss the girls at Wellington, gymnastics, tennis lessons. And those mothers, you'd have to stay on their good side. The girls can't be excluded if you don't show up at some important breakfast."

They both smiled at Travis's description, his regurgitation of everything Caroline had reported about having skin in the Palm Beach mothers' game.

"I'm not going away. I'll manage things, I'm acrobatic," Caroline said. She almost added that she would be inspired yet didn't dare.

Travis shifted in her direction. He came to where Caroline was pacing and lifted her, carrying her across the room. He tugged at the spaghetti straps, her night slip fell to her waist. He guided it over her hips, his tongue pressing against her mouth until she opened it. He tossed the covers off the bed. Each gesture made him stronger—a sizzle reel of Travis, in whom Caroline once utterly believed.

After he came inside her, he kissed her eyelids. "Imagine we're on the field in Kesgrave, my touchdown, your cheering. We've just won, Caro. We're back."

She was with him again. It had seemed a very long while apart.

CHAPTER TWENTY-NINE

Raleigh

The night belonged to no one. Raleigh was sure of it by Alex's silence. He didn't suggest they cut out as early, and enroute to the event, there were no usual Alex questions—"What's the cause, the occasion?"—something he did predictably before every one of these parties with a mission. At the moment, he was hanging at the bar, and Raleigh's sisters had already left the Wildlife Conservation dinner.

Raleigh hadn't wanted to come. All evening long, she and her sisters sat together, inimitable actresses. Lucinda noticed nothing, too busy eyeing the room, pleased with the location of their table, the totem pole crowd. Maribelle was cordial but frigid to Raleigh. Caroline was neutral to both of them. They excelled at the *all is well* gig for the public. Raleigh didn't attempt to speak to anyone in the family. Betrayal. Contrition. Repentance. Then, some thirty hours later, there they were at the Four Seasons while guests danced to Al Green's "Let's Stay Together."

In better times, with a lead singer this polished, Raleigh and Alex would have been drawn to the dance floor. Alex was good at getting lost in the music and ignoring that it was some Barrows *show-up*, as a family, as a business. Raleigh was always conscious of her husband's dancing skills. Until the accident, Samuel was there too. He and Maribelle, chicest in an older sister style, would have been close by on the parquet, spinning around. Samuel would have been eyeing Raleigh's dance moves. Had Raleigh not comprehended how utterly, completely flawed and ill-fated it was?

Once Maribelle, Caroline, and Travis excused themselves, Raleigh and Alex were left with Lucinda and William, Aunt Bryant, Mrs A and the Norrics. Lucinda quickly had the seating rearranged to pull everyone closer, to avoid a hole at the table. Now, Alex was lingering at the bar, Raleigh walked over.

"We should get going, too. It's late."

He stared at her. "How about we walk on the beach first?"

"I'm not sure, I mean we ought to get back and let Gabriella go home," she said. "Tomorrow, I have finishing touches on the Garrett girls' portrait. Aren't you delivering the Lucinda and William painting?"

"A short walk, it's a beautiful night," he said.

"Okay." Raleigh agreed, not wanting to.

Alex had been in a mood from the start tonight. While Raleigh was zipping into her dress, and Alex was putting Caleb to sleep, she sensed it. He ignored her when she stood at the nursery door, not inviting her in to hear Caleb squeal to his favorite lines from Robert Louis Stevenson's poem, "The Swing."

"We should hurry," he had said without glancing at her.

The lights from the hotel shone over the entire swath of beach-front. Raleigh carried her Manolo slides—Maribelle's cast offs—walking fast to keep up with Alex. The sand was smooth and damp. Alex took his loafers off, he was neither scowling nor smiling. Raleigh had not seen this expression on his face before. Only a few stars were out.

"Hey, Raleigh, do you remember the trip to New York for some wedding two Thanksgivings ago?"

"I do. Those friends of our family's from Longreens, the Dartens, their daughter. William set us up to fly privately. You were happiest to be in New York—hours at MoMA."

"Then we took Caleb to the Big Apple Circus after the museum. We were sitting in an overheated tent with little kids eating cotton candy. Caleb was delighted with the clowns. I thought how great life was with you and our son."

He slowed down stopped. Raleigh stopped too. They were under some sort of strobe light on the Four Seasons beach. Her husband was telling her something very important, life changing, really. Because what she remembered from that trip was how it could have been superb with Alex were it not for North—infiltrating and obliterating her chances.

Raleigh was sick inside, she wished he wouldn't speak. She said, "Caleb was thrilled with the circus."

Alex nodded. "He was. I kept looking at him on your lap, back on my lap, and thought, this is what it is. Life as pure bliss with our little family."

"I know," Raleigh said.

Alex sighed. "I don't think that anymore."

Wasn't it ironic, Raleigh realized too late, that the person who would have convinced her not to have an affair was Maribelle. She was the confidante who would have warned against collateral damage. She might have said, had she known, stop missing your lover so much, let him go. She had never considered an affair worth it. Raleigh imagined Maribelle phrasing it sweetly, *You have a lovely husband, be careful, be wise.* Like that? What was it Caroline's friends from the Academy whispered about their husbands? How they were the *right idea, wrong guy*. Did anyone exist who would believe Raleigh, that she hadn't set out to have an affair? That it was very specifically about North? In her sisters' eyes, in the eyes of the world, that made it worse.

A game of musical chairs, Raleigh thought, where she was upright when the music stopped. The lie had caught up with her; she was very alone. The wind blew at their faces, her dress billowed. She wanted to fall against Alex, her husband worth keeping. That meant he had to learn about North from her, not any other person.

"Alex, I was having an affair." Her words crashed into each other. "I'm not anymore."

"I know," Alex said.

"It's over," Raleigh said. Samuel and Alex were in a duel, thrashing around her brain, cluttering any clear memory of either one.

"Right," he said. There was a briny smell from the ocean tonight, like sea life was being brought in on the waves.

"I've been in some layer of outer space, circling above earth. I want to tell you how it happened . . ." she said.

"I don't want details," Alex said.

"I'm sorry, so sorry," Raleigh began to cry. "I never meant to hurt anyone."

Alex was facing the hotel while Raleigh stood in the opposite direction, the dark ocean behind him.

"We should go." Without waiting for her, Alex started back. Raleigh raced to be with him although she was afraid it was too late.

Neither of them spoke on the drive home. Along the A1A, parts of the road were well lit. Raleigh, as frightened as she was, watched the sliver moon, how the stars crowded the sky. She thought of her mother, who described their father as too preoccupied with Barrows to talk on car rides. Lucinda read or listened to books on tape or favorite songs by Led Zeppelin, The Rolling Stones, The Band. She taught her girls so much about music. When David Bowie died, Lucinda played *Heroes* over and over, mourning him. Raleigh's sorrow, in contrast, was over her own life. It had nothing to do with a global loss, a music icon adored around the world. She felt so alone it crept into her bones.

Inside the house, Gabriella sat in the den, her feet up on the couch, series surfing on Hulu. On a good night, Raleigh liked to ask what she had watched, how Caleb had been. None of this was in her now. Gabriella picked up on this—she gathered her things and exited the minute Alex Zelled her the money. She had left too many bright lights on outside Caleb's room. Raleigh switched them off. Alex appeared, having changed into jeans and a white button-front shirt. His hair was slicked back, more for the beginning of the day, not the end.

He headed into their shared studio. Raleigh followed. There was a cheerlessness that hadn't been there before. He started gathering his paint sets, his unstretched canvases. Passing by his landscapes and contemporary paintings, he closed in on the portraits that were his most recent work. When he paused at the Lucinda/William portrait, she knew she should say something. A project he had come to despise.

"Wow, you totally pushed that through. Proving you can paint fast, if need be," Raleigh said. "You only need the finishing touches."

"There are no more finishing touches. This is the final product," Alex said.

Raleigh wished she could start over, they could start over. If they began at this very moment, she believed none of the past would apply, every bit of it banished. Only Caleb existed, always their son, suspended in time.

"I see, well, you could unveil it tomorrow at Lucinda's," she said. "It's great. They'll be so pleased."

"I might do that, early in the morning on the road out of town," Alex said.

Raleigh's teeth began chattering.

"I'm not sure what you mean, Alex," she said. "Each of us has two commissioned paintings to hand in. The landscape for the Cross mother-in-law, the portrait for the family in Delray."

She tried to be friendly, like a normal wife would be. The room, the paint colors, his palette—she was nauseated. His eyes were fiery, his voice frosty. He was foreign, slipping from her, he had mulled things over.

"Alex, I'm . . ."

He held up his hand. "I'm taking a break, Raleigh, from you. From us."

She knew the impact; what she couldn't perceive was his plan.

"No, no, no." Raleigh rushed to Alex. He stepped back. "Alex, please, listen. I once read about a wife renegotiating her marriage after she had an affair. Her husband wanted to know what was missing so they could fix it together. He was willing to work with her. Let's work it out. I'll do better," she said.

All of her was high-pitched, desperate. He was sympathetic by nature. Raleigh had counted on that her entire marriage. Yet now he looked at her with pity.

"That's irrational, Raleigh. There is no 'we' here, there is no shared part to 'fix.' I'm not responsible for what's missing. Why would I work with someone who finds me deficient? Perhaps only someone else's husband works for you, Raleigh. Maybe someone's sister's husband," he said.

"No, Alex, let me explain. Not quite. I didn't want Samuel . . ."

"You didn't? Then what the fuck were you doing sleeping with him? Nothing . . . nothing is real to you except what you experience," Alex said.

Raleigh laid her hand on Alex's neck, touching his skin and the collar of his white shirt. She kissed him, he kissed her back. His mouth was stone, unkind. Still, he wasn't pushing her away, there was this modicum of hope, despite what he had just said.

Then he politely moved back. "No, Raleigh, it's not happening."

She bit her lip hard not to cry. "We could go to Kesgrave together like you had suggested. We could try again, hit the backroads, get out of Palm Beach. That's what we need to do."

Raleigh slipped out of her dress, a geometric print that Caroline called silly on anyone else except a few tall, lean friends. She stood in only her panties. North would have been pleased. She grabbed Alex's hand and put it on her collar bone. She knew he liked her taught skin around her neckline. He jerked away.

"Raleigh, don't."

Alex lifted her dress from the floor and handed it to her.

"Don't what?" Raleigh asked. "What about Caleb, how can you leave him?"

"I'm not leaving Caleb, we'll have an arrangement," Alex said. "Gabriella is available to work for both of us."

"You asked Gabriella before me?"

"Not to get ahead of you," he said. "I wanted to understand her schedule. Caleb really likes her, she's good with him."

"Where will you go, Alex?" Asking the question frightened Raleigh.

"I've got it worked out," he said.

Raleigh sensed it, the moment that shifted everything. What was precious wasn't retrievable. Not with her lover, her husband, her child, her life. Only Alex's profile was the same, but she felt it slipping out of her sight. He was taking that with him too. The rest of him was mannequin to her, a billboard. The light had gone out, the room was somber.

Raleigh wasn't able to bear it. She remembered Samuel and how safe it had seemed. False safeness.

"You should go this minute, Alex," she said.

He walked down the hall into Caleb's room and came out with tears in his eyes.

Then Alex started moving his pictures. When they were both in the entryway, Raleigh realized he had already placed a canvas tote and backpack there.

He opened the front door. "I'll FaceTime with Caleb in the morning."

Once Alex left, Raleigh tried to reach Aunt Bryant. First, she texted, then called when there wasn't an immediate text back. She started a text to Lucinda, decided to erase it. The part of her that was responsible knew how upset she would be. She didn't dare try Caroline or Maribelle, not tonight. Tomorrow, Raleigh prayed, would be better. People made mistakes daily, she told herself. She checked on Caleb and kissed his forehead, reshuffling her old Pooh bear that he clutched in his sleep.

In the bathroom, Raleigh found the light more jarring than ever before. She leaned into the mirror, *This will be the story of your dreams because you dreamed it.*

She decided to choose what to remember and what to let go. It wasn't too late. *Alex will come back.*

She repeated it, *Alex will come back.* There was nothing else to believe.

CHAPTER THIRTY

Maribelle

Ten o'clock on a weekday morning, and Maribelle was not at her desk at *PB Confidential*, a new and uncommon scenario. Her GPS, which fended off the traffic to work, corrected her when she turned onto Worth Avenue instead.

"Stop route guidance," Maribelle commanded.

Her GPS halted. She angled into a parking spot in front of Ta-boo. The clouds were spotty, the sky, a Palm Beach blue. Northern Parulas flew low, Maribelle felt hollow. The past two days, ever since Raleigh's reveal, it was as if Maribelle had been drugged. Or she had been bonked over the head and was now desperately trying to rearrange her thoughts and reality.

Lucinda's belief in *action as a reaction* was beginning to resonate, and so Maribelle was fifteen minutes early for an appointment at Vintage Tales. She was about to become a consignor. Although she not been to the floor where women brought their luxury goods to sell, she had heard enough about it. Nadia's article several years ago detailed the seller versus buyer at this high-end consignment shop without disclosing who fell into which category.

To be circumspect, Maribelle had packed three Hermes Kelly bags, one Birkin, and two Chanel Classic Flap bags into Samuel's favorite carryall. He used to comment on how easily it zipped, how the fabric breathed. Her dread that she might run into someone was at an all-time high. She had an explanation ready to go—that as a loyal Vintage Tales purchaser and fan, she hoped to experience the other side firsthand. Selling a few designer things and buying new was fresh, part of giving back to the ecosystem. Besides, Maribelle longed to be practical, shedding and reevaluating.

She glanced around Via Amore and dragged her carryall up the back stairs.

"Maribelle Walker! How good to see you," Eve Crane, the manager, said.

How unerring and blonde she was, sporting a simple off-white sheath and a pair of slides. Another one, thought Maribelle, who projected herself as seamless. Unless she, like many, was another pro at the con. *Lucinda 101.*

"I haven't seen you in an age," Eve added.

"Since Samuel's memorial," Maribelle said. To be certain, she had scanned the guest list last night.

"My condolences, once again," Eve smiled that polished, Palm Beach smile. "Samuel was a fine man. He loved to shop for you. He would come in and . . ."

"Thank you. We don't have to remember," Maribelle said. She waved her arm around to banish any more praise for Samuel. She wasn't able to handle it. "I've brought some classics to start."

"The timing works. Today should be quiet." Eve sets two crystal glasses of fizzy water at the edge of the desk. On the cabinet behind was an array of haute designer bags. Jewelry lay clumped together as if it hadn't been sorted.

Eve nodded patiently, sort of like the dentist before a root canal.

"Let's sit." She pointed to the Estrella sofa.

Eve lifted each bag out of the felt pouch to study. She picked up her iPad, snapping photos of each. Next, she began inventory, fingers flying.

"We have one Fuchsia Ostrich Birkin, a Rose Magnolia Kelly, a Gold Togo Kelly," Eve sighed, "and a Bleu Frida Epsom Kelly, two Chanel quilted double flaps, a black and a beige. I love it. You know the demand."

"I've more, other designers too—bags, belts, wallets, scarves— in the car," Maribelle said. "If you are interested, I could bring jewelry another time."

"Interested? We are enthused about *all* of it." Eve said.

Eve walked to the window. "Maribelle, if you are comfortable with it, tell me where you've parked. I'll give your car keys to my assistant, and she'll bring in the rest."

Against Maribelle's better judgment, Eve led her downstairs, claiming she might want to see where her consignment was to be placed.

"Over here, Maribelle," Eve pointed to the main cabinet. "Home to the best of the best."

"Perfect," Maribelle said.

Seriously, what did Maribelle care? What she liked was leaving a closet's worth of gorgeous stuff at Vintage Tales.

Then the voices rose, interrupting her thought. Fracas enveloped the room. Lucinda and Aunt Bryant had come into the store, coiffed and prepared to shop. Their bodies were close, complimentary, they were a purposeful duo.

Within seconds, Maribelle knew Lucinda had spotted her.

"Maribelle, are you having a meeting?" Lucinda asked. "Obviously you are, I wouldn't expect you to be shopping midday."

Her mother wore a beige-on-beige silk scarf tied under her chin, a Jackie Kennedy, Palm Beach circa 1960 effect. Maribelle assumed she had read the same articles—how the look was popular again. Not many women were doing it, yet today, as the wind kicked up from the east, it worked. Aunt Bryant's head was not covered in any way, her thick braid and rose gold eyeglasses, progressives, made her the librarian sidekick to Lucinda's glamour.

"Maribelle, what a treat to see you. How are you?" Aunt Bryant asked. "Did you find what you're looking for?"

Eve nodded at Maribelle. "I know what you like, Maribelle, I'll be in touch."

"I don't mean to be rude, except I'm dashing," Maribelle said.

But her mother and aunt were on the far side of Vintage Tales, looking at Gucci belts from the seventies. Lucinda waved a hazy wave. Aunt Bryant was staring at her.

Eve guided Maribelle to the door.

"And you will be pleased with the value—the money," she whispered. "I always say it is a form of shedding."

Shedding, Maribelle got that. As if her life was inverted, she had *appeared* a butterfly.

As soon as Maribelle was on the Avenue, her phone dinged: *5 pm today? I'll come to your house.*

Two hours later, Felicity of Felicity Consignors was hauling garment bags out of Maribelle's house. Felicity, at about fifty years old, in a tan, silk cardigan and tan cropped pants, was surprisingly good at it. Maribelle imagined the many house visits she had made for the inventory.

"Are you sure you don't want to give some of these dresses, skirts or blazers, shoes or booties to your sisters? I know you have two sisters. I love reading about your family. You don't have to consign everything."

"I'm sure," Maribelle said. "My sisters have their own collections."

"Well, I have three sisters, and we do share some great items, especially the dresses, back and forth." Felicity pressed.

"Oh, yes, I've done that," Maribelle said. She flashed back to Raleigh "shopping" in Maribelle's closet, what she chose was usually for a charity dinner—the kind where Samuel was seated between the two sisters. Fucking Samuel.

"I so appreciate your business," Felicity said.

"Of course," Maribelle said. She had considered calling the Real Real, but Felicity was someone she knew, through Aunt Bryant. Whomever she had called, it was the right decision.

After Felicity carted off eight large garbage bags worth of clothes, Maribelle was drained. Also, lighter and lighter. She started scrolling for Margot Damon's number, for an estimate on her house when Lucinda pulled up. It wasn't yet five o'clock, her mother was fifteen minutes early. She was still in society-lady mode, wearing the same get-up and scarf tied under her chin as she had at Vintage Tales. Either she hadn't gone home yet, or she had and was too preoccupied to change her clothes. Supy, who hadn't barked at Felicity once she walked inside, went berserk when Lucinda appeared.

"It's okay, Super Dog," Maribelle took a few biscuits from the pantry before she opened the door.

"No one is here today, is that correct—no cleaning crew?" Lucinda asked as she descended.

"No one," Maribelle said.

She understood her mother's request—without interruptions, other family members, or eavesdroppers—bordered on a clandestine meeting. At Lucinda's, Rosie was perpetually dusting when Maribelle and her sisters gathered around, trading secrets.

William occasionally showed up after golf or tennis, toward the end of one of their dramas.

While today was unlike any other in terms of Lucinda's behavior, she did do her exhaustive sixty-second take of the first floor. What she liked was intact furniture, working lights, impeccable order. Once reassured that all was in order and her daughter hadn't lost her mind completely, she motioned toward the living room,

"Well, Maribelle," Lucinda said as they sat facing the ocean.

What, what do you want, Maribelle wanted to shout. Instead, she looked out at the waves. It was much rougher than earlier in the day, the start of a Nor'easter, the kind of storm that lasted three days. Samuel relished them, so did Raleigh actually. The thought of them together was other worldly. As if they were never kindred, never sisters. Alternately, as if they were sisters first and sisters after. Was Samuel real?

On the couch, Lucinda appeared ragged, her legs weren't crossed properly. Splayed, old-lady style. The skin across her jawline was looser. Today, her mother wasn't beautiful, no matter what. She had been trampled on by her daughters. Maribelle wasn't sure how much had been divulged by Caroline. Whatever it was, she preferred Lucinda's tough exterior, not her emotions. No one's emotions, in fact, only her own.

"What were you doing at Vintage Tales? You weren't on a shopping spree, were you?" Lucinda asked.

"No, there's nothing for me there," Maribelle said. "I mean, look at this house, it's obscene for one person. It was obscene when Samuel was alive and it was for two people." She didn't elaborate how it was Samuel's fantasy. It felt like a decorated prison to her.

"Everyone knows Vintage Tales is a last stop when someone, a woman, is in dire straits," Lucinda said. "What if people see you heading upstairs? Readers of *PB Confidential*?"

"I was watchful," Maribelle said. "I'm really pleased to be selling some belongings, extravagances."

"Why would you do that, Maribelle?" Lucinda asked. "You have an assemblage. These bags, these collectables, are not replaceable. Especially now with no husband and Barrows in flux."

"Flux? Okay, because I don't want what a husband or a family company provides. What I can't sustain on my own. None of it counts anymore. If it ever did."

Maribelle got up and practiced breathing deeply.

"I've been trying to stop Nadia from writing a tell-all about Samuel. I've been trying to figure out how to pay Barrows back... I'm tired," she said. "I need a break."

Lucinda stood up. Supy ran to her, barking.

"Supy, stop, stop it!" Supy kept at it, higher pitched, unrelenting barks. "Stop!" Maribelle shouted.

Supy slowed down, slinking away while watching Lucinda.

"I've no clout to hold up the Nadia article," Maribelle said. "I've as much as offered her my position at *PB Confidential.*"

"Excuse me?"

Maribelle hesitated at her chance to come clean about how much she longed to leave Palm Beach. She knew her mother's grail.

"What is happening, Maribelle?"

"You know, the greater good. Barrows, the family, that's why the bargaining with Nadia," Maribelle said.

"Nadia will interview Julian. That can't be controlled." Lucinda began pacing.

"I'll speak with him," Maribelle said.

"Aunt Bryant knew you'd like him," Lucinda said.

Aunt Bryant looking after her. Had Maribelle ever thanked her? "What does she know?"

"Everything and nothing," Lucinda said. "She wanted to protect you as best she could. I did too, Maribelle. I kept thinking Travis knew something, that's partly why I wanted to look into it."

Samuel, Travis, Barrows, piled up in Maribelle's head.

"I look back and I'm not sure how much I loved Samuel, or maybe I didn't truly love him."

"It doesn't matter, Maribelle. This is where we are."

"Do you know the truth about Samuel?" Maribelle asked.

"Which truth? His truth, your truth, Raleigh's truth? I certainly know Raleigh's truth," Lucinda said.

The living room in the quasi-mansion that Samuel and Maribelle bought together to live the life that Barrows provided felt hellish, dizzying.

"Sit down, Maribelle." Her mother addressed her as if she were in grade school in Kesgrave, about to rearrange her schedule against her will.

Supy came over and put her face in Maribelle's lap. She touched her to be sure she existed. Lucinda sat beside her. They were too near one another, the feathery lines around Lucinda's mouth from decades ago, when she took long drags on Lucky Strikes, were visible. The kind of etched lines that Botox and filler only fixed to a degree. Daily, she painstakingly covered them, like much of her narrative.

"I know what happened that morning," Lucinda said.

That morning. "No matter what Samuel did, no matter who he was, he should be alive today." Maribelle began to cry.

"Of course," Lucinda said. "It was a bad hour to be on a boat. The wind squalls were terribly strong. I'm saying something else. I'm saying I know exactly what did occur. Raleigh was at the pier after you dropped Samuel off. There was no staff around, it was too early. The two of them talked briefly. The storm was kicking up. Samuel should have come in and tied up his Riva Rivamare."

A new kind of dread began for Maribelle, worse than the day Travis came to tell her that Samuel had drowned. Worse than the day Raleigh said she was Samuel's lover, the one Maribelle had been searching for.

"Because you were there too, is that it?" she asked. Suddenly she was trapped in mounds of seaweed, fighting to reach the shoreline.

"I got there when you were leaving. I was in William's sedan, directly behind you. I was parked and able to see them, the car was shielded by an empty van."

Lucinda at the pier between the two sisters, she had missed Maribelle and caught Raleigh.

"Why?" Maribelle asked. "Why the hell were you driving to my husband's boat slip at what you call an ungodly hour?"

"I'd been attempting to find out where the money was going from the business. I kept asking Samuel, Travis too. The day before, I had found out it was Samuel. I was going to speak with him before work, not at the office. I was incensed. I planned to confront him and insist he pay it back. Instead, there was Raleigh on the dock with him, the two of them kissing. She began shaking her head, and Samuel got into the boat. He tossed the rope to Raleigh. She didn't catch it, and it fell into the water. They were shouting, the wind picked up, I couldn't hear them. Raleigh walked away. Samuel went to the front of the *Vertigo* and took off at full speed, smashing into the waves. No one else was there, no boaters, no one. The storm came up too fast for anyone on the dock to have helped anyway."

Raleigh, dropping the line. Maribelle's heart squeezed.

"You could have told us, at least told me. What you knew about Raleigh all along, what you thought happened."

"What good would that do and for whom?" Lucinda asked. "I saw her face, Maribelle. We have to forgive her. Samuel didn't only fool you and Raleigh. What about Travis? What about me? He was the rising star at Barrows. For months, I was misled. He convinced me the books—all the records—were fine when I knew they weren't. Who was Samuel, Maribelle? A different man to each of us. Whatever you wanted to hear, he'd whisper in your ear. He was the most suave, smartest spoiler. He loved being adored, he was a thief in the night."

"But you could have run down to the dock!" Maribelle said. "Maybe you could have saved him—you and Raleigh together."

"Do you believe it would have made a difference?" Lucinda was dispassionate, cold, she had no remorse. "I was there because of what he'd done to the company."

Maribelle closed her eyes, there was Samuel on the open water in his beloved Riva Rivamare, the *Vertigo*. Samuel, alone with his secrets.

Lucinda walked to the wet bar and opened a bottle of Black Label Scotch. Maribelle hadn't seen her do this before—her mother didn't drink Scotch.

"Samuel's," Maribelle said. "A gift from a vendor."

"How fitting." She held up a picture of her and Reed at a party of some sort in Kesgrave. "Over twenty-five years ago."

"You adored Dad," Maribelle said. "What an example. That's why Caroline and Raleigh and I—we've strived with our husbands. Although we've failed, haven't we?"

Lucinda shook her head. "Reed. Your father. Well, I loved the idea of him. I adored the idea, maybe not the man."

Maribelle wasn't in the mood for this. "I'm sorry, Dad was incredible."

"Ah, an amazing father, sure. Not an amazing husband," Lucinda said. "Do you think I don't know what it feels like to be betrayed? All those business trips your father took without me? People betray one another, they have their reasons. Your father was . . ."

"I don't want to hear," Maribelle said. "I'm incapable of any more information."

"Your father was busy," Lucinda continued. "Busy with his mistress. Except in my situation, it was fine."

Her mother did her social, fake laugh, the one she was good at stopping abruptly. "Bryant helped out."

Maribelle frowned. "I'm sorry? What are we talking about?"

"Your father, Bryant, and I were, shall we say, a threesome. How else could I have gotten through? I was preoccupied with running Barrows. I treasured it. Bryant entertained your father, she kept him happy. I made the connections for Barrows and built up the company. I got us situated in Palm Beach while Bryant and your father, they were, like I said, busy. They loved restaurants, horizons, hotel suites."

"Aunt Bryant's our godmother, practically a fairy godmother," Maribelle said.

"Of course, she is." Lucinda went back to the bar and poured the Black Label. She took a swig. "And she is my dearest friend. We have quite a history together. I'm grateful to her. You see, Maribelle, we're not going to judge."

She was astonished, sickened. "I don't need to know any more about it," Maribelle said. "Lately, just too many surprises."

"Quite a triangle, Reed, Bryant, me. Barrows was growing quickly. I had no time for anything besides the business and my girls. Reed found Aunt Bryant available and sympathetic. She always is, isn't she? We cut a deal. I found it convenient. I didn't want a divorce. He was great arm candy, a dashing man in Palm Beach."

Maribelle considered a quick search for a tranquilizer, a sip of Scotch. Instead, she poured a Perrier.

"I will never forgive Raleigh," she said. "I shared everything with her, my hopes, my friends, my clothes. I don't know how you could share your husband. I couldn't share Samuel."

"Don't be so dramatic, Maribelle," Lucinda said. "Samuel was another husband. They come; they go. An example is William—what is there to say? He fills a chair nicely. They're fungible. Sisters, friends who are like sisters, aren't."

"I've been searching for Samuel's last lover, and Raleigh has fucking watched me, pretending she's on my side."

"All of us liars, to some extent," Lucinda said. "That's how we survive, alone and together."

"No, no," Maribelle said. "I've hit a wall."

"While I'm very against breaking up a family, as you and your sisters know, this is no longer about my desire for you to stay. Despite my efforts and what I've insisted on having, I can't keep my girls together, not in present time. I accept we are beyond that."

Supy came quietly to Lucinda's feet. Lucinda lightly tapped her head.

"In town people watch and measure others. I've kept us above the fray. We appear to be a praiseworthy family. Deep down, we Barrows are a bit cult-like, aren't we?"

Maribelle looked at her mother, unshakeable, determined, unbowed. Lucinda reached over and took her hand.

"Your father would want each of us happy," she said. "He would want us to have a good life."

Lucinda handed her a very thick manila envelope. Maribelle knew it was filled with cash.

"Start with this. Wire transfers will follow. From Bryant and me—we've decided it's best to let you go. Leave town, Maribelle. You haven't wanted to live as you do for a long while. Start again. Consider Raleigh your bridge to the other side, a banner for your escape."

After Lucinda was gone, Maribelle packed very little. She dropped Supy, the Tesla, and her house keys at Caroline's. Raleigh was there too, standing by the front door with Caleb. There was something in how Maribelle appeared, neither sister questioned her. Both noted how methodically and quickly she came and went. As she was rushing from Caroline's house, Maribelle looked back. Caroline and her girls were playing with Supy on the front lawn. Raleigh and Caleb were watching her as she moved farther out. Everyone waved in a slow, hazy motion.

In the dusk Maribelle was almost invisible. Only those she cared to see her, saw her. She headed quickly to the east, away from the Intracoastal.

At the end of her sister's street was Julian, waiting.

Discussion Questions
Maribelle's Shadow

1. Maribelle, a young widow, knows little about who her husband really was. Do you think this happens often in marriages? Why?

2. Lucinda runs the Barrows family like a corporation. Why are her daughters so beholden to her?

3. One's loyalty as wife, mother, sister, and adult daughter are themes in this novel. How do these relationships affect our daily lives? Do you see any of your own relationships reflected in the book?

4. Palm Beach is almost a character in the novel. What do you think the societal expectations are for those who live there? How might it determine their choices and actions?

5. Lucinda comes from humble beginnings and has had to work at being accepted. How do you think this endeavor shapes the experience of women in particular? Why?

6. Is there one character who most resonates with you? Is there a character you aspire to be like, or the reverse?

7. The Barrows sisters are a complicated threesome. Discuss how they treat one another and what their motivations are. Do you think the women will all be closer now, or more distant from one another?

8. How does the structure of witnessing each sister's point of view affect the reader's experience?

9. There is the mystery of what happened to Samuel. What do you suspect happened?

10. And of course, the surprise ending. Who were you rooting for, and why? How would you have ended the novel?

Acknowledgments

The story of the Barrows sisters and their mother has been with me for many years in various incarnations. Along the way, there are those who listened, suggested, advised and edited. I am so grateful for their input.

Meredith Bernstein, Alice Martell, Katinka Matson, Sally McElwain, Meryl Moss, Jim Parry, Jane Shapiro, Alexandra Shelley, Jonathan Stone, Jennifer Weis, Deb Zipf.

The insightful team at Beaufort Books: Eric Kampmann, Alicia Manning, Emma St. John, Megan Trank. For his amazing jacket design, John Lotte.

For his boating expertise, Robert Fagenson, for his financial knowledge, Tom Moore, for her editorial skills, Rebecca Stowe. Steadfast assistants: Lexie Lieberthal and Katie Schaffstall.

Treasured family and friends for endless support and patience. Muses: My daughters.
My late mother, who understood, as the youngest of three sisters, what limitless loyalty is. Howard Ressler, ever there.

About the Author

Author photo by James Maher

SUSANNAH MARREN is the author of *Between the Tides, A Palm Beach Wife* and *A Palm Beach Scandal* and the pseudonym for Susan Shapiro Barash, who has written over a dozen nonfiction books, including *Tripping the Prom Queen, Toxic Friends, You're Grounded Forever, But First Let's Go Shopping*, and *A Passion for More*. For her nonfiction she has been featured in *The New York Times, Wall Street Journal, New York Post, Chicago Tribune, Elle, Marie Claire*, and has appeared on national television including the *Today Show, Good Morning America, CBS, CNN*, and *MSNBC*. Barash has been a guest on national radio including NPR and Sirius Radio.

For over twenty years she has taught gender studies at Marymount Manhattan College and has guest taught creative nonfiction at the Writing Institute at Sarah Lawrence College.